PENGUIN CLASSICS

THE GREEK ALEXANDER ROMANCE

The *Greek Alexander Romance* has been one of the most long-lived and influential works of Greek literature. Wrongly attributed by early modern scholars to the contemporary historian of Alexander, Callisthenes, it was probably composed in its earliest form in the third or second century BC. It was rewritten and expanded several times in antiquity, with the result that there are at least three widely divergent Greek texts. The earliest version, now lost, was translated, with further variations, into Syriac, Ethiopic, Armenian and Pahlavi, whence it contributed stories to the Qur'an and inspired the Persian writers Firdausi and Nizami. A Latin version of the third century AD was the basis for the extensive Alexander traditions of medieval Europe, which are known from texts in more than a dozen languages as well as from the visual arts. The adventures which the Alexander of the *Romance* adds to the achievements of his historical original, the world conqueror, include an ascent into the air in a basket borne by eagles, a descent into the ocean in a diving bell, a meeting with the Amazons, an interview with the Brahmans or naked philosophers, and the search for the Water of Life, which ended in the transformation of Alexander's daughter into a mermaid. The *Romance* reflects Alexander's metamorphosis in legend from a consummate general to a sage and beloved of God.

Richard Stoneman is the author of several books on Greece and the classical tradition, including *A Literary Companion to Travel in Greece* (Penguin, 1984; reissued by the J. P. Getty Museum, 1994), *Land of Lost Gods: The Search for Classical Greece* (1987), *Aquarian Guide to Greek Mythology* (1991) and *Daphne into Laurel* (1982), a widely praised anthology of classical literature's reception into the English literary heritage through poetic translation and imitation. He has published *Legends of Alexander the Great* (Everyman, 1994) and is working on a general study of the Alexander traditions.

D0109140

THE
GREEK ALEXANDER
ROMANCE

TRANSLATED WITH AN
INTRODUCTION AND NOTES BY

RICHARD STONEMAN

PENGUIN BOOKS

PENGUIN BOOKS

Published by the Penguin Group
Penguin Books Ltd, 27 Wrights Lane, London W8 5TZ, England
Penguin Putnam Inc., 375 Hudson Street, New York, New York 10014, USA
Penguin Books Australia Ltd, Ringwood, Victoria, Australia
Penguin Books Canada Ltd, 10 Alcorn Avenue, Toronto, Ontario, Canada M4V 3B2
Penguin Books (NZ) Ltd, 182–190 Wairau Road, Auckland 10, New Zealand

Penguin Books Ltd, Registered Offices: Harmondsworth, Middlesex, England

This translation first published 1991
5 7 9 10 8 6 4

Copyright © Richard Stoneman, 1991
All rights reserved

The moral right of the translator has been asserted

Printed in England by Clays Ltd, St Ives plc
Filmset in Bembo (Monophoto, Lasercomp)

Except in the United States of America, this book is sold subject
to the condition that it shall not, by way of trade or otherwise, be lent,
re-sold, hired out, or otherwise circulated without the publisher's
prior consent in any form of binding or cover other than that in
which it is published and without a similar condition including this
condition being imposed on the subsequent purchaser

To Geoffrey de Ste Croix
and for my son Alexander

CONTENTS

ACKNOWLEDGEMENTS

I am grateful, as ever, to the various libraries I have used for the plenty of their resources – in particular, the London Library, indispensable support of the wandering scholar, and the Library of the Institute of Classical Studies. Especial thanks are owed to Professor Waldemar Heckel and Professor Peter Parsons, both of whom read the Introduction and made many valuable suggestions for its improvement. Any errors that remain are of course my own.

The book is dedicated to my undergraduate tutor, Geoffrey de Ste Croix, who first introduced me to the historical Alexander. He will, I am sure, have firm views as to which Alexander – the historical one or he of the *Romance* – is of the more abiding importance and interest.

INTRODUCTION

❦

ALEXANDER THE GREAT IN HISTORY AND LEGEND

When Marco Polo visited the city of Balkh, ancient Bactra, 'Mother of Cities, Paradise of the Earth', his hosts still spoke of the marriage that had taken place there between Alexander the Great and Roxane, the daughter of Darius, king of Persia. Not much further on, in Badakhshan, the Venetian traveller was told of horses for which was claimed a direct line of descent from Alexander's horse Bucephalus: 'They were all born like him with a horn on the forehead. This breed was entirely in the possession of one of the king's uncles, who, because he refused to let the king have any, was put to death by him. Thereupon his wife, to avenge her husband's death, destroyed the whole breed, and so it became extinct.'

It was not only the horses whose ancestry was legendary. Many of the kings of Bactria, Derwauz and neighbouring regions claimed descent from Alexander the Great.[1] One of them, the Mir (or Thum) of Nagir, Shah Sikander Khan, minted coins on which his profile bore a striking resemblance to that of his putative ancestor.[2]

These examples are chosen to illustrate the power of legend over the minds of men, the longevity of the name of Alexander over two millennia, and also the unimportance of historical fact for the endurance of a great name. Alexander never married the daughter of Darius, and the kings' claims could not be other than fiction. He did marry Roxane, but she was a Sogdian princess and not a Persian. No historian claims her for a daughter of Darius; that piece of legend is due directly to the *Alexander Romance*.

It is not only on such dynastic claims that the *Romance* had an impact. The legends of Alexander entered a common stock of central Asian lore through the manifold translations and retellings of the legend. Visitors to English cathedrals such as Wells and Gloucester will recognize in the *Romance* the source of frequent representations – on misericords, roof bosses and the like – of scenes of Alexander's flight into the heavens. His name is known in Malaya and in Russia, in Israel and in Spain.

It would hardly be an exaggeration to say that the legends of Alexander are as widely disseminated, and as influential on art and literature, as the story of the Gospels. Each age makes its own Alexander: the Hebrew tradition makes him a preacher and prophet, the later Christian Greek and Syriac versions emphasize his faithful obedience to God; in the European Middle Ages he is an exemplar of the chivalrous knight; for the Persians he is, in one tradition, the arch-Satan because he destroyed the fire-altars of the Zoroastrian religion,[3] while in the epic authors he is the legitimate king of Persia because he is really the son of Darius and not of Philip; for the modern Greeks he is one of the half-magical bearers of Romiosyni, lord of storms and father of the mermaids. The *Greek Alexander Romance* stands at the beginning of these traditions and is fundamental to the understanding of all of them. It is also not without interest for historians of Alexander. But it is above all a repository of excellent adventure tales, some of which will seem familiar to readers of the *Adventures of Sindbad* or of *Baron Munchausen*: the floating island that turns out to be a whale is common to all three; the Baron's horse is named Bucephalus; the use of small animals to defeat an army of elephants is common to the *Romance* and *Munchausen*. One can also discover interesting cross-fertilizations of the Arab and Greek legends: for example, the discovery of the Valley of Diamonds in the *Adventures of Sindbad* is in other Arab legends associated with Alexander,[4] and the talking trees called waq-waq trees in the Syriac versions share the name of the legendary islands of Waq-Waq in the Arab tales.

How did legends of this kind come to be attached to the historical figure of Alexander the Great? In sober fact, Alexander was born in 356 BC at Pella, the son of Philip II of Macedon and his wife the Epirote princess, Olympias.[5] He was educated by the philosopher Aristotle, who seems to have instilled in him a taste for discovering the secrets of distant lands – he took numerous scholars and scientists with him on his expedition to Asia; and his taming of the horse Bucephalus is mentioned even in the least extravagant historians.

In 336 Philip was murdered and Alexander became king of Macedon. He swiftly put into action a plan, which may have been already outlined by his father, for a war against Persia 'to avenge the wrongs of the Greeks' suffered in the Persian wars of a century and a half before. (Though the Macedonians were not Greeks, and the common people did not speak Greek, their kings claimed Greek nationality and direct descent from the hero Heracles.)

In 334 Alexander crossed the Hellespont with an army of 40,000 men, and for the next eleven years he advanced steadily across Asia, defeating the Persian army in the three great battles at the river Granicus, at Issus and at Gaugamela, finally occupying the capital city of Persepolis and confiscating the king's treasure. In the course of this expedition, he made a detour to the oracle of Ammon at Siwa in the Egyptian desert, where he seems to have been told by the priests that he was the son of Ammon. At this time he also founded the city of Alexandria in Egypt.

Once king of Persia, Alexander's ambition grew in grandeur. Tension was caused among his Greek and Macedonian courtiers by his adoption of oriental clothing and customs such as greeting by prostration, and by his insistence on plunging further and further into Asia – over the Hindu Kush, into Khwarizm, and as far as the Indus – on a voyage of exploration and conquest the like of which had never been seen before. Botanists, ethnographers, and historians travelled with Alexander to record both his exploits and the customs and geography of the lands they traversed.

Eventually a mutiny of his troops at the river Hyphasis forced him to abandon plans to march to the Ganges, and he returned to Babylon. For this journey part of the troops were sent with the admiral Nearchus down the Indus and followed the coastal route to Mesopotamia, and part marched with Alexander through the Gedrosian desert – a disastrous episode in which most of the participants died, and which contemporaries attributed simply to his desire to emulate a similar march by the legendary Queen Semiramis.

At Babylon Alexander fell ill, perhaps as the result of a heavy drinking bout (a typically Macedonian practice), and died. Among his papers were controversial documents including his Last Plans – for conquest of the West. Almost at once dissension between his generals resulted in the division of the Empire into several separate, and often warring, kingdoms.

Assessments of the historical Alexander have differed widely. Some see in him the wild and youthful adventurer, hounded on by his own *pothos* (yearning) to ever more discoveries. This is essentially the view of Arrian (a historian of the second century AD, generally regarded as the most reliable account), and this romantic vision of the youthful explorer is central to the treatment of more recent biographers such as Robin Lane Fox. Other sources were more critical and emphasized his intolerance, his bouts of murderous rage and his ruthlessness. Much of this comes across in Quintus Curtius Rufus (first century AD), and for a modern historian like Ernst Badian[6] there is little to choose between Alexander and Hitler. W. W. Tarn saw him as a visionary who believed in the brotherhood of man and a world state; this view receives some slight support from the possibly authentic letter of Aristotle to Alexander on the World State,[7] but is generally rejected as a view of Alexander's own motivation. Lately the military genius of Alexander, for whom the establishment and consolidation of political rule was always a foremost objective, has been stressed again by Donald W. Engels.[8]

There will never be a definitive portrait of Alexander. The legends began to crystallize around his person even as the catafalque bearing his body rolled across the desert from Babylon en route to Siwa – until it was hijacked by Ptolemy and re-routed to Memphis, and later Alexandria, where the king's tomb became a talisman of Ptolemy's own kingly rule in Egypt.

The *Greek Alexander Romance* as we have it represents an advanced stage of development of this kind of legendary material, and the historical framework has itself become very shaky, as well as being overlaid by many layers of fabulous material.

*

The plot of the *Greek Alexander Romance* is as follows. Nectanebo, the last Pharaoh of Egypt, foreseeing by his magic arts the defeat of his country by the Persians, flees to the Macedonian court (I.1–3). Falling in love with Olympias, the wife of King Philip, he devises a way to make love to her by disguising himself as the god Ammon (4–7). When in due course Olympias becomes pregnant, Nectanebo explains that the child will be the son of a god and the avenger of his father. Philip's suspicions of Olympias' pregnancy are allayed by Nectanebo who sends a magic sea-hawk to him in a dream to explain the situation, a proceeding that is supported by other omens (8–11). But Philip remains suspicious of the child.

When Alexander begins to grow up, one of his first actions is to dispose of Nectanebo in a murder whose motivation is obscure. As he dies, Nectanebo tells him the truth about his paternity (9–14).

Alexander grows up, is educated by Aristotle, tames the horse Bucephalus and goes to compete at the Olympic Games (15–20). On his return he nearly murders Philip in a quarrel (21–2). In his father's absence on campaign he receives ambassadors from Persia who have come to collect their usual tribute, and treats them to a display of youthful intransigence (23). Philip dies (24). A series of campaigns in Greece and elsewhere is followed by the invasion of Asia. The chronology of the *Romance* – or perhaps its geography – is so confused that this campaign is interrupted by a further series of campaigns in Greece and Italy: clearly the author had no idea where these places were (25–9).

Alexander then goes to Egypt, where an oracle of the god Ammon gives him instructions on where to found the city that will be Alexandria. Its construction is described in detail – especially Alexander's erection of an altar at the sanctuary of Sarapis. The god Sarapis predicts to Alexander the prosperity of Alexandria (30–33). Alexander continues to Memphis, where he is received as the reincarnation of Nectanebo (34).

Alexander now marches into Asia, conquers Tyre (35) and begins the long campaign against the Persian king, Darius, in the course of which he and Darius exchange a series of diplomatic letters. The historical events of this campaign are given in some detail and with passable accuracy (36–42), but are interrupted by a reprise of the campaigns in Greece (43–II.6) including the sack of Thebes (I.46) and the resistance in Athens (II.1–6).

The story of the Persian campaign resumes (7–11) and Darius seeks the assistance of the Indian king, Porus (12). Alexander uses various tricks to demoralize the Persians (13) and visits the Persian court in disguise (14–15), crossing for this purpose the mysterious river Stranga which can freeze and unfreeze in a moment. The battle on the Stranga (16) corresponds to that at Arbela in the historical accounts. Alexander burns the palace at Persepolis – although the city is not named in the text (17). The murder of Darius by his satraps (20) is followed by Alexander's proclamation to his subjects and execution of the murderers (21).

Alexander now prepares to marry Darius' daughter Roxane (22) and writes a letter to Olympias with a long account of his adventures, starting with a reprise of what has already been described in the text and continuing with travels in strange regions (23–44). His adventures include meeting strange beasts, magic trees and stones; he tries to explore an island but an unseen voice tells him to return (38). He explores the sea in a diving bell and marches into the Land of Darkness towards the Land of the Blessed; the stratagem of taking mares without their foals enables them to return safely, led by the mares' instinct. Alexander discovers the Water of Life but fails to drink it (39). Two birds with human heads appear and tell him to turn back. An attempt to explore the heavens in a basket carried by eagles is also unsuccessful (40). He meets Sirens and fights Centaurs (41).

Then Alexander advances to India and the City of the Sun, where he receives an oracle foretelling his death (44). The campaign against Porus is interrupted by a mutiny of the soldiers (III.1), but Alexander defeats Porus in single combat (4). Then he visits the Brahmans (5–6). Here follows the Letter of Alexander to Aristotle about India (7–16).

He visits the trees of the Sun and Moon (17), and then conceives a desire to see the palace of Semiramis, now inhabited by Queen Candace of Meroe. He visits her in disguise, and gets into her good graces by rescuing her son Candaules from his enemies (18–23). Candaules brings him to the Dwellings of the Gods, where the Pharaoh Sesonchosis warns him of his inevitable death (24).

Alexander visits the Amazons and makes them his subjects (25–6). A second letter to Olympias repeats this account and then describes his visit to the City of the Sun and the Palace of Cyrus with its golden ornaments (27–9).

When he reaches Babylon, a monstrous birth is interpreted as an omen of his death (30). Meanwhile, Antipater (the acting ruler of Macedonia) sends his son to poison Alexander. The poison is served to him by his cupbearer Iolaus,[9] and Alexander falls ill (30–31). He makes his will and says farewell to his comrades, appointing rulers for all the provinces of his Empire (32). He then dies (33) and Ptolemy has the body brought to Memphis, where the priests order it to be transferred to Alexandria (34). The work concludes with a list of the cities he founded (35).

These legends became enormously important in later tradition.[10] The Greek *Romance* was translated into Latin in the fourth century AD, and this was in turn translated during the Middle Ages into every major language, including English, Scots, French, German, Swedish, Italian, Bulgarian, Serbian, Rumanian, Czech, Polish, Russian, Magyar, Spanish-Arabic and Hebrew.

The Greek tradition is important too. The story of the *Romance* continued to be retold throughout the Byzantine period, in both verse and prose, and the legends of Alexander creep into works on other subjects too. The latest of the Greek retellings was published in Venice in 1529 by Demetrios Zenos.[11]

A Syriac translation from the Greek was the source of all the oriental versions of the tale.[12] It both influenced Arabic literature, including the Qur'an, and became a fundamental source for the epics of the kings of Persia, notably the important *Sikandernameh* of Nizami (1140–1203)[13] and the *Book of Kings* of Firdausi (941–1019).[14] It was from here that the tales seeped into the common lore of Afghanistan and its rulers.

At the same time the legend spread via the Syriac version to Christian Ethiopia, and a version of the Christian legend was brought – probably by Nestorian missionaries – to central Asia, originating a Mongol version no later than the fourteenth century.[15]

THE FORMATION OF THE ROMANCE

The formation of the legend as it was known to the Middle Ages was a gradual process. The circumstances of its origin are a matter of some controversy. One red herring may be quickly dealt with. Several fifteenth-century MSS of the *Romance* attribute the work to Alexander's court historian, Callisthenes. This is impossible for the simple reason that Callisthenes was disgraced and executed before Alexander's expedition to Asia was over, while the *Romance* covers the whole of Alexander's life and death. For this reason the work is sometimes known as Pseudo-Callisthenes. However, this obscures the main question surrounding the origin of the earliest form of the *Romance*, and its date.

The *Greek Alexander Romance* as we have it survives in three major versions (the scholarly term used is 'recensions'), each containing material that differs considerably from that in the other two.[16] None of these is securely dated, though it is easy enough to place them in a relative chronology. The first is quite close to being a conventional, if somewhat rhetorical, historical account. The second has incorporated a large amount of legendary material deriving from a series of letters purporting to have been written by Alexander to his mother, Olympias, and to his tutor, Aristotle. The third is a considerably expanded version of the second, containing much additional legendary material, a good deal of which can be firmly associated with a Jewish–Christian milieu.

The most difficult question to answer is at what date the earliest version of the work as we have it was written down. The first manuscript dates from the third century AD. Thus composition must have taken place between this date and the death of Alexander in 323 BC – a period of 600 years. Its popularity in the third century AD coincides with a period when there was considerable interest in the lives of sages, holy men and wonder-workers, and a flourishing literature developed around these subjects. Some scholars therefore argue that the *Romance* was first composed at this date by an 'editor' from a variety of sources. More recently argument has tended to set the composition of the *Romance* quite early in this 600-year period.[17] Can we tie it down to a particular literary milieu?

There is no doubt that most of the component elements of the *Romance* were already in existence in the third century BC. Even in the decades after Alexander's death the historical accounts competed with pure legend, as well as carefully structured reinterpretation and perhaps even forgery (for example, Alexander's will) in the interests of one or other of the successors. None of the work of the first generation of Alexander historians survives today, and what we read are reinterpretations by later writers of what they wrote. The contemporary historians of Alexander were his general, Ptolemy, and a member of his scientific staff, Aristobulus; the historian Arrian regarded these as the best sources. But Quintus Curtius Rufus and the rest of the so-called Vulgate tradition, including Plutarch (who wrote both a life of Alexander and two essays on his Fortune), placed more reliance on the extravagant tales of the official court historian Callisthenes and of Cleitarchus (who wrote after Alexander's death and did not go with him to Asia). For the wonders of India the historian Onesicritus, who was trained as a Cynic philosopher, was a major source. Even in these accounts one can see the seeds of what will later become the legends or tall stories of the *Romance*. As Strabo put it: 'All who wrote about Alexander preferred the marvellous to the true' (2.1.9).

At the same time literature of a very different kind was already beginning to circulate. Papyrus finds in this century have proved beyond a doubt that many of the elements of the *Romance* were current as early as a century after Alexander's death. The most important discovery is part of a cycle of letters between Darius and Alexander which is closely similar to, though not identical with, the correspondence in the *Romance*.[18]

A separate Jewish tradition on Alexander, which described his visit to Jerusalem among other things, was also formed at an early date, and is known to us from the writings of Josephus[19] rather than from the nature of any material in the *Romance*.

Other elements to infiltrate the tradition at this early date include, most notably, the part of Nectanebo in the story and the details of the founding of Alexandria, both of which clearly originate in an Egyptian, Alexandrian milieu. The miraculous adventures were probably in circulation early, but the date at which they were integrated into the *Romance* is the most difficult question about its composition.

The Alexandrian context of the *Romance* is important. The *Romance* is the product of a process of accretion, and a question that remains unanswered is whether the basic framework was already established in Ptolemaic Alexandria. My opinion is that it was.[20] It can be shown that most of the elements of the *Romance* were already circulating then – the historical part, the Egyptian elements, the correspondence with Darius – and I believe it can be argued that the wonder-letters were also current. If so, it seems likely that they were combined into a single narrative by the end of the third century BC. If the *Romance* is to be dated so early in substantially its present form, it is not by any means a bizarre document for its context, though it certainly is unique.

The first of the early elements drawn on by the *Alexander Romance* is a Hellenistic poetic history, perhaps that of Cleitarchus, perhaps another otherwise unknown work: this would be the source of the most historical parts of the work, especially Book I of the A recension. In addition to this historical narrative in Book I, other pieces of genuine historical information are embedded in the *Romance*. They include the order of events around the foundation of Alexandria, and, perhaps, the list of guests at Alexander's last supper, and even the hatred of Pausanias for Philip the doctor.[21] Tales such as the taming of Bucephalus, the crows that led the way to the oracle of Ammon, and Alexander's retort to Parmenio,[22] also correspond to this historical or quasi-historical tradition.

Another element of the *Romance* is an 'epistolary novel' containing the correspondence of Alexander and Darius, which we know to have been circulating early. The letters containing the fabulous adventures constitute another cycle, and the letter on India belongs to yet another independent tradition. To these must be added a discrete account of the meeting with the Brahmans; a separate document on the last days and will of Alexander; and an admixture of local Alexandrian tradition for the Egyptian material.

Though the episodes in these letters are quite unhistorical in character, they still derive their inspiration from matters of historical record – even such surprising details as Alexander's penchant for disguises and the honey trees of Hyrcania (vouched for by Onesicritus, as well as later travellers).[23] The narrative and correspondence in the *Romance* seem alike to have been devised by authors familiar with Alexander's history but with no interest in using it other than as a starting-point for romance. The historical element, therefore, is often as fanciful as such Hollywood epics as *Spartacus*: characters who lived centuries apart meet cheek by jowl (for example, the ten orators in Athens), or fictional characters (Alexander's friend Pheidon) mingle with real people (Ptolemy, Callisthenes) and join in remarkable adventures. One cannot overstress the aspect of popular entertainment in the *Romance*.

Many of the non-historical elements of the *Romance* show clear signs of early origin.

The Egyptian Tales: One of the few episodes of the *Romance* that not only is unhistorical in character but also has no basis in the historical record is the paternity of Alexander. In the historians' accounts Alexander is the son of Philip, and perhaps of Ammon also, but never of Nectanebo. The idea that Alexander was Nectanebo's son belongs essentially to Egyptian tradition, and is related to Egyptian nationalist beliefs in the return of a king to Memphis.[24] Such beliefs must belong to the period soon after the overthrow of the last pharaoh, Nectanebo. In addition, the tale has a distinctly novelistic flavour, and resembles other stories in Egyptian tradition in which a god may beget a child on a mortal woman.[25] It is notable that the *Romance* makes it very clear that Nectanebo is a mere trickster in this respect, even if his magical powers are genuine, and no sympathy is shown when Alexander murders him. The Greek author has taken the Egyptian tale but turned it into one of a somewhat ludicrous deceit, rather than the nationalist parable it would have been for the

Egyptians. It provides an interesting contrast to the seriousness with which other Egyptian traditions are taken, such as the Return to Memphis or the foundation legends of Alexandria. Other features of the Nectanebo story, such as his use of wax models and divination by bowls of water, were also common in Egyptian literature of the first millennium BC.

The establishment of the cult of Sarapis by Alexander (I.30–33) is not historical, but probably a later invention of Ptolemy I or Ptolemy II to legitimate his state religion.[26] The episode thus belongs to the earliest stage of the formation of the Alexander legend.

The Debate in Athens (II.1–5): This long and highly rhetorical episode appears only in the A-text of the *Romance* (see Note on the Text, pp. 28–32), where it is in parts corrupt, making the level of argument even lower than it may originally have been. Yet the motif of the Ten Orators being sent as hostages to Alexander appears already in Plutarch, and certainly has a historical basis.[27] It will have appeared in the early histories of Alexander written in his lifetime and soon after. The identity of these ten orators is of course entirely the invention of the author of the *Romance*, and – on the *Spartacus* principle – includes characters who flourished in the late sixth century (Heraclitus) as well as the mid fourth century (Plato, Demosthenes) and the early fourth century (Lysias). A phrase or sentence of history has been turned into a fictional extravaganza.

Alexander's Last Days and His Will: The provenance of the first section of Alexander's will (III.32) is very plain from the heavy emphasis given to his bequests to the Rhodians. There can be no doubt that this document – in a clotted officialese quite unlike the preceding and following parts of the narrative and will – was composed in Rhodes to bolster the justice of their case in expelling the Macedonian garrison after Alexander's death. Its function as a piece of political propaganda is sufficient to explain its omission from later versions of the *Romance*. A narrative that includes this essentially third-century-BC material is likely to belong to the third century BC.

The Wonders of the East: Much of the detail on India already appeared in Onesicritus, one of the historians who accompanied Alexander on his expedition, and was worked up in what was originally a separate work, the *Letter to Aristotle on India*. It is likely that the *Letter* originally adhered more closely to history, and its fabulous nature increased over time and was incorporated into the *Romance* only at a late stage of composition.[28] The Land of Darkness seems to derive from accounts of the Hindu Kush[29] or the Zagros Mountains.[30] The duel with Porus seems based on an account of a duel with Porus' son apparently related in some unknown source.[31] Even the meeting with the Amazons is said to have been told by Onesicritus,[32] though when Onesicritus gave a public reading of this episode, Lysimachus asked him, 'Where was I at the time?'

The meeting with the Brahmans or Gymnosophists (Naked Philosophers) is treated in different ways by our sources. In Onesicritus, the fundamental source for all the Indian adventures, Alexander is represented as learning from their wisdom. In Plutarch he bullies them. In the *Romance*, a riddle contest, which they have no difficulty in answering successfully, is succeeded by their begging him for immortality. The picture is complicated by the insertion, in our first version and also in the third, of a work by the Christian writer Palladius, *On the Brahmans*,[33] which has the purpose of lauding the Brahmans' philosophy in a Christian light. But there is no doubt that this episode had a place in the earliest accounts of Alexander: a papyrus of the second century BC is now our earliest independent source.[34]

The Fabulous Adventures: Though many of these have no historical basis and take us into the different world of romance, some details can be traced to historical fact. The fabulous adventures may be related to Quintus Curtius' allusion to Alexander 'battling with woods and rivers' (7.8.13), but in detail they derive from the Letter to Olympias, which is very brief in the earliest version of the *Romance*. In later tellings the letter quality of the adventures is forgotten, and the narrative becomes a third person one (though not always consistently!). Even such outlandish details as the river of sand may correspond to Arrian's description of the river Polytimetus. The fundamental idea, that Alexander is proceeding beyond the boundaries of the known world, is expressed even in Alexander's lifetime by the Athenian orator Aeschines: 'Meanwhile Alexander had withdrawn to the uttermost regions of the North, almost beyond the borders of the inhabited world.'[35]

Discussion of the tales occurring solely in the third recension – the visit to Jerusalem, the unclean nations, the preaching of one god in Alexandria – may be omitted as these belong to the later accretions of an obviously Jewish milieu. The reference to the Book of Daniel in Josephus' account of Alexander's visit to Jerusalem makes clear that this legend at least could not have originated earlier than 180 BC. As a corollary, the absence of this episode from the first version increases the likelihood that that version had acquired essentially its present form *before* 180.

All this suggests that the main outlines of the narrative could have been fully formed as early as 50–100 years after Alexander's death. A dating of the *Romance*, in substantially its present form, in third-century-BC Alexandria, can be supported by consideration of the literary context of the period, with which it might at first sight seem out of keeping.

For most students and readers, Alexandrian literature means the highly cultivated, recondite and mannered poetry of Callimachus (c. 305–c. 240 BC), the highly-wrought pastoral of Theocritus (c. 300–c. 260 BC), the epic narrative of the *Argonautica* of Apollonius (c. 295–215 BC), and perhaps the arcane inscrutabilities of the *Alexandra* of Lycophron (b. c. 320 BC). Equally important for the cultural context of these works was the writing of scholars such as Eratosthenes the geographer, Manetho the historian of Egypt, and his contemporary Hecataeus of Abdera, author of *Aegyptiaca*. All these (except perhaps Manetho) were working in a purely Greek tradition of literature and science, under the patronage of the Macedonian king Ptolemy II Philadelphus (283–245 BC). It is easy to forget how cosmopolitan a place Alexandria was even in the mid third century BC, less than a century after its foundation. As in most major cities, high culture was only one aspect of a complex and varied society. From the beginning there was a sizeable Jewish community with its own districts and, to an extent, its own laws, and native Egyptians also played an important part in the city's affairs. The researches of recent years[36] have shown how the different nationalities of Ptolemaic Egypt commingled and intermarried: most Egyptians and many Greeks were bilingual. If Greek was the dominant culture, it nevertheless offered a mouthpiece and not a muzzle to writers of other racial origins.

Much important Jewish Alexandrian literature of this period was written in Greek. Several historical works are known from the third and second centuries BC,[37] and there is poetry too: Philo the Elder's epic on Jerusalem, Ezekiel's tragedy *Exodus* composed in rigorously classical form. But the major work of Alexandrian Judaism is the translation of the Hebrew Bible, the Septuagint, some sections of which were translated as early as 250 BC.

There are even signs of a direct influence of Jewish and other oriental literature on Greek writing. Callimachus shows some slight signs of acquaintance with other literatures.[38] The very form of Lycophron's *Alexandra*, a history cast as riddling prophecy, recalls the style of the Hebrew prophets. Jewish tales about Alexander must have been circulating in the third century BC though we do not see their influence on the *Romance* until the composition of the γ-version some time after AD 900 (see Note on the Text, p. 29). Conversely, Jewish writing also began to adopt the form and conventions of the Greek romance or romantic novella – as, for example, in *Joseph and Aseneth* (perhaps as early as 100 BC) as well as some of the books of the Apocrypha.

Given the amount of writing by Jews in Greek, it is not surprising that native Egyptians too turned to Greek as a natural literary medium. The amount of Egyptian literature surviving from the second century BC may reflect the more prominent role in Egyptian affairs taken by native Egyptians from about 205 in the reign of Ptolemy V. The Egyptian history of Manetho has already been mentioned. Plutarch[39] remarked on the predilection of the Egyptians for stories about the heroic deeds of Sesostris – a predilection for heroic tales that ancient peoples generally shared. But most Greek writing of the Egyptian tradition is of a

very different kind, knowledge of which we owe almost entirely
to the discovery and decipherment of papyri in the last forty
years. There are some commonplace hymns, but also folk tales,
romances, and resistance pamphlets in the form of oracles. (Important examples are the *Dream of Nectanebo* of the second century BC, and the *Oracle of the Potter*, probably of the third,
possibly very soon after the foundation of Alexandria.)

There is no dividing line between the kind of material written
in Greek and in demotic Egyptian; the *Demotic Chronicle* of the
third century BC, written in demotic Egyptian, is essentially a
Romance-type history of Egypt.[40] Some works circulated in
both languages.[41] We also find in both languages works which
have interesting resemblances to the *Alexander Romance*. These
include the *Romance of Sesonchosis*,[42] and the story of Amenophis
– fighting the gods reminds us strongly of Nectanebo's similar
position in the *Alexander Romance*.[43] A Ptolemaic tale of an
Egyptian army in the Land of the Amazons also recalls the
atmosphere of our work.[44] Similarly the story of King Thulis,[45]
who asked the oracle of the god Serapis, 'Has there ever been
another king as powerful as I? or will there ever be?', reminds us
very much of Alexander's own questions to the same god regard-
ing his death. Unfortunately few of these legendary texts can be
firmly dated.

The figure of Nectanebo recurs several times in these texts.[46]
As the last Pharaoh of Egypt (his Egyptian name is Nekhthorheb)
before the Persian conquest, he was regarded to some extent in a
Messianic aspect, as the king who would return to drive out
foreign rule. Hence the significance of Alexander's reception in
Memphis as the son of Nectanebo or the Pharaoh incarnate. It
seems clear that folk tales of this kind were familiar in early
Ptolemaic Alexandria, and, furthermore, that they had an impact
on Greek literary works even of a quite sophisticated kind.

The same point may be made concerning the *Romance*'s account of the foundation of Alexandria (I.31). This reflects Egyptian tradition, but also corresponds to a stylistic feature of Greek
literature that involved the explication of obscure monuments.
This literary technique began with Herodotus in Egypt and
continued to the eighth-century collection of legends concern-

ing the monuments of Constantinople.[47] Aetiology – 'giving accounts of causes' – is one of the major literary forms of Alexandrian literature, and is intimately connected with the Alexandrian poets' project to humanize and make approachable the heroic myths.[48]

These considerations suggest that the *Alexander Romance* would by no means be out of place in the literary context of third-century-BC Alexandria. It is of course impossible to state that the *Romance* in precisely its present form dates from that period. Much of the material that clearly was added later – notably that from the Jewish tradition – had certainly begun to circulate at this time. One must imagine a continuous process of rewriting up to the composition of our earliest manuscript in the third century AD, and beyond. The reason for its acquiring a canonical form at this time must be connected with the growing interest in the lives of great men, already noted. This point can be sharpened by a consideration of the literary character of the work in terms of genre.

THE GENRE OF THE *ALEXANDER ROMANCE*

What kind of a work is the *Alexander Romance*? The title we give to it begs a considerable question. There is no Greek word for romance, and the nature and the genesis of the genre have been a matter of some controversy. In 1876 Erwin Rohde argued, in an influential work,[49] that romance was a creation of the Second Sophistic – the period of revival of Greek literature in the second and third centuries AD – and that it resulted from a convergence of the picaresque adventure tale or travel account with a love story. At that time the only ancient romances known belonged to that period: Heliodorus' *Aethiopica* (probably *c.* AD 220–50), Achilles Tatius' *Clitophon and Leucippe* (second century AD), and perhaps Longus' *Daphnis and Chloe* (date uncertain).

Rohde's view of the origins of romance was exploded by the discovery of a number of papyri of substantially earlier date than these works, containing Hellenistic works with a similar subject matter. Now that romance had to be given an origin in the Hellenistic period, it was not difficult to find analogues in existing

Hellenistic literature:[50] the love tales of Hellenistic poets, which utilized obscure local legends for the purposes of piquant narrative, seemed to be closely similar in content though they were written in verse. The only difference lay in the greater length of the prose romances. Their characters are epic heroes newly clad in bourgeois dress and with their emotions tailored to fit a more domestic world.

But a definition of romance primarily as a love story does not fit the *Alexander Romance* at all. It is more illuminating to see this work as a descendant of the adventure narrative, which goes back – who could expect otherwise? – to the roots of Greek literature, the poetry of Homer. Some of Odysseus' adventures have a love interest, others do not. The only essential difference between what are usually called romances and Homer, is that the latter is in verse, the former in prose. The unhistoricity of the narratives of romance is made explicit by the fabulous character of many of the events. This is a feature that goes back to Homer with his one-eyed giants, to Hesiod's Long-heads, Dog-heads and Pygmies, and to some of the taller tales of Herodotus. The traveller's tale became a recognizable genre as early as the fifth century BC, but was easily contaminated with tall stories. A good example is the tale of Iambulus (undated, but probably third century BC) and his journey to the Paradise Islands.[51] Such tales were satirized by Lucian (second century AD) in his *Icaromenippus*, the story of a man whose many adventures include, like Baron Munchausen's, a visit to the moon. Lucian's *True History* also picks up some typical tall stories, some of which recall the *Alexander Romance*: for example, the Pillars of Heracles and Dionysus (Lucian, I.7) or the men in the Moon who, having no mouths, feed on smells (Lucian, I.23).

What distinguishes the *Alexander Romance* from wonder tales of this kind is its use of a historical figure as hero. Narrative inevitably aspires, or at least pretends, to the condition of history. That is why so many authors of romance called themselves Xenophon: the simple one-thing-after-another narrative of Xenophon was a highly appropriate model for the picaresque.

Setting was at least as important in the plot as the characters. There is a quasi-nationalist aspect to these romances, consonant with the origins of the genre in local legends. This aspect of

Hellenistic romance facilitated its adoption by Jewish writers in those numerous works that aim to identify Jewish interests and to establish their independence and dignity against their Greek masters – 'to promote cultural survival'.[52] Many of the books of the Apocrypha fit this description – the books of Esther, Tobit, Judith, Daniel, Ruth and Susanna – as well as some of the Pseudepigrapha – for example, III Maccabees and the Testament of Joseph. In many of these an adventure story, often with a love element, serves to clarify and confirm Jewish self-consciousness, and establishes – for example, with Daniel or Esther – the type of the wise man or clever champion of his/her own culture.

The influence of romance in this form on Jewish writing took a further step in the development of the Apocryphal Gospels and Apocryphal Acts of the early Christian period.[53] These combined a series of travel and wonder tales with an account of the life of a single character. In doing so they drew also on the traditional forms of ancient biography, the purposes of which were neatly summarized by Plutarch.[54]

> I am writing biography, not history, and the truth is that the most brilliant exploits often tell us nothing of the virtues or vices of the men who performed them, while on the other hand a chance remark or a joke may reveal far more of a man's character than the mere feat of winning battles in which thousands fall.

His purpose was above all to illustrate character, and he followed Aristotle in believing that the best way to understand character was to look at acts or actions (*praxeis*).[55] In this connection it is striking that some MSS of the *Alexander Romance* refer to the work as the 'Acts' or 'Life and Acts' of Alexander.

There is another strand to ancient biography that has been called aretalogy[56] – literally, a 'description of virtues'. Though the ultimate model is Plato's account of the last days of Socrates, generally this kind of biography has a higher proportion of miraculous elements. Again, the confluence of Jewish and Greek traditions is important: a good example of such a life is Philo's *Life of Moses*, which follows closely the Biblical narrative while presenting it in a form suitable for Greeks, with discussion of such miracles as that of the Burning Bush.

These models provide us with all the fundamental features of the apocryphal lives of the Apostles: a prolonged wandering by the hero, the performance of miracles, the regular presence of a companion as foil, sea journeys, fights with dragons, discovery of sunken cities and great treasures, the worship of the hero as a god, the encounters with cannibals and monsters, wondrous plants, strange races and talking animals, struggles to escape erotic entanglements, the help of God given at crucial moments, and the incidence of oracles, prophetic dreams and divine orders. All these features can easily be paralleled in the *Alexander Romance*. The Acts of Thomas include several specific parallels, including a visit to India. The Acts of Andrew and Matthias include a visit to the Anthropophagi. And so on. These Apocryphal Acts belong of course to the Christian era, two to three centuries later than the date at which we have argued the earliest form of the *Alexander Romance* was composed. But it is precisely the romance elements that are least in evidence in the first recension of the *Romance*, the one that clings most closely to the form of Hellenistic history. The development of Hellenistic romance in the Christian period has in turn influenced the successive rewritings of the *Romance*.

The development we should thus envisage is as follows: in the decades after Alexander's death a history was composed, on a broadly biographical framework, with extensive rhetorical passages such as the Debate in Athens. To this was added, perhaps as an integral part of the very composition of the history, a series of letters that characterize the clever man and diplomat (some of the most successful writing is in the correspondence of Alexander and Darius). A second series of letters, included in only brief form in the earliest version, gave the opportunity for continued expansion of the romance elements and an increasing assimilation of the work to the form of the Apostolic Acts, in consonance with which the work eventually comes to be referred to as the Acts of Alexander. This process can probably be imagined as continuing from the third century BC right up to the dates of the two later recensions. The writing down of the first recension in the third century AD ties in very neatly with the new enthusiasm for *Lives* of saints, sages and holy men which was then gaining momentum. The *Alexander Romance* approximated to this genre but was found not to be extravagant enough, and so was gradually adapted to meet the expectations of that genre.

This development went still further with the increasing importance of the fabulous element in the later versions. Such aspects of Alexander's character as his desire to go beyond the limits of the known world and to discover the precise date of his death (or, perhaps, to be assured of his immortality) receive growing attention. Episodes such as the descent in the diving bell, the ascent into the air, the admonitions not to seek for immortality and the search for the Water of Life are precisely the elements that are completely absent in the earliest version, and must, therefore, have been introduced into the narrative well after the beginning of the Christian era. Many of them have a heavily Christian colouring which becomes even more pronounced in the Syriac versions, and which may also be directly related to such themes in Babylonian literature as Gilgamesh's search for the secret of immortality in the *Epic of Gilgamesh*.[57]

The dominant theme of the wonder tales is the quest for immortality. This motif is combined with the historically attested – though controversial – facts of Alexander's seeking to be worshipped as a god. Soon after his conquest of Persia, Alexander began to demand the treatment and honours appropriate to a god, prompting Demosthenes to say, 'Let him be a god if he wants to.' This was partly manifested in the controversial insistence on prostration before him in the Persian style, and partly in outright demands for worship. The dividing line between man and god was less absolute in antiquity than it is now, and Alexander would not have been the first mortal to ascend the skies: apart from his ancestor Heracles, the Spartan general Lysander had recently been accorded cult status at Samos.[58] Alexander's achievements made him godlike, and this was acknowledged in contemporary and later writers.[59]

But by the time the *Romance* was written, Alexander's achievement was less easy to define. The Empire he had conquered was fragmented again; the god's achievement had proved impermanent. So the search for immortality reflects the tragedy as well as the wonder of Alexander, the impermanence of his conquest as

well as its immensity. Each succeeding version makes more of
Alexander's relation to God, his dependence on and trust in
'Providence above', and his eventual submission to the divine
commands to 'go no further'. In the Brahman episode we see the
motif stood on its head. When the Brahmans ask Alexander for
immortality, he states plainly that it is impossible for any man to
give that. Alexander in the later versions of the *Romance* has
become a sage more than a conqueror, an exemplar of virtue
specifically in his continence. (The latter trait is, however, docu-
mented also in Plutarch's *Fortune of Alexander*, pp. 328 f.[60])

By the second century AD the man of influence is already
beginning to be not the one who has political power but the one
who is in touch with the gods. The fictional Alexander of the
later versions looks not only back to the yearning fanatical youth
and conqueror, but forward to the Holy Man of the fourth
century.[61] In his adaptability as a figure of legend lies the secret
of his endurance through the centuries.

The two closest parallels from antiquity to the *Romance* may
help us to characterize the respective ends of this development.
One of these is a popular work, the anonymous *Life of Aesop*; the
other much more literary, written in the second century AD,
just about the time of our earliest recension of the *Romance*, the
Life of Apollonius of Tyana by Philostratus.

The *Life of Aesop*[62] has been dated to every century from the
fifth century BC (soon after Aesop's death) to the fourteenth
century AD. Papyri now show that it cannot be later than the
third century AD. It is very probable that it originated in early
Hellenistic Alexandria. It resembles the *Alexander Romance* in a
number of ways: Aesop, like Alexander, is represented as a
clever inventor; both works have in common the ascent in an
eagle-chariot and the involvement of Nectanebo; and the *Life of
Aesop*, like the *Romance*, is an example of a Greek work borrowing Egyptian ways of thinking and writing.

Stylistically, the *Life of Apollonius of Tyana*[63] is a complete
contrast – a highly polished literary encomium of a remarkable
sage and wonder-worker, who shows interesting similarities to
Jesus Christ. It, nonetheless, contains numerous parallels with –
perhaps borrowings from – the *Alexander Romance*, including a

visit to the Brahmans, a visit to Meroe, and a visit to the Great King's palace. It is a secular or pagan analogue to the Christian Gospels. It belongs to the literary life of the imperial court circles of the early third century AD, when considerable interest was being shown in oriental religions.

The *Alexander Romance* is a popular, uneducated version of the same kind of work. Although it concerns a conqueror and not a wise man like Aesop or Apollonius, Alexander has, as we have seen, taken on important characteristics of the sage. The best modern analogy is not with literature but with film. The *Alexander Romance* is Cecil B. de Mille's Gospel of Alexander.

NOTES

In these notes the following abbreviations are used. *FGrH* = *Fragmente der griechischen Historiker*; *POxy* = *Papyrus Oxyrhynchus*; *PSI* = *Pubblicazioni della Società italiana per la ricerca dei papyri greci e Latini in Egitto*.

1. W. W. Tarn, *The Greeks in Bactria and India* (Cambridge, 1951), p. 302.
2. Tarn, op. cit., p. 408.
3. S. K. Eddy, *The King is Dead: Studies in the Near Eastern Resistance to Hellenism 334–31 BC* (Lincoln, Nebraska, 1961), chs. 2 and 3; James Darmesteter 'La Légende d'Alexandre chez les Parses', *Essais Orientaux* (Paris, 1883), pp. 227–50.
4. L. Boulnois, *The Silk Road* (London, 1966), p. 161.
5. The main historical accounts of Alexander are those of Arrian, Quintus Curtius Rufus and Plutarch. Among modern biographies one may mention those of U. Wilcken (New York, 1967); W. W. Tarn (Cambridge, 1948); Robin Lane Fox (London, 1973); and A. B. Bosworth, *Conquest and Empire: The Reign of Alexander the Great* (Cambridge, 1988).
6. The articles of Badian are too numerous to list here. There is an excellent bibliography of Alexander studies in Bosworth, op. cit.
7. S. M. Stern, *Aristotle on the World State* (Oxford, 1968).
8. D. W. Engels, *Alexander the Great and the Logistics of the Macedonian Army* (Berkeley, 1978).
9. In L Iolaus is called Ioullos; in A, Iollas.
10. See in general G. Cary, *The Medieval Alexander* (Cambridge, 1956) and D. J. A. Ross, *Alexander Historiatus* (London, 1963).

11. See David Holton, *The Tale of Alexander: The Rhymed Version* (Thessaloniki, 1974).

12. See in general A. Abel, *Le Roman d'Alexandre* (Brussels, 1955); T. Nöldeke, *Beiträge zur Geschichte des Alexanderroman, Denkschriften der kaiserl. Akad. der Wissenschaften, phil-hist. Klasse 38* (Vienna, 1890).

13. *The Sikander Nama* (London, 1881), tr. H. Wilberforce Clarke; W. Bacher, *Nizamis Leben und Werke* (Leipzig, 1871).

14. *The Shahnama of Firdausi*, tr. A. G. Warner and E. Warner (1912), vol. 6. For other Persian Alexander works see *Iskandernameh*, tr. Minoo S. Southgate (New York, 1978); J. A. Boyle, *Bulletin of the John Rylands Library*, 60 (1977), pp. 13–27.

15. J. A. Boyle, *Zentralasiatische Studien*, 9 (1965), pp. 265–73.

16. See the Note on the Text, pp. 28–32.

17. See Reinhold Merkelbach, *Die Quellen des griechischen Alexanderroman* (Munich, 1954; 2nd edn 1977); D. J. A. Ross, op. cit:

18. Dino Pieraccioni, *Lettere del Ciclo di Alessandro in un Papiro Egiziano* (Florence, 1947); re-edited by M. Norsa and V. Bartoletti, *PSI*, XII, no. 1285 (Florence, 1951).

19. Josephus, *Antiquities of the Jews*, XI.8.

20. This is also the view of M. Braun, *History and Romance in Graeco-Oriental Literature* (Oxford, 1938).

21. See A. E. Samuel, 'The Earliest Elements in the Alexander Romance', *Historia*, 35 (1986), pp. 427–37; C. B. Welles, 'The Discovery of Sarapis and the Foundation of Alexandria', *Historia*, 11 (1962), pp. 271–98. See also R. Bagnall, 'The Date of the Foundation of Alexandria', *American Journal of Ancient History*, 4 (1979), pp. 46–9; *POxy* XVI, 1798; Lionel Pearson, *The Lost Histories of Alexander the Great* (Chico, California, 1960), pp. 255 f.

22. *Alexander Romance*, II.17; cf. Quintus Curtius, 4.11.14, Plutarch, *Alexander*, 29.

23. Engels, op. cit., p. 84, n. 67.

24. The *Alexander Romance* mentions the return of Nectanebo to his country at I.34; a similar idea appears in the Oracle of the Potter (*POxy* 2332; L. Koenen, *Zeitschrift für Papyrologie und Epigraphik*, 2 (1968), pp. 178–209), which probably reflects the anti-Greek feelings of 'poor white' Graeco-Egyptians, though it may date from any time between the fourth and the late second centuries BC: see Dorothy Thompson, *Memphis under the Ptolemies* (Princeton, 1988), pp. 82 and 152–3 nn.; Eddy, op. cit., p. 293.

25. O. Weinreich, *Der Trug des Nektanebos* (Leipzig and Berlin, 1911).

26. P. M. Fraser, *Ptolemaic Alexandria* (Oxford, 1972), p. 267.

27. *Demosthenes*, 23.4. Cf. Diodorus Siculus, 17.5.1; Adolf Ausfeld, *Der griechische Alexanderroman* (Leipzig, 1907), p. 152. A piece of Hellenistic tragic history (*FGrH* IIB, no. 153 F 8; *POxy* II, 216) in which an Athenian orator speaks against Alexander may represent a source, or a parallel, for this episode.

28. Merkelbach, op. cit., pp. 193 ff.

29. Quintus Curtius, 7.3; 7.4.29.

30. Quintus Curtius, 5.6.12–14; Engels, op. cit., pp. 74 f.

31. Arrian, 5.14.3–5. Lucian, *How to Write History*, 12, says that this source was Aristobulus; but Arrian implies that it was *not* in Aristobulus. Lucian is in error. Waldemar Heckel points out to me that the source is not Onesicritus either because the latter gives a different version from these writers of the death of Bucephalus.

32. Arrian, 7.13.2; Plutarch, *Alexander*, 46.4–5; W. W. Tarn, *Alexander the Great* (Cambridge, 1948), p. 329.

33. ed. W. Berghoff, *Palladius de gentibus Indiae et Bragmanibus* (Meisenheim, 1967). There is a Latin translation ascribed to St Ambrose: V. Scheiwiller, *De moribus Brachmanorum liber Sancto Ambrosio adscriptus* (Milan, 1956).

34. Pearson, op. cit., p. 259.

35. Aeschines, *Against Ctesiphon*, 165; cf. Plutarch, *Alexander*, 63; Quintus Curtius, 9.2.9; 9.3.8; 9.6.22; 5.6.12–14; Arrian, 5.26.2; Engels, op. cit., pp. 74 f. The region was always a repository of legend: W. W. Tarn, *The Greeks in Bactria and India*, pp. 105–9. Aristotle thought that Ocean was visible from the Hindu Kush (*Meteor*, 1.13.15): see F. C. Holt, *Alexander the Great and Bactria* (Leiden, 1988), pp. 71–2. Plutarch (*Theseus*, 1) remarks on the propensity of writers to fill ill-explored regions with fabulous beasts and plants.

36. N. Lewis, *Greeks in Ptolemaic Egypt* (Oxford, 1986); Alan K. Bowman, *Egypt after the Pharaohs* (Oxford, 1986); Dorothy Thompson, op. cit.; A. E. Samuel, *The Shifting Sands of History: Interpretations of Ptolemaic Egypt* (Lanham, MD, 1989).

37. Titles include Demetrius' work *On the Kings of Judaea*, Artapanus' *Romance of Moses* (*FGH*, 726 – a nationalist romantic aretalogy of about 100 BC, designed to combat the anti-Jewish accounts of Manetho known to us from Josephus, *Contra Apionem*, 1.228 ff.; Philo the Elder's *Life of Moses*, Aristobulus' *Commentary on Moses* (written under Ptolemy VI, 181–145 BC), Pseudo-Hecataeus, *On the Jews* (200–150 BC), Eupolemus, *On the Kings in Judaea* (150 BC), and the work of the late-second-century historian Jason of Cyrene, which was utilized by the author of II Maccabees.

38. Epigram 54 may echo Isaiah 14.12, and his Iambus IV describes a contest of talking trees, a form familiar in Middle Eastern literature.

39. *De Iside et Osiride*, 360 B.

40. ed. W. Spiegelberg, *Die sogenannte demotische Chronik* (Leipzig, 1914).

41. For example, the Tale of Tefnut: J. V. Powell, *New Chapters in the History of Greek Literature*, 3rd series (Oxford, 1933), p. 227. S. West, *Journal of Egyptian Archaeology*, 55 (1969), pp. 161 ff.

42. *POxy* 1826, 2466, 3319 – all papyri of the third century AD.

43. *POxy* 3011 (third century AD). Cf. Josephus, *Contra Apionem*, 1.243 ff.; M. Braun points out the resemblance.

44. E. Bresciani, *Letteratura e poesia dell' antico Egitto* (Turin, 1969).

45. Suda, s.v., Thoulis. The god's reference in his reply to 'god, word and spirit' suggests a date in the Christian period for this tale. The punchline comes with Thoulis' departure from the sanctuary, upon which he is immediately murdered.

46. See B. E. Perry, 'The Egyptian Legend of Nectanebus', *Transactions of the American Philological Association*, 97 (1966), pp. 327 ff.

47. Averil Cameron and Judith Herrin, *Constantinople in the Early Eighth Century: the Parastaseis Syntomai Chronikai* (Leiden, 1984).

48. On some similar folk-tale aetiologies, see S. West, 'And it came to pass that Pharaoh dreamed', *Classical Quarterly*, 37 (1987), pp. 262–71.

49. E. Rohde, *Der griechische Roman* (Leipzig, 1876).

50. B. Lavagnini, *Studi sul Romanzo greco* (Messina–Florence, 1950).

51. Diodorus Siculus, II.55–60.

52. Moses Hadas, *Aristeas to Philocrates* (New York, 1951), p. 127.

53. Rosa Söder, *Die Apokryphen Apostelgeschichten* (Stuttgart, 1932).

54. Plutarch, *Alexander*, 1.

55. cf. Aristotle, *Poetics*, 1450a1–2 and *Rhetoric*, 1359a, where it is argued that one can generalize from *praxeis*, and that they are therefore a useful object of study.

56. R. Reitzenstein, *Hellenistische Wundererzählungen* (Leipzig, 1906).

57. Bruno Meissner, *Alexander und Gilgamos* (Leipzig, 1894; Berlin, 1928).

58. See Ch. Habicht, *Gottmenschtum und griechische Städte*, 2nd edn (Munich, 1970), pp. 3–7.

59. W. Kroll, *Historia Alexandri Magni recensio vetusta* (Berlin, 1926).

60. cf. T. Nöldeke, *Beiträge zur Geschichte des Alexanderroman, Denkschriften der Kaiserl. Akad. der Wissenschaften, phil.-hist. Klasse 38* (Vienna, 1890).

61. Peter Brown, 'The Rise and Function of the Holy Man in Late Antiquity', *Journal of Roman Studies*, 61 (1971), pp. 80–101.

62. B. E. Perry, *Aesopica* (Urbana, Illinois, 1952), dates it to the first
    century AD.
63. tr. C. P. Jones (Penguin Classics, 1970).

A NOTE ON THE TEXT

The textual history of the *Alexander Romance* is an unusually complicated one, and cannot be ignored in approaching the translation. There are three major traditions or recensions, each of which contains material differing substantially from the other two. Our earliest version, known as A, is a single MS of the third century AD.[1] Of the extant versions, this most closely resembles a conventional historical work, with a detailed account of Alexander's activities in Greece, and formal rhetorical debates in the classical manner to illuminate the issues. It contains virtually none of the fabulous elements prevalent in later versions, though it is precisely these elements that are the most conspicuous and familiar from the post-Greek and non-literary traditions.

The single MS of A represents the closest approach to what may be posited as the original form of the *Romance*. This hypothetical original is known as α.[2] A contains several large and small lacunae. These lacunae may be supplemented from two early translations of A, a Latin one by Julius Valerius (after AD 300), and an Armenian one perhaps by Moses of Khoren (fifth century AD).[3] In particular, the Armenian version gives a fuller version of Alexander's letter to Aristotle about India (III.7–16; see Supplement I, pp. 181–5) of which a yet fuller version is the independent Latin Epistula.[4]

Deriving from α is β, a fuller version known in several MSS and probably dating from between AD 300 and 550.[5] In this version the verse passages have been recast as prose, and some (unsuccessful) attempts have been made to restore the confused chronology in the first book.

β is the source of a further recension λ, represented by five MSS, in which the adventures recounted in the letter to Olym-

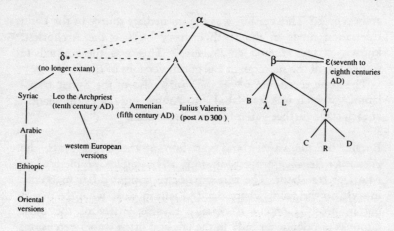

The recensions of the *Alexander Romance*
Note: Greek letters indicate recensions, upper-case letters indicate
manuscripts. A dotted line indicates uncertain origin.

pias (II.38–41) are greatly expanded. In particular, this is the only
β-version to include the descent in the diving bell and the flight
into the air. Very close to the λ-recension is another MS of β,
L,[6] which contains some additional unique material (for example,
the letter to Olympias in III.33).

In about the eighth century a new version, ε, was compiled
from a combination of the original α and some material from β,
as well as from parts of the letter to Aristotle on India, from
Palladius on the Brahmans (ε.30–31) and Pseudo-Methodius on
the Unclean Nations (ε.39 and 45.2).[7] This last addition gives us
a *terminus post quem* for the recension, as Pseudo-Methodius is to
be dated *c.* AD 640. Both ε and β were then combined in the
composition of the latest and longest version, γ.[8] This version is
characterized by a markedly inferior style, inept metres and
some notably tasteless passages. γ has a heavy admixture of Jewish
and Christian material, which probably originated many centuries before its use in this recension.

δ★, a fourth version of the *Romance* which is now no longer
extant, was based either on A or on another version of the

archetype α.[9] This version was the immediate source of the Latin translation made in the tenth century by Leo the Archpriest, known as the *Historia de Proeliis*.[10] This was the immediate source for all the subsequent European versions of the *Romance*.

The same recension, δ*, is the source also of the Syriac translation,[11] which was translated into Arabic and then Ethiopian;[12] at each stage further variants were introduced.

Because of the variety and variation of the Greek texts, the *Alexander Romance* presents an unusually complex problem to an editor or translator. The three major recensions differ markedly in style, to the point where one (A) tells in verse what the others tell in prose. Content is equally diverse: many of the most famous episodes occur only in the late and often crass γ-recension, while the debate in Athens and the conquest of Thebes, as well as Alexander's will, appear in full only in A. Different readers will seek different things from a translation: the historian will look for the possibly historical material of A, the medievalist or orientalist will wish to trace the originals of the wonder tales in the texts familiar to him, while the general reader will simply want to read as much of the Greek legendary material about Alexander as possible.

The only solution seemed to be to provide a composite text. No way of doing this can be completely satisfactory: some events are told in a different order in different recensions (the meeting with the Brahmans); others are displaced historically and occur twice even in a single recension (the sack of Thebes in L). Several passages of A are lost in the single MS and have to be restored from the Armenian translation or from Julius Valerius. The spelling of proper names varies from one recension to another also. Editors of the Greek recensions have used a single system of chapter-numbering for all versions, so that some chapter numbers are absent in some of the recensions.

What I have done is to translate the whole of L, being the fullest version of the β-recension, and to insert into the narrative, where practicable, the extra material that occurs in the other recensions. These passages are enclosed within bold square brackets and their source is indicated at the end of each passage. In some cases the narratives diverge too widely for this to be possible, and here I have given the versions of A or γ as supplements to be found together on pp. 161–88 the points at which they would have occurred are noted in the main text. Angle brackets indicate passages that are lost in the Greek MS, but have been restored by comparison with the Armenian version. Where a passage of A was restored by Kroll from the Armenian, I have used the modern English translation of the Armenian text by A. M. Wolohojian,[13] though I have changed proper names from their uncouth Armenian forms into ones consistent with the rest of the narrative.

The long section on the meeting with the Brahmans posed a particular problem. Both A and γ insert here (III.7–16) the bulk of a separate work by Palladius, a fourth-century writer, *On the Brahmans*. Despite its intrinsic interest, I have omitted this as it is in many respects a doublet of the *Romance*'s own narrative and is not strictly part of the same work. (Kroll did likewise in his edition of the A-text.)

Consistency in the Anglicization of Greek names is impossible and I have aimed to be clear and not to confuse or to jolt the reader.

The *Alexander Romance* is not a literary masterpiece. It is definitely popular literature. That at least eases the task of the translator. The importance of the *Romance* lies in the rich store of fabulous material that it drew together and bequeathed to the civilizations of both East and West. This I hope to have made more accessible to the general reader, in what is to date the only full translation into English.

NOTES

1. W. Kroll, *Historia Alexandri Magni* (Berlin, 1926).
2. Adolf Ausfeld, *Der griechische Alexanderroman* (Leipzig, 1907), is an attempt to reconstruct on *a priori* principles the hypothetical α; there is an English translation of Ausfeld's reconstruction by E. H. Haight (New York, 1955).
3. A. Wolohojian, *The Romance of Alexander the Great by Pseudo-Callisthenes* (New York, 1969).

4. F. Gunderson, *Alexander's Letter to Aristotle about India* (Meisenheim am Glan, 1980).

5. Leif Bergson, *Der griechische Alexanderroman, Rezension β* (Uppsala, 1965).

6. Helmut van Thiel, *Leben und Taten Alexanders von Makedonien nach der Handschrift L* (Darmstadt, 1983).

7. J. Trumpf, *Vita Alexandri Regis Macedonum* (Stuttgart, 1974).

8. *Der griechische Alexanderroman Rezension γ*: vol. 1, ed. Ursula Lauenstein (Meisenheim, 1962); vol. 2, ed. Hartmut Engelmann (Meisenheim, 1963); vol. 3, ed. F. Parthe (Meisenheim, 1969).

9. The existence of δ* is taken as a datum by A. Ausfeld, *Der griechische Alexanderroman* (1907), F. Pfister, *Historia de Proeliis* (Heidelberg, 1913) and G. Cary, *The Medieval Alexander* (Cambridge, 1956).

10. ed. F. Pfister, op. cit.; Michael Feldbusch, *Die Historia de Proeliis Alexandri Magni* (Meisenheim am Glan, 1976).

11. E. A. Wallis Budge, *The History of Alexander the Great* (Cambridge, 1889).

12. E. A. Wallis Budge, *The Life and Exploits of Alexander the Great* (Cambridge, 1896), and *The Alexander Book in Ethiopia* (Cambridge, 1933).

13. See note 3.

THE
GREEK ALEXANDER ROMANCE

THE LIFE AND DEEDS OF
ALEXANDER OF MACEDON

BOOK I

1. In our opinion, Alexander the king of the Macedonians was the best and most noble of men, for he did everything in his own way, finding that his foresight always worked in harness with his virtues. When he made war against a people, the time he spent in his campaigns was not sufficient for those who wished to research the affairs of the cities. We are going now to speak of the deeds of Alexander, of the virtues of his body and his spirit, of his good fortune in action and his bravery; and we will begin with his family and his paternity. Many say that he was the son of King Philip, but they are deceivers.[1] This is untrue: he was not Philip's son, but the wisest of the Egyptians say that he was the son of Nectanebo,[2] after the latter had fallen from his royal state.

This Nectanebo was skilled in the art of magic, and by its use overcame all peoples and thus lived in peace. If ever a hostile power came against him, he did not prepare armies, nor build engines of war nor construct transport wagons, he did not trouble his officers with military exercises, but took a bowl and carried out a divination by water. He filled the bowl with spring water and with his hands moulded ships and men of wax, and placed them in the bowl. Then he robed himself in the priestly robes of a prophet and took an ebony staff in his hand. Standing erect, he called on the so-called[3] gods of spells and the airy spirits and the demons below the earth, and by the spell the wax figures came to life. Then he sank the ships in the bowl, and straightaway, as they sank, so the ships of the enemy which were coming against him perished. All this came about because of the man's great experience in the magic art. And thus his kingdom continued in peace.

2. After some time had gone by there came men on reconnaissance, whom the Romans call *exploratores* and the Greeks *kataskopoi*, and they informed Nectanebo of a black cloud of war, a force of innumerable armed men advancing on Egypt. Nectanebo's general came to him and said: 'O King, live for ever! Put aside now all the ways of peace and prepare yourself for the manoeuvres of war. For a great storm cloud of barbarians is threatening us: it is not one people that advances against us, but a horde of 10,000. Those who are coming against us are the Indians, the Nocimaeans, the Oxydorcae, the Iberians, the Kauchones, the Lelapes, the Bosporoi, the Bastranoi, the Azanians, the Chalybes and all the other great peoples of the East,[4] and their massed army of countless armed men is advancing on Egypt. Set all else aside and consider your position.'

This is what the general said to Nectanebo. But the king laughed and said to him: 'You have spoken well and fittingly for one to whom our protection has been entrusted, but you speak like a coward and not like a soldier. Strength does not lie in numbers, but the issue of war depends on zeal. One lion may overcome many deer, and one wolf may shear many flocks of sheep. Go with the soldiers who are under your command and get ready for battle. But I, with a single word, shall overwhelm this huge horde of barbarians in the sea.' And so saying, Nectanebo sent his general away.

3. Nectanebo stood up and went into his palace, and when he was alone he made all his usual preparations and gazed into the bowl. There he saw the gods of Egypt steering the ships of the barbarians, and the armies under the command of the same gods. Nectanebo, being a man experienced in magic and accustomed to talk with his gods, realized that the end of the Egyptian kingdom was at hand. He filled his garments with gold, and shaved his hair and beard. Thus transformed in appearance, he fled to Pelusium. From there he sailed away to Pella in Macedonia, and settled there as an Egyptian prophet, and foretold to many people events that were hidden in the stars.

Meanwhile, the Egyptians asked their so-called gods what had become of the King of Egypt, since all of Egypt had been overrun by the barbarians. And the self-styled god in the sanctuary of the Serapeum spoke an oracle to them: 'This king who has fled will return to Egypt not as an old man but as a youth, and he will overcome our enemies the Persians.' They asked one another what the meaning of this saying might be; but, finding no answer, they wrote down the oracle that had been given to them on the pedestal of the statue of Nectanebo.

4. Nectanebo soon became a familiar figure to everyone in Macedonia. [King Philip happened to be childless by his wife, Olympias, and as he was going to be away at war for a long time, he called her to him and said, 'Take note of this: if you do not bear me a son after I return from the war, you shall never know my embrace again.'

When the day ended, Philip went off to war with his entire army. One of Olympias' servants, realizing why her mistress was so sad, said to her, 'Lady, I have something to tell you; I will say it, if you will not hold it against me.'

'Speak,' replied the queen, 'I shall not hold it against you. If it is what I want to hear, I shall certainly owe you my thanks.' Then the maid went on, 'There is in the city a man from Egypt who is able to fulfil everything that the soul desires, if you will only allow him to see you.' Olympias did not hesitate but sent for him right away and ordered him to come in to her. *γ-text*]

When Nectanebo saw her, he began to lust after her beauty. He held out his hand and said, 'Greetings, queen of the Macedonians.'

'Greetings to you too, most excellent of prophets,' she replied. 'Come in and sit down.

'You are the Egyptian teacher,' she went on, 'in whom those who have tried you have found nothing but truth. I too was persuaded by you. What art of prophecy do you use to foretell the truth?'

'There are many and diverse methods of prophecy, O queen,' he replied. 'One may interpret horoscopes, or signs, or dreams; one may utter oracles from the belly or prophesy from the fleece of a lamb; and there are casters of nativities, and the so-called Magi, who are the masters of prophecy.'

So saying, he gave Olympias a sharp look.

'Prophet,' she said to him, 'have you turned to stone as you look at me?'

'Yes, madam,' he replied; 'for I remembered an oracle given to me by my own gods – "you must prophesy to a queen" – and see, it has come true. So tell me what you wish.'

Then he placed his hand in a fold of his garment and took out an extraordinary little writing tablet, constructed from gold, ivory, ebony and silver, and engraved with three zones. [On the first circle were the thirty-six decans, on the second the twelve signs of the zodiac, and on the inner one the Sun and Moon. He put it on a chair. Then he opened a small ivory box, revealing the seven stars and the ascendant made of eight precious stones, which lit up the pictured miniature heaven. The Sun was of crystal, the Moon of diamond, the Mars of haematite, the Mercury of emerald, the Jupiter of air-stone,[5] the Venus of sapphire, the Saturn of ophite and the pointer of white marble. *A-text*]

Olympias was full of wonder at the precious object; she ordered everyone to go away, sat down beside him and said, 'Prophet, cast a nativity for myself and Philip.' (There was a rumour going around that if Philip returned from the war, he would reject her and marry another.) Nectanebo said to her: 'Put down the hour of your birth, put down that of Philip.' What else did Nectanebo do? He placed his own nativity next to that of Olympias; then he made some calculations and said to her, 'The rumour which you have heard concerning you is no lie. I, as an Egyptian prophet, can help you to avoid rejection by Philip.'

'How can you do that?' she asked.

He replied: 'You must have intercourse with an incarnate god, become pregnant by him and bear his son and bring him up. He will be your avenger for the wrongs Philip has done you.'

'Who is the god?' asked Olympias.

'Ammon of Libya,' he replied.

Then Olympias asked him, 'What form does this god take?'

'He is a man of middle age,' replied the prophet, 'with hair and beard of gold, and horns growing from his forehead, these also made of gold. You must make yourself ready for him as befits a queen. This very day you will see this god come to you, in a dream.'

'If I see this dream,' said Olympias, 'I shall reverence you not as a magician, but as a god.'

5. So Nectanebo left the queen's chamber and collected from a desert place certain herbs which he knew to be reliable in dream-divination. He made an infusion with them, then moulded a female figure out of wax and wrote on it the name of Olympias. He lit torches ⟨and sprinkled on them the infusion⟩ of herbs, and called with the appropriate oaths on the demons whose function this is, to bring an apparition to Olympias. That very night, she had a vision of herself being embraced by the god Ammon. As he rose to leave her, he said to her, 'Woman, in your womb you now carry a male child who will avenge you.'

6. When Olympias awoke she was amazed. She sent for Nectanebo and said to him, 'I had a dream and saw the god Ammon whom you spoke of. I beg you, prophet, make him make love to me again, and be sure to let me know in advance when he is coming, so that I may be better prepared for the bridegroom.'

'First of all, lady,' he replied, 'that was a dream you saw. When he comes to you again, he will require something of you. But if your highness commands it, give me a room where I can sleep, so that I can make prayers to him on your behalf.'

'Very well,' she answered, 'you may make your resting place in my apartments. Then, if I become pregnant by the god, I will give you the great honours that a queen can, and shall treat you as if you were the father of the child.'

'You must know,' went on Nectanebo, 'that the following sign will be given before the god enters your room. If, as you rest at evening in your chamber, you see a serpent creeping towards you, order everyone to go outside. But do not put out the lamps, which I have prepared to give proper honour to the god, and which I will light and give you; no, go to your bed and make yourself ready, cover your face and do not look directly at the god whom you saw come to you in your dream.'

So saying, Nectanebo went away. The next day Olympias gave him a bedroom immediately adjoining her own.

7. Nectanebo, meanwhile, procured a fleece of softest sheep's wool, with the horns still attached to its temples. The horns shone like gold. He also procured an ebony sceptre, a white robe and a cloak resembling a serpent's skin. Wearing these, he entered the bedroom, where Olympias was lying under the coverlet, just peeping out. She saw him come in, but was not afraid, because he looked just as the god had done in her dream. The lamps were lit, and Olympias covered her face. Nectanebo, putting aside his sceptre, climbed on to the bed and made love to her. Then he said, 'Be calm, woman, in your womb you carry a male child who will avenge you and will become king and ruler of all the world.' Then he left the room, taking the sceptre with him, and hid all the pieces of his disguise.

The next morning when Olympias woke, she went into the room where Nectanebo was sleeping and roused him.

'Greetings, your majesty,' he said to her, rising from his bed, 'what news do you have for me?'

'I am amazed that you do not already know about it, prophet,' she replied. 'But will the god come to me again? For it was very sweet with him.'

'Listen, your majesty,' replied the prophet, 'I am the prophet of this god. If you will,' give me this place where I may sleep undisturbed, so that I can make the appropriate spells for him, and then he will come to you.'

And she replied, 'You may have this room from now on.' She gave orders that he should be given the key to the room. Then he hid his disguise in a secret place, and went in to her as often as Olympias wanted. And all the time she thought it was the god Ammon who came to her.

Day by day Olympias' belly grew, until one day she said to Nectanebo, 'What shall I say if Philip comes home and finds me pregnant?'

'Have no fear, queen,' replied the wizard. 'Ammon will come to your aid in the following way: he will appear to Philip in a dream and relate to him all that has occurred, so that Philip will not be able to make any accusation against you.'

In this way Olympias was taken in by the magic powers of Nectanebo.

8. Then Nectanebo took a sea-hawk and cast a spell on it: he instructed it in all the things he wished to tell Philip, and, when it was fully prepared by his black arts, sent it off to fly to Philip. The sea-hawk came by night to the place where Philip was, and spoke to him in a dream. When Philip saw the hawk speaking to him, he woke up in great disturbance of mind. At once he sent for a certain Babylonian dream-interpreter, who had a good reputation, and described the apparition.

'I saw in a dream some god, of great physical beauty, with grey hair and a grey beard; he had horns on his temples, which looked as if they were of gold, and in his hand he held a sceptre. I saw him go into my wife, Olympias, by night, and lie down with her and make love to her. Then the god stood up and said, "Woman, you have conceived a male child who will make you fruitful[6] and will avenge the death of his father." Then I saw myself sewing up her body with papyrus fibres and sealing it with my own ring.[7] The ring was of gold, with a stone in it, and on the stone were engraved the sun, a lion's head and a spear. While I watched this, I seemed to see a sea-hawk standing beside me, who roused me from sleep with the beating of his wings.

'Tell me, what does this signify?'

'Long live King Philip!' the dream-interpreter replied. 'What you saw in the dream is true. The sealing-up of the body of your wife is a reliable sign that she is pregnant; for no one seals up an empty vessel, but only one that has something in it. As for your sewing her up with papyrus – well, papyrus grows nowhere but in Egypt. The seed then is of Egyptian origin, and not humble, but glorious and of great fame, as the gold ring indicates. For what is more glorious than gold, with which we make our honours to the gods? And the seal portraying the sun, the lion's head and the spear shows that the child will fight against all peoples like a lion, and make their cities captive even as far as the place where the sun rises. The god whom you saw with ram's horns and grey hair is the Libyan god Ammon.'

Such was the dream-interpreter's answer, but Philip was not pleased when he heard it.

9. Olympias, for her part, was in a state of great anxiety, because she had no confidence in Nectanebo and his arrangements concerning Philip. When Philip came back from the war, he saw the disturbed state his wife was in and asked her, 'Wife, why are you so disturbed about what has happened? The sin was another's, as was made clear to me in a dream; so you cannot be faulted. We kings are all-powerful in respect of everyone, but not in respect of the gods. It was no common man who was your lover, but one of those far superior in comeliness to us.'

So saying, Philip put Olympias' mind at rest. She was full of gratitude to the prophet, who had informed Philip of all that had happened.

10. Some days later Philip said to Olympias, 'You were deceiving me, wife. You were not ravished by a god but by some other; and you may be sure he will not escape me.' Nectanebo took due note.

Soon there was a great feast in the palace, and everyone was celebrating with Philip the king's return. Only King Philip was cast down because of his wife's pregnancy. Suddenly Nectanebo turned himself into a serpent, larger than the previous one, and crept into the dining-room, hissing in a most fearsome way, so that the very foundations of the palace shook. When those who were dining with the king saw the serpent, they leapt from their places in fright; but Olympias, who recognized her special lover, extended her right hand to him. The serpent raised himself up and placed his head on her lap; he then coiled himself up and lay on her knees, popping his forked tongue in and out to kiss her – which the onlookers took as an indication of the serpent's affection for her.

Philip was at the same time annoyed and amazed, and could not take his eyes off the apparition. Suddenly the snake changed itself into an eagle and disappeared, no one could say where.

When Philip had recovered from his shock, he said, 'Woman, I have seen a sign of the god's concern for you, for he came to help you when you were in danger. But still I do not know which god this is. For he appeared to me in the form of Ammon, and Apollo and Asclepius.'

'He made clear to me when he lay with me,' Olympias replied, 'that he is Ammon, the god of all Libya.'

Then Philip congratulated himself on the god's favour, since the offspring of his own wife was to be the seed of a god.

11. Some days later, Philip was sitting in one of the palace gardens, where a great number of birds were pecking about for food. Suddenly, one of the birds leapt on to his lap and laid an egg there; but the egg rolled out, fell on to the ground and broke. At once a small snake shot out of it, made a circuit of the egg and then tried to re-enter by the way it had just come out. But when it had managed to get its head inside, it died. King Philip was disturbed by this and sent for an interpreter of signs, and recounted what he had seen. The interpreter, inspired by a god, announced to him, 'Your majesty, you will have a son, who will go round the world subduing all the peoples to his power, but then will return to his own kingdom and die a very short time afterwards. For the snake is a royal beast, and the egg, from which the snake emerged, resembles the world. So, having circled the world, and wanting to return to his origin, he was unable to do so and died.' The interpreter received rich gifts from Philip for interpreting the omen, and went away.

12. When the time had come for Olympias to give birth, she sat down on the birth-stool and went into labour. Nectanebo stood by her, measuring the courses of the heavenly bodies; he urged her not to hurry in giving birth. At the same time he jumbled up the cosmic elements by the use of his magic powers,[8] discovered what lay hidden in them, and said to her: 'Woman, contain yourself and struggle against the pressure of Nature![9] [Get up from your chair and take a little walk. Scorpio is dominating the horoscope, and the bright Sun, when he sees the beasts of heaven yoked together and going backwards, will turn one who is born at this hour altogether out of heaven.

'Take a grip of yourself, your majesty, and wait for this star as well. Cancer dominates the horoscope, and Saturn, who was the victim of a plot by his own children, and who cut off his genitals at the root and hurled them to Neptune, lord of the sea, and Pluto, god of the dead, making way for the majesty of Jupiter. ⟨If you give birth now⟩ your son will be a eunuch.

'Hold on a little longer. The horned Moon in her bull-drawn chariot has left the zenith and come down to earth to embrace the beautiful herdsman Endymion. Whoever is born now will die by fire.

'The next sign is not auspicious either. Bed-loving Venus, mother of archer Cupid, will kill the swineherd Adonis. Whoever is born in this hour will take the lustre of the women of Byblos and raise a great commotion around himself.

'Next is the lion-like rage of Mars. He is a lover of horses and war, but was exhibited naked and unarmed by the Sun on his adulterous bed. So whoever is born at this hour will be a laughing-stock.

'Wait also for the passing of Mercury, your majesty, the goat-horned next to the ill-omened one: or you will give birth to a quarrelsome pedant . . . Your son will be a monster.

'Sit down now, your majesty, on the chair of benefaction, and make your labours more frequent and energetic. Jupiter, the lover of virgins, who was pregnant with Dionysus in his thigh, is now high in the clear heaven, turning into horned Ammon between Aquarius and Pisces, and designating an Egyptian as world-ruler. Give birth NOW!' *A-text*]

And as the child fell to the ground, there were great claps of thunder and flashes of lightning, so that all the world was shaken.

13. Next morning, when Philip saw Olympias' new-born child, he said: 'I wished him not to be raised because he was not my own offspring, but now that I see that he is the seed of a god and the birth has been signalled by the heavens, let him be raised in memory of my son by my previous wife, who died, and let him be called Alexander.'[10]

After Philip had said this, every care was lavished on the child.

There were celebratory processions throughout Macedonia, and in Pella and also Thrace.

In order to make short the long story of the childhood of Alexander – he was weaned and reached puberty. When he was grown up, his appearance in no way resembled that of Philip or Olympias or the one who had sired him, but was quite unique. In shape he was a man, but his hair was that of a lion and his eyes were asymmetrical – the right one being downward-slanting and the left one clear;[11] his teeth were as sharp as nails, and his movements were as swift and violent as a lion's. His nurse was Lekane[12] the sister of Melas,[13] his tutor and attendant was Cleonides, his grammar teacher was Polynices, his music teacher Leucippus of Limnae, his geometry teacher Melemnus, a Peloponnesian, his teacher of rhetoric Anaximenes of Lampsacus, the son of Aristocles; and his philosophy teacher was Aristotle of Stageira, the son of Nicomachus.[14]

When Alexander had finished his education, which included astronomy, and had left school, he gave instruction to his fellow students in his turn. He used to draw them up in ranks for war and send them into battle. Whenever he saw one side being worsted by the other, he took the part of the losing side and helped them until they were winning again. This made it clear that he himself was Victory. He also went on military exercises with the troops, springing on to a horse and riding with them.

One day, Philip's grooms brought from the stables an exceptionally large colt and led him before the king. 'O lord king,' they said, 'we found this horse just born in the royal stables; and because his beauty excels even that of Pegasus, we have brought him before you, O king.' Philip was amazed when he saw the beauty and the stature of the horse, which had to be forcibly restrained and kept under guard, because, the grooms said, he was a man-eater. To this King Philip answered: 'Truly then the proverb of the Greeks is fulfilled, that good grows very close to evil. But since you have brought the horse to me, I will take him.'

Then he ordered his attendants to build an iron cage and to lock the colt inside, unbridled. 'And whoever is insubordinate to my rule, and has broken the law or been taken in the act of robbery, shall be thrown to the horse.' At once it was done as the king had ordered.

14. Alexander, meanwhile, was growing up, and when he was twelve years old he accompanied his father to a review of the troops. He wore armour, marched with the troops and leapt on to the horses, prompting this remark from Philip: 'Alexander, child, I love your character and your nobility, but not your appearance, because you in no way resemble me.'

All this was very irksome to Olympias. She called Nectanebo to her and said, 'Find out what Philip's intentions are concerning me.'

Alexander was sitting by them, and when Nectanebo took his tables and examined the heavens, he said, 'Father, what you call the stars, are they not the ones in heaven!'

'Of course, my child,' replied the wizard.

'Can I not learn them?' asked Alexander.

'Yes, child,' came the reply, 'when evening comes, you can.'

That evening, Nectanebo took Alexander outside the city to a deserted place, where he looked up into the sky and showed Alexander the stars of heaven. But Alexander, seizing him by the hand, led him to a deep pit and pushed him in. Nectanebo wounded his neck severely in the fall, and cried out, 'Dear me, child Alexander, what possessed you to do that?'

'Blame yourself, mathematician,' Alexander replied.

'Why, child?'

'Because, although you do not understand earthly matters, you investigate those of heaven.'

Then Nectanebo said, 'Child, I am fearfully wounded. But no mortal can overcome destiny.'

'What do you mean?' asked Alexander.

'I myself,' replied Nectanebo, 'have read my own fate, that I was doomed to be destroyed by my own child. And I have not escaped my fate, but have been killed by you.'

'Am I then your son?' asked Alexander.

Then Nectanebo told him the whole story of his kingdom in Egypt and his flight from there, his arrival in Pella and his visit to Olympias to cast her horoscope, and how he came to her disguised as the god Ammon and made love to her. With these words, he breathed his last.

Alexander believed what he heard and, realizing that he had killed his own father, was grief-stricken. He was afraid to leave the body in the pit, lest the wild beasts should come and tear it apart, since it was dark and the place was deserted. Touched now with a feeling of affection for his sire, he tied his belt around Nectanebo's corpse, lifted him on to his shoulders and carried him back to his mother, Olympias.

Olympias was surprised when she saw him and asked him what had happened. 'I am a second Aeneas,' replied Alexander, 'carrying my Anchises.' And he told her the whole story in detail, as he had heard it from Nectanebo. Olympias was astounded, and berated herself for having been made a fool of by Nectanebo's magic arts and tricked into adultery. But she too was seized by affection for him, and had him buried fittingly,[15] as father of Alexander. She built a monument and placed it by the grave.

It is a remarkable proof of divine Providence, that Nectanebo the Egyptian was laid to rest in Macedonia in a Greek grave, while Alexander the Macedonian was to be laid to rest in an Egyptian one.

15. When Philip returned from campaign, he went to Delphi to inquire of the oracle who would be king after him. The Pythia at Delphi, taking a sip from the Castalian spring, spoke as follows from her underground chamber: 'Philip, he who is to rule the whole world and bring all peoples under the power of his spear, will be the one who leaps on to Bucephalus and rides him through the middle of Pella.' (The horse was called Bucephalus, because he had on his haunch a mark shaped like an ox's head.)[16] When Philip heard the oracle, he began to anticipate a second Heracles.

16. Alexander, meanwhile, now had only one teacher, Aristotle. There were a number of other children in his school, including several sons of kings. One day Aristotle said to one of them, 'When you inherit your father's kingdom, what favour will you show me?'

The boy replied, 'You shall be my sole companion and authority, and I shall make you famous everywhere.'

Then he asked a second boy, 'When you inherit your father's kingdom, how will you treat me your teacher?'

The reply was, 'I shall make you a minister, and my personal adviser in all my judgements.'

Then he asked Alexander, 'And if you, child Alexander, inherit the kingdom from your father Philip, what will you do for me your teacher?'

Alexander replied, 'Are you already asking me about things that will happen in the future, when you have no certainty about what will happen tomorrow? I will give you a present when the time and the occasion arise.' Then Aristotle said, 'Hail, Alexander, ruler of the world: you will be the greatest king.'

Alexander was well loved by everybody because of his intelligence and warlike prowess, but Philip had mixed feelings. He rejoiced in the military spirit of the boy, but grieved because he did not resemble him in appearance.[17]

17. Alexander reached the age of fifteen. One day he happened to be passing the place where the horse Bucephalus was locked up, and he heard his terrifying whinny. He turned to his attendants and asked where the neighing came from.

'My lord,' replied Ptolemy the general, 'this is the horse Bucephalus, whom your father had caged up because he is a man-eater.'

When the horse heard Alexander's voice he whinnied again, but not in the terrifying tones he usually used, but gently and tamely, as if a god were directing him. When Alexander approached the cage, the horse immediately stretched out both his forefeet towards the prince, and licked him with his tongue, acknowledging him as his own master.

When Alexander saw how remarkable the horse was, and saw also the pieces of dismembered human corpses lying around him, he elbowed the horse's guards aside and opened the cage. Then he grabbed the horse by his mane and leapt on him, bridleless as he was, and rode him through the middle of Pella. One of the grooms ran to Philip, who was outside the city at that time. The king at once remembered the oracle, and he went to Alexander and embraced him with the words, 'Hail, Alexander, ruler of the world!' From that day on Philip was full of joy over his son's future.

18. One day, when Alexander found his father relaxing, he kissed him and said, 'Father, I beg you to allow me to go to Pisa to the Olympic Games; I want to take part.'[18]

'For what event have you been training,' Philip asked him, 'that you want to do this?'

'I want to take part in the chariot race,' replied the prince.

Then Philip said, 'Child, I will provide you with suitable horses from my own stables. They will be well looked after. You devote your energies to your training, for the event has great prestige.'

But Alexander replied, 'Father, please just give me permission to go to the contest. I have horses of my own which I have raised since they were young.'

Then Philip kissed Alexander, amazed at his enthusiasm, and said, 'Child, if that is what you want, go, and good fortune go with you.'

So Alexander went to the harbour and ordered a new ship to be built, and his horses and his chariot to be loaded on board. Then he embarked with his friend Hephaestion, sailed away and arrived at Pisa. On arrival he was showered with gifts; he ordered his slaves to rub down the horses, while he went for a walk with Hephaestion.

They encountered Nicolaus, the son of Andreas, king of Acarnania, who exulted in his wealth and good fortune, those two unstable gods, and placed great confidence in his own bodily strength. He came up to Alexander and greeted him, 'Greetings, young man!'

And Alexander replied, 'Greetings to you, too, whoever you may be and wherever you come from.'

'I am Nicolaus, the king of Acarnania.'

Alexander replied, 'Do not pride yourself so, King Nicolaus, and glory in the assumption that your life will last to the morrow; for fate is not accustomed to stay in one place, but a turn of the balance makes mock of the boastful man.'

'Your words are true,' replied Nicolaus, 'but not so your thoughts. Why are you here? As a spectator or as a competitor? I know who you are; you are the son of Philip of Macedon.'

'I am here,' said Alexander, 'to compete with you in the horse-chariot race, even though I am still young.'

'Surely,' said Nicolaus, 'you should have come rather as a wrestler, or pancratiast, or boxer.'

Alexander said again, 'I have come for the chariot race.'

Nicolaus began to boil with rage, and to despise Alexander because of his youth, knowing nothing of the extent of his mettle. He spat at him and cried, 'Bad luck to you! See to what a pass the Olympic Games have now come.'

But Alexander, to whom it came naturally to control his feelings, wiped away the insulting spittle and said, with a murderous smile, 'Nicolaus, before long I shall defeat you, and I shall take you prisoner in your homeland of Acarnania.' And the two parted as enemies.

19. Some days later the appointed time for the Games arrived. There were nine who entered for the chariot race, four of them the sons of kings: Nicolaus the Acarnanian, Xanthias the Boeotian, Cimon the Corinthian and Alexander the Macedonian; the rest were the sons of generals and satraps. Then everything was made ready for the contest and the lots were drawn from an urn. The first track went to Nicolaus, the second to Xanthias, the third to Cimon, the fourth to Clitomachus, the fifth to Aristippus of Olynthus, the sixth to Pierius of Phocis, the seventh to Cimon of Lindos, the eighth to Alexander of Macedon, and the ninth to Critomachus[19] of Locri. So they lined up for the race, and the trumpet sounded the fanfare for the start; the starting-gates were raised, and they all bounded forth with the utmost energy. They went one, two, three and four times around the turning-post. [Behold, Nicolaus was clothed in heavenly garb, and his companion Cimon of Corinth was dressed like him. After these was the Olympian, Laomedon, and Alexander, like the rising sun. There was a tremendous clamour as the partisans of the Olympian cried out to Laomedon, 'Why do you want to throw away your life, Laomedon? Have you come to

fight with a mere youth? Do not agree to drive the chariot.'

But Laomedon replied to them, 'You of Olympus, leave me alone: I shall win a garland from this youth by the grace of Zeus the Kindly. An oracle foretold that I should win my father's kingdom as a result of this contest.'

Then Alexander took his hand and said, 'Behold the new Oenomaus.'

Meanwhile, each of them was getting ready. Alexander yoked two dappled horses to his chariot, while the outriders were chestnuts, Bucephalus on the right, Petasios on the left. They looked so fine and noble that everyone said Alexander's horses must have been born on Olympus. The standard-bearer was ready, the spectators were ready, the supporters were shouting, Zeus was looking down from above, and the priest of Zeus in charge of the Games was seated on the Capitol.[18] The crowd was eager for the show to start; they were looking not at the Olympian but at Alexander, to see how he would fare. There were tens of thousands there, and every eye was on Alexander.

Then Alexander gave the signal, the standard-bearer signalled to the crowd with his hand, and the starting-gates were raised. Everyone was agog. Nicolaus and Callisthenes came out together, with Alexander jammed between them; both of them were casting about to see how they could kill him. *γ-text*] Those who were in the rear soon lost ground because their horses began to tire. Alexander was in fourth place, and behind him was Nicolaus, less keen to win than to destroy Alexander. (Nicolaus' father had been killed in battle by Philip.) Alexander was intelligent enough to realize this, and when the leading chariots crashed and overturned one another, he let Nicolaus overtake him. Nicolaus, unaware of the trap, drove past expecting to win the garland.

And it was Nicolaus who was in the lead, when, after two rounds of the turning-post, Alexander urged his horses on and drew level with him. As he went by, he caught Nicolaus' axle from behind: the chariot was entirely overturned, the charioteer was thrown out and Nicolaus was killed. So only Alexander was left in the race. The dead man had been a victim of the proverbial truth: 'Who makes a trap for another, will fall in it himself.'

Alexander was crowned as victor and, wearing the olive

garland of victory, he approached the temple of Olympian Zeus. There the prophet of Zeus said to him, 'Alexander, this is the prophecy of Olympian Zeus: as you have conquered Nicolaus, so you will conquer many others in war.'

20. [Alexander accepted the acclamation and returned victorious from Rome.[18] Many people – almost all the city in fact – came out with him, as well as Laomedon, his driver; being a good young man, and deserving of the gods, Alexander did not want to abandon him. Anyhow, they came home. Full of wonder at the bravery and intelligence of Alexander, the Macedonians composed a hymn of celebration:

'Boast Philip, Rejoice Macedonia,
The one for being the father of Alexander,
The other for being the country of this most glorious man.
Welcome him with garlands,
The unconquered victor, the great ruler:
He rose up in glory at Rome,
When he competed like the sun in the stadium,
And blotted out all the other stars.
Welcome him now, shining Macedonia.
Hand over his enemies to him:
Alexander is king of all the world.'

Singing this song, they marched around the city holding branches of bay in their hands. γ-text]
    With this excellent omen in his mind, Alexander returned victorious to Macedon. There, he found that his mother, Olympias, had been rejected by King Philip, who had taken a new wife, the sister of Lysias,[20] Cleopatra by name. The marriage was being celebrated that very day. Alexander, still wearing his crown of victory, went into the banqueting hall and said to Philip, 'Father, receive this crown of victory, the reward of my first efforts. And when I give my mother, Olympias, in marriage to another king, I shall invite you to the wedding.' So saying, Alexander took his place opposite Philip, but Philip was angry at his words. [Those who were sitting with him noticed from his face that he was angry, and sent a cup to Philip; but he refused to drink. γ-text]

21. Lysias, who was also reclining at the table, turned to Philip. 'King,' he said, 'ruler of the whole city, we now solemnize the marriage to you of our virtuous sister Cleopatra, from whom you shall breed legitimate children, no sons of adulterers, and resembling you in appearance.' When Alexander heard this he was very angry; at once he hurled his goblet at Lysias, struck him on the temple and killed him. When Philip saw what had happened, he leapt up, drew his sword, and rushed at Alexander in a rage; but he tripped on the edge of his couch and fell over.

Alexander laughed and said to Philip, 'You are eager to conquer all Asia and to destroy Europe to its foundations, yet you are unable to take a single step.' Then he in turn seized the sword from his father, and laid about him till all the guests were battered and bleeding. It was just like the battle of the Lapiths and Centaurs: some were hiding under the couches, others were using the tables as weapons, and yet others were scurrying away into dark places to watch this new Odysseus destroying the suitors of Penelope.

Alexander went and brought his mother, Olympias, to the palace, having thus avenged her marriage. He sent Lysias' sister Cleopatra into exile. The guards lifted up Philip, who was in a very poor way, and laid him on his bed.

22. Ten days later, Alexander went to Philip's room and sat down beside him. 'King Philip,' he said, '– I shall call you by this name, since you will no longer take pleasure in hearing me call you Father – I have come to you not as a son but as a friend and intermediary, on account of the wrong you have done your wife.'

'It was a wicked thing you did,' said Philip, 'to kill Lysias because he had made an unseemly remark.'

But Alexander replied, 'Did you then do well to leap up with your sword drawn against your own son, meaning to kill me, because you wanted to marry another woman, although your first wife, Olympias, had given you no cause for complaint? Get up then, and have confidence in yourself – for I know why your body is so weak – and let us forget our past misdemeanours. Now, I will call my mother Olympias here to be reconciled with you. She will be persuaded by her son, even though you wish not to be called my father.'

So Alexander went out and went to Olympias and said, 'Mother, do not be angry at what your husband has done. He knows nothing of your sin, while I, being the son of an Egyptian father, am a constant accusation. Go then and beg for a reconciliation. It is right that a woman should be ruled by her husband.'

He then led his mother to King Philip, his father, and said, 'Father, turn now to your wife. Now I shall call you Father, because you obey your child. Here is my mother; I have besought her to come to you and to forget what is past. So, embrace each other: it is not shameful for you to do so before me, since I was born of you both.'

Thus Alexander brought his parents to a reconciliation, and everyone in Macedon marvelled at him. Thereafter people who get married avoid mentioning the name of Lysias, for fear his mention should set up a division between them.

23. The city of Methone had rebelled against Philip. So Philip sent Alexander with a great army to make war on it. But when Alexander reached Methone, he used subtle arguments to persuade Methone to return to obedience to Philip.

[Supplement A]

When Alexander returned from Methone and went to his father, Philip, he saw with him some men dressed in barbarian garments. When he asked who they were, Philip replied that they were satraps of Darius, the king of Persia. Then Alexander asked them why they had come. 'To demand of your father the accustomed tribute,' was the reply.

'On whose behalf do you demand this tribute?' asked Alexander; and they said, 'For the country of king Darius.' Then Alexander said, 'Seeing that the gods have given the earth to men for their sustenance, how can Darius demand contribution of the gift of the gods?' And he asked them, in order to test them, 'How much do you want from us?'

'One hundred golden eggs,' was the reply, 'each weighing 20 pounds of solid gold.'[21]

Alexander said, 'It is not right for Philip, the king of the Macedonians, to pay tribute to the barbarians: one cannot rule over Greeks just by wanting to.' So he replied to the satraps, 'Go and tell Darius as follows: Alexander, the son of Philip, says this to you: as long as Philip was alone, he paid tribute to you, but now that he has sired a son, Alexander, he will not pay you tribute, but I myself shall come and take back from you in person all that you took from us.' So saying, he sent away the ambassadors, and did not even do Darius, who sent them, the honour of writing a letter. Philip, the king of the Greeks, was delighted when he saw how audaciously Alexander had handled the matter.

The ambassadors, however, gave some money to a certain Greek friend of theirs, a painter, and got him to make for them a miniature image of Alexander. This they took with them to Darius in Babylon; and they told him everything that Alexander had said to them.

Now another Thracian city revolted against Philip, and he again sent Alexander with a great number of soldiers to make war on it.

24. There was a certain man named Pausanias, a rich and powerful man and ruler of all the Thessalonians. This man conceived a desire for Olympias, the mother of Alexander, and sent some powerful men to persuade her to leave Philip and to marry himself; he also sent a good deal of money. When Olympias would not agree, Pausanias came to where Philip was, in the middle of a theatrical performance. He knew that Alexander was away on campaign. Philip was taking part in the contests in the Olympic theatre when Pausanias came in, armed and accompanied by several of his nobles, with the intention of murdering Philip and seizing Olympias. He stepped straight up to him and struck him in the chest with his sword, but did not kill him. There was a tremendous uproar in the theatre. Then Pausanias rushed off to the palace to seize Olympias.

It happened that on this very day Alexander returned victorious from the war. Seeing the turmoil in the city, he asked what had happened. He was told that Pausanias had gone to the palace to seize his mother, Olympias. At once Alexander went in with some of his bodyguard, who were with him, and caught Pausanias holding on to Olympias with great force, while the latter screamed. Alexander wanted to run him through with his lance, but was afraid that he might injure his mother at the same time, since they were so closely entangled. So Alexander tore Pausanias away from his mother, and ran him through with the lance he had in his hand. Then, learning that Philip was still alive, he went to him and asked, 'Father, what do you want me to do with Pausanias?'

'Bring him to me here,' replied Philip. So they brought him. Alexander took a sword, placed it in Philip's hand and stood Pausanias before him. Philip took hold of Pausanias and killed him. Then he said to Alexander, 'Child Alexander, I do not mourn that I am dying; for I have had my revenge in thus destroying my enemy. It was well, what Ammon the Libyan god said to your mother, Olympias: "You carry in your belly a male child, who will avenge his own father's death."'

With these words, Philip died. He was given a royal burial, attended by all the people of Macedonia.

25. When the city of Pella had settled down again, Alexander went up on to the memorial of his father, Philip, and cried in a loud voice, 'O Sons of Pella and Macedon, of Greece and of the Amphictyons,[22] of the Lacedaemonians and Corinthians, come now and bring me your allegiance and entrust yourselves to me; let us make an expedition against the barbarians and free ourselves from enslavement to the Persians. It is not right for Greeks to be the servants of barbarians.' So saying, he sent royal envoys to all the cities; and of their own free will the men from every place gathered together in Macedonia, as if summoned by the voice of a god, and made ready for the campaign. [At once he gathered together all those who were skilled in crafts of any kind, workers in iron, bronze or wood. He ordered the bronze-smiths to make breastplates and helmets and decorated swords, and to fashion spears, barbs and daggers. He ordered the carpenters to make shields and arrows and spear-hafts. *γ-text*] Alexander opened his father's arsenal and gave the young men their armour and

weapons. Then he assembled all his father's champions, who by now were getting old, and said to them: 'Venerable sirs, brave veterans, will you deign to adorn the Macedonian army and to march with us to war?'

'King Alexander,' they replied, 'in our youth we marched out to fight with your father, King Philip, and our bodies are no longer strong enough for combat; we beg you to excuse us from military service.'

Then Alexander said to them, 'I, however, would prefer to march with you, old though you are, because age is much tougher than youth. Often fresh youth, trusting in its bodily energy, is tempted into rash behaviour which results in running great risks; but an old man reflects before he acts, and thus avoids danger. Therefore, fathers, join us on the campaign, not so much in order to fight the enemy, as to inspire the younger ones with courage. Both of you have a part to play. Yours is to strengthen the army with discretion; for even in war brains are necessary. It is plain that your own security depends on the victory as much as does your country's. If we are defeated, the enemy will not spare the old and useless; but if we win, the victory will be attributed to the wisdom of the counsellors.' With these words Alexander persuaded all the superannuated soldiers to join his expedition.

26. Alexander was eighteen when he took over the kingdom of his father, Philip. Antipater, an intelligent and cunning man, put an end to the uproar occasioned by Philip's death in the following way. He led Alexander into the theatre, wearing his breastplate, and, with a long speech, filled the Macedonians with favour towards Alexander.

[Supplement B]

Alexander seemed to be luckier than his father, Philip; and he immediately embarked on a great enterprise.

He assembled all his father's soldiers and counted them. There were 20,000 men, 8,000 armoured horsemen, 15,000 foot soldiers, 5,000 Thracians, and 30,000 Amphictyons, Lacedaemonians, Corinthians and Thessalonians. When he had counted the whole assembly, the total came to 70,000[23] men, and there were, in addition, 6,950 bowmen.

[He hastened with his army to Thessalonica. When the ruler of that place heard that Alexander was approaching his borders, he sent ambassadors to ask for peace; they brought with them gold and silver as well as his son. He also sent a letter, as follows:

'Polykratos, the unworthy suppliant, sends greetings to Alexander the Godlike, the ruler of the world. Since nothing is impossible for Providence, we must of necessity submit all our affairs to Fortune. We know that you are our most godlike king, through the grace of Providence: Fortune has easily accomplished everything that you wished. Therefore, those who dwell beneath heaven must, like slaves, pay homage to your power, even if they do not want to. I know all about your great successes in conquering countries; that is why I have sent you this humble letter to express my enslavement to you. As a pledge of my willingness to submit to your power, I have sent you my son, the only one whom Fortune has blessed me with, accompanied by my most pitiful gifts. Accept my humble supplication in full, if it is pleasing in your eyes. Farewell, my lord: do whatever you wish with us your servants.'

When Alexander had read this letter, he yielded to Polykratos' supplication: he treated his ambassadors kindly and sent Polykratos a letter in return, as follows:

'What you say is true: divine Providence has given us authority to rule, and one must yield to Fortune. I have been a faithful pupil of Providence above. Now you have mollified my intentions towards you, and have extinguished the inordinate pride shown by your father Anaxarchus – not by your gifts, but by the humble tone of your letter and by the sending of your son. Your son Charimedes shall remain with us as a reminder of your good intentions towards me. Farewell.'

After subduing Thessalonica, he made a campaign against the Scythians beyond. After three days' march, ambassadors came from Scythia offering their submission as his slaves, and asking him not to attack them. Alexander said to them: 'Go away to your own country and send me as many thousand skilled bowmen as you wish, to be my allies. You see, I am marching against the Lacedaemonians. Your allies are to join me within sixty days. If the appointed day arrives and the soldiers I expect have not arrived, I shall send my army against you and I shall not be turned back.'

The Scythians promised to do everything he ordered, like slaves; so he treated them kindly and sent them away to their homes.[24]

27. Alexander marched against Lacedaemon. When the Lacedaemonians learnt of his advance, they were struck with fear and trembling, and were at a loss what to do. The leaders of the cities gathered in Athens, which was the capital at that time, and twelve orators held the fate of all Greece in their hands. They gathered together to discuss what they should do about Alexander. After three days they had reached no conclusion on the best course of action, and were unable to reach a unanimous decision. Some were in favour of resisting Alexander, others argued the opposite. Fate was against them. When they determined to fight Alexander, Diogenes opposed them. 'How can we hope for a victory? How can we do other than yield to Alexander?' But the partisans of Antisthenes and Parmenides said, 'Remember the story of our ancestors. When Dionysus attacked our city and subdued our whole country, the Athenians opposed him and raised up great trophies and sent him back empty-handed, like a mere weakling. Alexander is certainly not stronger than Dionysus.' When he had heard this, Diogenes came forward and said, 'Tell me, you rulers of the Athenians, who at that time was the champion of the Thebans and who were that city's generals?'

'Atreus was the champion,' they replied, 'and among their generals was the wondrous Hyllus who was the first king of the Lacedaemonians.' Then Diogenes[25] laughed and said, 'Well, if only you can get Hyllus on your side, then I will advise you to resist Alexander. But if you cannot do this, you will not only fight Alexander but you will destroy Thebes.' With these words he went away. But his arguments did not persuade them to a sensible decision; they decided to prepare for war.

Alexander arrived and drew up his line. When he asked them to surrender, they became all the bolder and sent back his messengers after abusing them severely. At that, he retreated a little from their city, and spoke to them as follows: 'Now, if you change your minds at the last, it will do you no good.'

Alexander pitched his camp a mile away and waited for the Scythian allies to arrive. A few days later the expected troops appeared, all dressed in decorative breastplates, carrying white shields of chain-mail as well as arrows and quivers, daggers and spears. He reviewed them and found that there were 80,000 of them. Then he drew up his lines against Athens, marched on the city and began to besiege it. The archers were innumerable, and the sun could not be seen for their arrows. *γ-text*]26

He led a campaign against the Illyrians, Paeonians and Triballians, who had revolted from his rule. During this campaign, there was unrest in Greece. A rumour reached Greece that Alexander the king of Macedon was dead, whereupon, it is said, Demosthenes led a wounded man into the Athenian assembly, who claimed to have seen with his own eyes Alexander lying dead. When the Thebans heard this, they murdered the garrison, which Philip had installed in the Cadmeia after the battle of Chaeronea. It is said that Demosthenes put them up to it.

Alexander was very angry and led an expedition against Thebes. Omens of the coming catastrophe were seen in Thebes: a spider wrapped the sanctuary of Demeter in a web, and the water of the spring called Dirce ran red with blood. The king took the city and razed it to the ground, preserving only the house of the poet Pindar. It is said that he compelled the Theban musician Ismenias to play his pipes while the city was being demolished. The Greeks, terrified by this, voted Alexander their leader and gave him the rule over Greece.

[When the war was over, Alexander went to look at the dedications. He found Diogenes sitting in a sunny place and said, 'Who are you?'

Those around him replied, 'This, your majesty, is Diogenes the philosopher, who so often advised the Athenians to fight against your power.'

When Alexander heard this, he went up to the place where Diogenes was sitting sunning himself (it was morning, and he was leaning on his barrel), and said to him, 'Diogenes, what favour can I do you?'

'Nothing,' replied the other, 'except to go away and leave me the sunshine, so that I can warm myself.'

People found Diogenes amazingly indifferent to earthly things. γ-text]

[Supplement C]

28. When he returned to Macedonia, Alexander began preparations for the invasion of Asia. He built swift sailing ships, triremes and men-of-war in large numbers. He put all his troops on board with their wagons and equipment of all kinds. Then he took 50,000 talents of gold and set off for Thrace; there he conscripted 5,000 men and took away 500 talents of gold. All the cities welcomed him with garlands.

When he reached the Hellespont, he went on board ship and set off from Europe for Asia; striking his spear into the ground, he claimed Asia as spear-won territory. From there, Alexander marched to the river called Granicus, which was guarded by the satraps of Darius. There was a fierce battle, in which Alexander was victorious; he sent the spoils he took from the Persians as gifts to the Athenians and to his mother, Olympias. He decided to conquer the coastal cities first. He occupied Ionia, and then Caria, after which he took Lydia and the treasure of Sardis. He captured Phrygia and Lycia and Pamphylia. In the latter a miracle occurred: Alexander had no ships, but part of the sea drew back so that his army could march past on foot.[27]

29. Soon he came to the place where his navy was. From here he sailed over to Sicily. He quickly defeated those who opposed him and landed on Italian ground. The Roman generals sent him a crown of pearls via their general Marcus, and another inlaid with precious stones, accompanied with this message: 'We too shall crown your head, Alexander, king of the Romans and of all the earth.' They also brought him 500 pounds of gold. Alexander accepted their gift and promised to make them great and mighty; he took from them 2,000 bowmen and 400 talents.

30. Next, Alexander crossed over to Africa. The African generals met him and begged him to stay away from their city of

Carthage. But Alexander despised them for their cowardliness and said: 'Either become stronger yourselves, or pay tribute to those who are stronger than you.'

Then he set off and crossed the whole of Libya until he came to the sanctuary of Ammon. But he put most of his army on the ships, telling them to sail on and wait for him by the island of Proteus. He himself went to make sacrifice to Ammon, on the grounds that he was the god's son.[28] He prayed and said: 'Father Ammon, if it is true what my mother told me, that I am your son, give me a sign!' And Alexander had a vision of Ammon embracing his mother, Olympias, and saying to him, 'Child Alexander, you are born of my seed.'

When Alexander thus learned of the power of Ammon, he repaired his sanctuary and gilded the wooden image of the god; and he dedicated it with this inscription of his own: 'Alexander erected this to his father, the god Ammon.' He wanted to receive an oracle from him, to indicate where he should found a city to be named after himself, so that it should endure for ever, and he had a vision of Ammon as an old man, with golden hair and ram's horns on his temples, saying:

'O King, thus Phoebus of the ram's horns says to you:
If you wish to bloom for ever in incorruptible youth,
Found the city rich in fame opposite the isle of Proteus,
Where Aion Ploutonios himself is enthroned as king,
He who from his five-peaked mountain rolls round the endless
    world.'

When Alexander received this oracle, he set about finding out which island was that of Proteus, and who was the god who presided over it. Thus engaged, he sacrificed again to Ammon and made his way to a certain village in Libya where he had left his troops to rest.

31. As he was walking there, a very large hind ran by and disappeared into a cave. Alexander called to one of his archers to shoot the creature. But when the archer loosed his bow, he missed the hind. 'Fellow, your shot went wide,' said Alexander. And thereafter that place was called Paratone[29] because of Alexan-

der's remark. He founded a small city there, and settled some of
the most distinguished of the natives in it, and called it Paratone.

Then he came to Taphosirion. He asked the local people
why it had that name, and they replied that the sanctuary was
the grave of Osiris.[30] After sacrificing there also, he approached
the goal of his journey and reached the site of our present city.
He saw a great open space, stretching into the infinite distance,
and occupied by twelve villages.[31] [Their names were Steiram-
pheis, Phanenti and Eudemos, Akames, Eupyros, Rhakotis,
Hegiosa, Ypones, Krambeitai, Krapatheis and Lyidias, Pases,
Teresis or Nephelites, Menuia, Pelasos. Rhakotis was the most
well-known and was the capital of the group. In the twelve villages
were twelve rivers running to the sea. Their outlets were
dammed up, and the rivers filled in to become the streets and
squares of the city. Only two continued to have an unhindered
passage to the sea, of which one is the river Rhakotis, now the
street of the great god Sarapis. Another canal is the site of the
main square. The largest river, called Xylero, is now Aspendia.
Another canal is the site of the temple of Fortune. Then there is
the great river Kopronikos; then the large canal and river Nepher-
otes, where now the dedications are and the shrine of Isis of
Nepheros, the first temple built in Alexandria. The largest river
of all is the Argeos, where the Argeion now is. Then there is the
canal of Areios where the statue of Areios is. Then there is the
canal that comes out at the Canopic estuary by the Zephyrion.
Another major river is the Heracleotic estuary.[32] *A-text*]

Alexander marked out the plan of a city, stretching in length
from the place called Pandysia as far as the Heracleotic mouth of
the Nile, and in width from the sanctuary of Bendis to little
Hormoupolis (it is called Hormoupolis, not Hermoupolis, because everyone who sails down the Nile puts in[33] there). These
were the dimensions of the city Alexander laid out, so that up to
this day it is called 'the territory of the Alexandrians'.

Cleomenes of Naucratis and Nomocrates of Rhodes advised
Alexander not to build such a large city. 'You will be unable to
find the people to fill it,' they said. 'And if you do fill it, the
ships will be unable to transport sufficient food to feed them.
Those who live in the city will make war on one another,

because the city is too big, endless. Small cities are harmonious in debate and take counsel together to their mutual advantage; but if you make this city as great as you have sketched it, those who live here will always be at odds with one another, because the population will be so huge.'

Alexander was persuaded, and ordered his architects to build a city on the scale they preferred. On receiving these orders, they marked out a city extending in length from the river Dracon opposite the promontory of Taphosirion as far as the river Agathodaimon, which is beyond Canobus, and in width from the sanctuary of Bendis as far as Europhoros³⁴ and Melanthios. Then Alexander ordered all those who lived within 30 miles of the city to leave their villages and move to the city; he presented them with parcels of land and called them Alexandrians. The chief officials of the boroughs were Eurylichos³⁵ and Melanthos, which is how those districts got their names.

Alexander took advice also from other builders, including Numenius the stone-mason, Cleomenes of Naucratis, the engineer, and Karteros of Olynthus. Numenius had a brother by the name of Hyponomos. He advised Alexander to build the city on stone foundations, and to construct water channels and drains running to the sea. So such canals are called Hyponomos after him, because of his advice.

32. [Looking out to sea from the land, Alexander spied an island, and inquired what its name was. The natives told him, 'Pharos, where Proteus used to live. His tomb is now there, on a very high mountain, at which we make regular observance.' They brought him to the hero's shrine and showed him the coffin. Alexander sacrificed to Proteus the hero; seeing that the shrine had collapsed because of the passage of time, he ordered it to be restored at once. *A-text*]

Then Alexander gave orders for the perimeter of the city to be marked out so that he could get an impression of it. The workmen marked out the limits with wheat flour, but the birds flew down, ate up the meal and flew away. Alexander was very disturbed at the possible meaning of this omen; he sent for interpreters and told them what had happened. Their reply was:

'The city you have ordered to be built, O king, will feed the whole inhabited world, and those who are born in it will reach all parts of the world; just as the birds fly over the whole earth.'

So he gave orders for building work to begin.

When the foundations for most of the city had been laid and measured, Alexander inscribed five letters: ABGDE. A for 'Alexander'; B for *Basileus*, 'king'; G for *Genos*, 'descendant'; D for Dios, 'Zeus'; and E for *ektisen*, 'founded an incomparable city'. Beasts of burden and mules helped with the work. As the gate of the sanctuary was being put in place, a large and ancient tablet of stone, inscribed with many letters, fell out of it; and after it came a large number of snakes, which crept away into the doorways of the houses that had already been built. Nowadays the door-keepers reverence these snakes as friendly spirits when they come into their houses – for they are not venomous – and they place garlands on their working animals and give them a rest day. Alexander was still in the city when it and the sanctuary were being built, in the month of Tybi, which is January. For this reason the Alexandrians still even now keep the custom of celebrating a festival on the twenty-fifth day of Tybi.

33. High in the hills Alexander discovered a cult image, and the Helonian columns and a hero-shrine. He searched for the Sarapeum according to the oracle that had been given to him by Ammon in the following words:

'O King, thus Phoebus of the ram's horns says to you:
If you wish to bloom for ever in incorruptible youth,
Found the city rich in fame opposite the isle of Proteus,
Where Aion Ploutonios himself is enthroned as king,
He who from his five-peaked mountain rolls round the endless
     world.'

So Alexander searched for the all-seeing one and built a great altar opposite the hero-shrine, which is now called the Grand Altar of Alexander, and made a sacrifice there. He prayed and said: 'That you are the god who watches over this land and looks across the endless world, is plain. Accept then this sacrifice of mine and be my helper against my enemies.' So saying, he placed the gifts on the altar. Suddenly a huge eagle swooped down and seized the entrails of the sacrifice, carried them off into the air, and then dropped them on another altar. Alexander noted the place where they landed, and went to it and saw the entrails lying on the altar, which was one built by the men of old. There was also a sacred precinct, and within it a seated cult-image holding in its right hand a three-headed beast[36] and in its left a sceptre; beside the image stood a very large statue of a maiden. He inquired of those who lived there what god dwelt in this place. They told him that they did not know, but that they had heard from their forefathers that it was a sanctuary of Zeus and Hera.[37]

Here Alexander also saw the obelisks that now lie in the Sarapeum, outside the present perimeter wall. On them were engraved hieroglyphic letters. [Alexander asked whose the obelisks were, and they told him, 'King Sesonchosis's, the ruler of the world.' The inscription in priestly lettering ran: 'King Sesonchosis of Egypt, the ruler of the world, erected this to Sarapis, the renowned god of the universe.' Then Alexander turned his eyes to Sarapis and said, 'O great Sarapis, if you are god of the universe, give me a sign.' The god appeared to him in his sleep and said, 'Alexander, have you forgotten what you said when you made the sacrifice? Did you not say, "Whoever you are who watch over this land and the endless world, receive my sacrifice and be my helper in my wars?" Suddenly an eagle flew down, seized the entrails, and placed them on the other altar. Did you not realize that I am the god who watches over all things?'

Then in his dream Alexander prayed to the god: 'Tell me if this city of Alexandria that I have founded in my name will remain, or if my name will be changed into that of another king.' He saw the god holding him by the hand and bringing him to a great mountain.

'Alexander,' the god said, 'can you move this mountain to another place?'

'No, lord, I cannot,' he seemed to say.

'Even so your name cannot be changed into that of another king,' replied the god. 'Alexandria will grow and receive great

benefits, and will increase also those cities that were there before
it.'

Then Alexander said, 'Lord, show me also, when and how I
am going to die.'

The god replied:

'It is better for a mortal man, and more honourable
And less painful, not to know in advance
The time appointed for his life to end.
Men, being mortal, do not understand
That this rich, varied life is endless, as long
As they have no knowledge of its misfortunes.
You too I think will find it better
To choose not to know the future in advance.
But since you ask to learn about your fate,
You may: I will tell it you in brief.
By my command, you shall subdue while young
All the races of the barbarians; [and then,
Dying but not dying, you shall come to me.]
This city you found will be the apple of the world's eye.
As the years and the ages go by, it will grow
In greatness, and it will be adorned
With numerous temples, magnificent sanctuaries,
Exceeding all in their beauty, size and number.
Everyone who comes to dwell in it
Will forget the land that bore him.
I myself shall be its protector,
Unaging and uncorrupted, and shall establish it
So that it remains firm for ever.
I shall level its deeps and inspire its flames,
I shall forbid the unhealthy south wind to blow upon it,
So that the evil influence of the wicked spirits
Will be unable to trouble the city at all.
There shall be earthquakes only for a short time,
Famine and plague will be brief also
And war will bring but little slaughter,
Drifting rather like a dream through the city.
Many people from many lands will worship you,

Even in your lifetime, as a god.
After death you shall be deified and worshipped
And will receive the gifts of kings. You shall live in it
For all time, dead and yet not dead.
The city you have built shall be your tomb.' *A-text*]

'Work out, now, Alexander, who I am: put together two hundred and one, then a hundred and one again, then eighty and ten; then take the first letter and put it at the end, and thus you shall know who I am who have appeared to you.'

With this oracular pronouncement he disappeared. Alexander remembered the oracle and recognized the name of Sarapis.[38]

The administration of the city remains just as Alexander drew it up, and the city, once founded, grew day by day in strength.

34. Then Alexander hastened with his army towards Egypt. When he reached Memphis, the Egyptians put him on the throne of Hephaestus[39] as king of Egypt. In Memphis Alexander saw a very tall statue of black stone which was treated as holy. On its base was this inscription: 'This king who has fled will return to Egypt, no longer an old man but a young one, and will subject our enemies the Persians to us.' Alexander inquired whose statue this was, and the prophets told him: 'This is the statue of the last king of Egypt, Nectanebo. When the Persians came to sack Egypt, he saw, through his magic art, the gods of the Egyptians leading the army of the enemy, and the land of Egypt being ravaged by them. So, knowing what was to come as a result of their betrayal, he fled. We, however, searched for him, and asked the gods where our king, Nectanebo, had fled to. They gave us this oracle: "This king who has fled will return to Egypt, no longer an old man but a young one, and will subject our enemies the Persians to us."'

When Alexander heard this, he sprang up and embraced the statue, saying: 'This is my father, and I am his son. The oracle that was given you did not lie. I am amazed only that you were overcome by the barbarians, when you have these invincible walls, which could not be thrown down by any enemy. But this is the affair of Providence above and the justice of the gods, that you, with a fertile land and a river to nourish it – blessings not made with hands – should be subdued by those who do not have these things, and should be ruled by them. For without their help the barbarians would have perished.'

Then Alexander demanded of them the tribute they had formerly paid to Darius. 'It is not so that I may transfer this to my own treasury,' he said, 'but so that I may spend it on your city of Alexandria which lies before Egypt, and is the capital of the whole world.' At this the Egyptians gladly gave him a great deal of money, and escorted him with great pomp and honour out of the country via Pelusium.

35. Alexander now led his army on to Syria, where he raised a force of 2,000 armoured warriors and marched on Tyre. The Tyrians resisted, and refused to let him enter their city, because of an ancient oracle that had been given to them in these terms: 'When a king comes against you, people of Tyre, your city will be levelled with its foundations.' Therefore, they made every effort to prevent his entry into their city. They built a wall round the whole city and prepared to resist. In a ferocious battle the Tyrians killed a great many of the Macedonians. Alexander, defeated, withdrew to Gaza. When he had recovered himself, he began to prepare for a siege of Tyre. In his sleep he had a vision of a figure saying to him, 'Alexander, do not think of going yourself as a messenger to Tyre.' When he rose from sleep, he sent ambassadors to Tyre, bearing letters whose contents were as follows:

'King Alexander, the son of Ammon and of Philip the king, also supreme king of Europe and all Asia, Egypt and Libya, to the Tyrians who are as nothing. I wished in the course of my march through the regions of Syria to make my entrance into your city in peace and good order. But since you Tyrians are the first to resist me in the course of my march, it must be from you that the other cities shall learn how much stronger the Macedonians are – by the example of your foolishness – and be terrorized into submission. The oracle that was given you is true: I shall destroy your city. Farewell, then, if you will be wise; but if not, then farewell in misery!'

As soon as the leaders of the council had read the letter, they ordered the messengers sent by Alexander to be strappadoed, and they asked them, 'Which of you is Alexander?' When they replied that none of them was, the Tyrians crucified them.

Now Alexander began to look for a way to make an entry and overthrow Tyre; he regarded his first defeat as inconsiderable. He saw in a dream a satyr, one of the attendants of Dionysus, giving him a curd cheese; he took it from him and trampled it underfoot. When he awoke, Alexander related his dream to an interpreter, who told him: 'You will rule over all Tyre, and it shall become subject to you, because the satyr gave you the cheese, and you trampled it underfoot.'[40]

Three days later Alexander took his army and the men of three neighbouring villages who had fought bravely on his side. They opened the gates of the city by night, entered and killed the guards. Alexander sacked the whole city, and levelled it to its foundations. To this day 'the miseries of Tyre' is a proverbial expression. The three villages that had fought on his side were united by Alexander into a single city and given the name of Tripolis.

[Supplement D]

36. Alexander established a satrap in Tyre to rule over Phoenicia and marched on down the Syrian coast. Presently he was met by ambassadors from Darius, who brought him letters, a whip, a ball and a chest of gold. Alexander took the letter of Darius, the king of Persia, and read as follows:

'The king of kings, of the race of the gods, who rises into heaven with the sun, the very god Darius, to Alexander my servant. I order and command you to return home to your parents, to be my slave and to rest in the lap of your mother, Olympias. That is what suits your age: you need still to play and to be nursed. Therefore I have sent you a whip, a ball and a chest of gold, of which you may take what you prefer: the whip, to show that you ought still to be at play; the ball, so that you may play with your contemporaries instead of inducing such numbers of arrogant young men to come with you like bandits and terrorize the cities. Even if the whole world becomes united under a single ruler, it will not be able to bring down the Persian Empire. I have so many troops that one might as well count the sand on the seashore as attempt to number them, and I have enough gold and silver to fill the whole world. I have sent you a chest full of gold, so that if you are unable to feed your fellow-bandits you can now give them what they need to return each to his country. But if you do not obey these orders of mine, I shall send my soldiers to pursue you until you are captured. Then you will not be treated like a son of Philip, but crucified like a rebel.'

37. When Alexander read this out to his army, they were all terrified. Alexander observed their fear and said, 'Men of Macedon and fellow-soldiers, why are you so scared at this letter of Darius? Do you think there is any truth in his boastful words? There are some dogs which, though weak in body, bark very loudly as if they could make an impression of strength by their barking. Such a one is Darius: though he can do nothing in practice, he pretends in his letters to be a somebody, just like a barking dog. But let us suppose his threats are realistic; he has thereby only given us an indication of how bravely we must fight for victory, in order not to be shamed by defeat.' So saying, he ordered the messengers of Darius to be tied up and carried off for crucifixion.

'What harm have we done you, Alexander?' they pleaded. 'We are messengers only; why do you wish us to be killed so cruelly?'

'Blame Darius, not me,' replied Alexander. 'It was he who sent you here, bearing letters more suitable for a bandit than a king. So I will treat you as if you had come to a desperado and not to a king.'

They replied, 'Darius wrote what he did in ignorance; but we can see your magnificent army, and recognize that you are a great and intelligent king, the son of King Philip. We beg you, lord, great king, spare our lives.'

Alexander replied, 'Now you are terrified at your punishment and are begging not to die: so I will release you. It is not my intention to kill you, but to show the difference between a

Greek king and a barbarian one. You may anticipate, therefore, no harsh treatment from me: a king does not kill a messenger.'

When Alexander invited them to sit down to dinner with him, the messengers proposed to tell him how he could capture Darius in an ambush; but he said, 'Tell me nothing! If you were not returning to him, I would be willing to be instructed by you. But since you will soon be going back to him, I have no wish for one of you to betray to Darius what you said to me; I should then be deserving of punishment too. Be silent then, and let us pass the matter over.' The messengers of Darius made many laudatory remarks, and the whole army joined in their acclaim.

38. Three days later Alexander wrote a letter to Darius and read it aloud to his army, in the absence of the messengers. It ran as follows:

'King Alexander, the son of King Philip and of Olympias, greets the king of kings, who is enthroned with the gods and rises with the sun, the great god of the Persians. It is shameful that one so swollen with greatness, who rises with the sun, should fall into miserable slavery to a mere mortal like Alexander. The names of the gods, which are common among men, give them also great power and wisdom. How then can the names of the gods dwell in corruptible bodies? See now, we have found out that you are powerless in comparison with us, but you borrow the names of the gods and go about on earth wearing their powers like a garment. I come to make war on you as against a mortal; but the balance of victory is in the hands of Providence above.

'Why did you write to me that you possess so much gold and silver? So that we should fight all the more bravely to win it? Well, if I conquer you, I shall be famous and a great king among both Greeks and barbarians for conquering a ruler as great as Darius. But if you defeat me, you will have done nothing outstanding – simply defeated a bandit, as you wrote to me. I, however, shall be defeating the great king of kings and god, Darius.

'You sent me a whip, a ball and a chest of gold to mock me;

but I regard these as favourable omens. I accepted the whip, so as to flay the barbarians with my own hands, through the power of my spears and weapons, and bring them to submission. I accepted the ball, as a sign that I shall be ruler of the world — for the world is spherical like a ball. The chest of gold you sent me is a great sign: you will be conquered by me and pay me tribute.'

39. When King Alexander had read out this letter to his own troops, he sealed it and gave it to Darius' messengers. He also gave them the gold that they had brought with them. They, having gained a very good impression of Alexander's nobility of spirit, returned to Darius. When the latter read Alexander's letter, he saw its force. He questioned them closely about Alexander's intelligence, and his preparations for war. Then, somewhat disturbed, he sent the following letter to his satraps:

'King Darius greets the generals beyond the Taurus. It is reported to me that Alexander, the son of Philip, is in rebellion. Capture him and bring him to me; but do him no physical harm, so that I may remove his purple robe and beat him and send him back home to his country to his mother, Olympias. I shall give him a rattle and knucklebones, such as Macedonian children play with. I will send with him men of wisdom to be his teachers.

'You are to sink his ships in the depths of the sea, to put the generals who accompany him in irons and send them to me, and to send the rest of his soldiers to live on the Red Sea. I make you a gift of his horses and transports. Farewell.'

The satraps wrote back to Darius:

'Greetings to the god and great king, Darius. We are amazed that you have not noticed before now that so many men are marching against us. We have sent you some of those whom we found roaming about, not daring to interrogate them before you. Come now quickly with a great army, lest we be plundered by the enemy.'

Darius was in Babylon, in Persia, when he received this letter. He replied as follows:

'The king of kings, the great god, greets all his satraps and generals. Demonstrate now the extent of your bravery without expecting any help from me. A great river has burst its banks in your country and has terrified you who are the thunderbolts that should be able to quench it; and you have been incapable of standing up to the thunder of a fresh-faced youth. What have you got to show? Has any of you died in battle? What am I to think of you, to whom I have entrusted my kingdom, when you give the advantage to a mere bandit and make no attempt to capture him? Well then, as you suggest I will come and capture him myself.'

40. When Darius learnt that Alexander was close at hand, he pitched camp by the river Pinarios.[41] Then he sent Alexander the following letter:

'The king of kings, the great god Darius and lord of all nations, to Alexander the plunderer of the cities. You seem to think that the name of Darius is an insignificant one, although the gods have honoured him and judged him worthy to be enthroned alongside them. It was unlucky for you that you supposed you could get away with being king in Macedon without heeding my orders, and went marching through obscure lands and foreign cities, in which you pronounced yourself king; you gathered together a band of desperadoes like yourself, attacked cities inexperienced in war – which I in my discretion had regarded as not worth ruling, the merest detritus – and you attempted to gather tribute from them like some beggar.

'Do you suppose that we are at all like you? Make no boast of the places you have captured. You made the wrong decision about them. You should, before all, have corrected your ignorance and come to me, Darius your lord, rather than accumulating your robber band. I ordered you in writing to come and pay homage to Darius the king. If you do so, I swear by Zeus the most high god, my father, that I will grant you an amnesty for your actions. But if you persist in your foolishness, I shall punish you with an unspeakable death. Even worse will be the fate of those who failed to instil any sense into you.'

41. Alexander, when he received this letter, would not allow himself to be goaded by Darius' boastful words. Meanwhile,

Darius gathered together a great force and marched forth, accompanied by his sons, his wife and his mother. With him were the 10,000 troops called the Immortals; they were called this because their number was preserved by introducing new men to replace any who died.

Alexander crossed the Cilician Taurus and arrived at Tarsus, the capital of Cilicia. There he saw the river Cydnus which runs through it; and, as he was dripping with sweat from the march, he threw off his breastplate and went for a swim. Unfortunately he caught a chill; his condition became very grave and he only just survived. Philip, one of the most distinguished doctors of the day, cured him. When he had recovered his strength he continued the march against Darius, who meanwhile had pitched camp at Issus in Cilicia.

Alexander raced ahead to battle, full of enthusiasm, and drew up his troops against Darius. When those around Darius saw Alexander leading his troops towards the quarter where he had heard that Darius was positioned, they halted their chariots and the rest of the army. Both sides were ready for the fight. Alexander was determined not to allow the enemy to break through his phalanx, or to ride it down or to come on it from the rear; instead, when the chariots charged, most of them were cornered and destroyed or scattered. Then Alexander mounted his horse and ordered the trumpeters to sound the call for an infantry charge. At once the armies clashed with tremendous noise and the battle was very fierce. For some time they attacked each other's wings, which swung hither and thither as they were forced back by each other's spears. Eventually the two sides separated, each thinking it had gained the victory.

Then Alexander's men forced Darius' back and made a fierce assault on them, so that they crushed and fell over each other in the mêlée. There was nothing to be seen but horses lying on the ground and slaughtered men. The clouds of dust made it impossible to distinguish Persian from Macedonian, satrap from ally, horseman from infantryman. The very sky and the ground were invisible through the gore. The sun itself, in sorrow at the event, refused to look longer on this pollution and hid behind the clouds.

In the end there was a great rout of the Persians, who fled

precipitately. With them was Amyntas of Antioch, who had been a prince of Macedon and had sought refuge with Darius. When evening came, the terrified Darius was still in fast retreat. Because his commander's chariot was too conspicuous, he dismounted and fled on horseback. But Alexander considered it a point of honour to capture Darius, and made all speed to catch up with him, for fear someone should kill him first. After pursuing him for 7 miles Alexander captured Darius' chariot and weapons, as well as his wife, daughters and mother; but Darius himself was saved by the onset of darkness, and because he had obtained a fresh horse. And so he escaped.

Alexander passed the night in the captured tent of Darius. Although he had defeated his opponents, he disdained to make a great boast of it, and did not behave arrogantly towards them. He gave orders for the bravest and most noble of the Persian dead to be buried; Darius' mother, wife and children he took along with him, treating them with all respect. He also consoled the remaining captives with conciliatory words.

The number of Persian dead was very great. The Macedonians were found to have lost 500 foot soldiers and 160 horsemen, and there were 308 wounded; but the barbarians had lost 20,000 men, and 4,000 were led into slavery.

42. Darius, having saved himself by his flight, at once set about assembling an even greater army. He wrote to all the subject nations, requiring them to join him with their troops. One of Alexander's scouts learnt of this new army being assembled, and sent the information to Alexander. On receiving the news, Alexander wrote to his general Scamander:

'Alexander the king greets General Scamander. Come here as soon as possible with your phalanxes and all your forces; the barbarians are said to be not far off.'

Then Alexander took the forces he had with him and marched ahead. When he had crossed the Taurus range, he thrust a great spear into the ground and said, 'If any strong man among the Greeks, barbarians, or any of the other kings, touches this spear, it will be an evil omen for him: for his city will be destroyed down to its foundations.'

Then he came to Hipperia, a city of the Bebryces. Here there was a temple and a statue of Orpheus, around which stood the Pierian Muses and wild beasts. When Alexander looked at it, the statue broke out in a sweat. Alexander inquired the meaning of this omen, and Melampus the interpreter told him, 'You will have to struggle, King Alexander, with toil and sweat, to subdue the nations of the barbarians and the cities of the Greeks. But just as Orpheus by his music and song won over the Greeks, put the barbarians to flight and tamed the wild beasts, so you by the labour of your spear will make all men your subjects.' When Alexander heard this, he gave the interpreter a large reward and sent him away.

Then he came to Phrygia.[42] When he reached the river Scamander, into which Achilles had sprung, he leapt in also. And when he saw the seven-layered shield of Ajax, which was not as large or as wonderful as the description in Homer, he said, 'Fortunate are you heroes who won a witness like Homer, and who became great as a result of his writings, but in reality are not worthy of what was written about you.' Then a poet came up to him and said, 'King Alexander, we shall write better than Homer about your deeds.' But Alexander replied, 'I would rather be a Thersites in Homer than Agamemnon in your poetry.'[43]

43. From Phrygia he went to Pyle.[44] Here he collected together the Macedonian army and those whom he had taken prisoner in the war against Darius, and marched to Abdera. The Abderites promptly closed the gates of their city. Alexander was angry at this, and ordered his general to set fire to the town. But they sent envoys to him, who said, 'We did not close our gates in a gesture of opposition to your rule, but through fear of the kingdom of Persia. We were afraid that Darius, if he remained in power, would sack our city because we had received you. So you must conquer Darius, and then you may come and open the gates of our city; we shall obey the stronger king.'

Alexander smiled when he heard this, and said to the envoys they had sent, 'Are you afraid that Darius will come and sack your city hereafter, if he remains in power? Go now and open your gates and live in peace. I shall not enter your city until I have conquered this King Darius whom you are so afraid of; then only will I make you my subjects.' With this message to the envoys, he went on his way.

44. Two days later he arrived at Bottiaea and Olynthus, laid waste the Chaldaeans' entire country and destroyed the neighbouring peoples. Next he reached the Black Sea and made all the cities on its coast his subjects.

It was at this time that the Macedonians' provisions ran out, so that they were all dying of starvation. Alexander had a brilliant idea: he rounded up all the cavalry's horses and slaughtered them; after skinning them he ordered his men to roast and eat them. Thus they satisfied their hunger and were revived. But they said, 'What is Alexander doing, slaughtering our horses? For the moment, to be sure, we have satisfied our hunger, but without our horses we are now defenceless in battle.' When Alexander heard this, he went into the camp and said, 'Fellow-soldiers, we slaughtered the horses, vital though they were for the prosecution of the war, in order to satisfy our hunger. The removal of an evil by a lesser evil leads also to less suffering. When we come into another land, we shall easily find other horses; but if we were to die of hunger, we should not find other Macedonians for some time.'

Thus he calmed the soldiers down and marched on to the next city.[45]

45. [Ignoring the other cities, he came to that of the Locrians, where the army camped for one day. Then he came to the people of Acragas. Here he entered the temple of Apollo and demanded an oracle from the prophetess. She replied that the god would give him no oracle. Alexander became angry and said, 'If you are unwilling to prophesy, I shall carry off the tripod as Heracles carried off the prophetic tripod of Phoebus,[46] which was dedicated by Croesus, the king of the Lydians.' Then a voice was heard from the inner sanctuary: 'Heracles, O Alexander, committed this act as one god against another; but you are mortal: do not oppose yourself to the gods. Your actions are talked of even as far away as heaven.' After this utterance had

been heard, the prophetess said, 'The god has addressed you himself, by the mightiest of names. "Heracles, O Alexander," he called you, thus indicating to you that you are to exceed all other men by your deeds and to be remembered through the ages.'

46. When Alexander arrived at Thebes he asked them to supply 4,000 of their best warriors; but the Thebans closed their gates and did not even send ambassadors to him; neither did they receive his, but drew up their army to fight him. They sent 500 armed men up on to the walls to order Alexander either to fight or to leave the city.

'Brave Thebans,' said Alexander with a smile, 'why do you shut yourselves up inside your walls and command those outside either to fight or to go away? I am going to fight not as if I were fighting a city, or brave men, or warriors experienced in battle, but as if against civilians and cowards. I shall subdue by my spear all those who shut themselves inside their walls. Brave men should fight on the open plain; only women shut themselves in for fear of what is to come.'

With these words, he ordered 4,000 horsemen to surround the walls and shoot down those who stood on them, and another 2,000 to dig away the foundations with mattocks, pickaxes, long hooks and iron crowbars. The stones of those walls had been fitted together in accompaniment to the music of the lyres of Amphion and Zethus; but he ordered his men to tear them apart. He ordered them to bring fire within the gates and to batter the walls with the so-called rams to destroy them (these are machines built of wood and iron, which are pushed along on wheels by the soldiers; they are released against the walls from a distance and by their momentum can break down even the most closely built walls). Alexander himself circled Thebes with another 1,000 archers and spearmen.

All parts of the city were bombarded with fire, stones, slingshots and spears. The Thebans fell wounded from the walls, and as the slingstones hit home they died as if struck by thunderbolts. Presently their resistance began to lessen as they found themselves unequal to the onslaught.

Within three days the whole of Thebes was in flames. The first breach was made at the Cadmean Gate, where Alexander had his position. At once the king made his entry, alone, through a narrow opening. Many of the Thebans who met him retreated in terror; Alexander wounded some of them, others he drove wild with fear. Then the rest of the soldiers, both infantry and cavalry, broke in through the other gates, 3,000 in number, and slaughtered everyone in the city. The walls were already shaking and crumbling; the Macedonian army had been assiduous in carrying out Alexander's orders. The ancient foundations of the Cadmeia were spattered with human gore and the bodies of numerous Thebans were crammed into that narrow area; Mount Cithaeron rejoiced at their laments and exulted in their struggle. Every house was pulled down and the whole city put to the torch. The hand of the Macedonian did not tire of bloodying its greedy iron; and the helpless, deluded Thebans were destroyed by Alexander.

There was a Theban called Ismenias, a clever man and an expert at playing the pipes. When he saw Thebes being torn down and razed to the ground, and all its youth destroyed, he groaned for his country and decided to make himself a hero through his skill on the pipe. He decided to take his pipe and fall as a suppliant at the feet of the king, and to play a heart-rending, pleading and piteous melody, in the hope of persuading Alexander to show mercy by his music and its lamenting tones. First he decided to make a speech in supplication to the conqueror. He stretched out his hand and, weeping, began to speak:

'Alexander, now we revere you, for we have learnt that your strength is like that of a god. Draw back your unconquerable hands from the Thebans, ⟨do not in your ignorance commit such impiety against your compatriots. Dionysus and Heracles were Thebans⟩, those glorious gods, the first offspring of the ancient race of Thebes. Dionysus, son of Zeus, was born of Semele by the thunderbolt in Thebes; Heracles was the son of Zeus and Alcmene. These have always been helpers of men and gentle guardians of peace; and furthermore, Alexander, they are your ancestors, whom you should imitate and to whom you should do good. As the son of a god, do not allow Thebes, the

nurse of Dionysus and Heracles, to be destroyed; do not tear
down the citadel founded by the ox.[47] If you do, you will be a
disgrace to the Macedonians. Do you not know, Alexander, that
Thebes, not Pella, is your home? The whole land of Thebes
beseeches you in my words, bringing before you your ancestors
– Lyaeus the reveller in dance and ecstasy, Heracles the just in
deed and helper of men. Now imitate your ancestors, good men
for the most part, and turn your wrath to benefaction. Hold pity
more ready to hand than punishment.

'Do not make a desert of the gods who bore you,
Do not destroy the city of your ancestors.
Do not in your ignorance destroy your own country.
Do you see these walls, built by the shepherd Zethus
And the lyre-player Amphion,
The sons of Zeus, secretly borne by the nymph,
The daughter of Nycteus,[48] when in an ecstasy of dance,
Cadmus built these foundations
And these wealthy homes. He took to wife
Harmonia, the daughter of foam-born Aphrodite
After she mated with the Thracian adulterer.
Do not unthinkingly make your country a desert.
Do not burn down the walls of Thebes.
This is the house of Labdacus. Here the unhappy mother
Of Oedipus bore the murderer of his father.
Here was the shrine of Heracles, formerly
The house of Amphitryon: here Zeus slept,
Joining three nights into one.[49]
Do you see those burnt-out houses
Still dripping with the wráth of heaven?
There Zeus once blasted with his thunderbolt
Semele, whom he desired; and in the midst of the flames
She gave birth to Eraphiotes, who is called Lenaeus.[50]
Here Heracles went mad; in his frenzy
He killed his wife, Megara, with his arrows.
This altar which you see is that of Hera;
Here Heracles devoured his flesh with a robe
Soaked in poison from the hands of Philoctetes.

This is the house of Tiresias, the mouthpiece of Apollo.
Here dwelt the thrice-old prophet,
Whom Athena once turned into a woman.
Here Athamas in his madness killed with his arrows
The boy Learchus who had been turned into a deer.
Here Ino in her madness leapt into the ocean depths
With her new-born son Melicertes.
From here blind Oedipus was driven out
On Creon's orders, his daughter Ismene his only staff.
This river which flows down from Cithaeron
Is the Ismenus, and its water is Bacchus'.
Do you see that fir-tree whose branches reach to heaven?
On that tree Pentheus, who spied on the women's dancing,
Was torn apart, wretched man, by his own mother.[51]
Do you see that spring bubbling with blood-coloured water,
From which the lowing of an ox echoes around?
This is the blood of Dirce who was dragged to death.
Do you see that furthest mountain ridge,
Which stands out prominently above the road?
There used to crouch the monstrous Sphinx,
Issuing her orders to the people of the city,
Until Oedipus solved her riddle and destroyed her.
This is the spring and sacred well of the gods,
From which emerge the silvery nymphs.
Artemis came once to its waters
And washed her limbs; and here the unholy Actaeon
Saw what was not permitted, the bath of Leto's daughter.
He was changed into a deer, and his body was devoured
By his own dogs, because he saw her bathing.
Then there was a great war against Thebes,
When the dazzling general Polynices led the people of Argos
Against the seven fortress-gates of Thebes.
Here Capaneus was set ablaze as far as his lips.
This gate is called the Electran Gate.

⟨'By the Proetid Gate, which was open, the earth swallowed up
the invulnerable Amphiaraus. At the third gate, the Ogygian,
Hippomedon was pent and killed by the son of Hipposthenes.

Before the Neistan Gate Parthenopaeus went into the earth, the
destroyer of thousands. Tydeus the Calydonian stood at the
Homoloian Gate. Here Adrastus fled and died.⟩

'They buried the dead leader of the Argives.
Have pity, the holy Cadmeia[52] begs it of you.
This is the city of Lyaeus, this Thebes
Which you are ordering to be razed to its foundations.
Do you see the precinct of Heracles, your ancestor
And ancestor of your father Philip, now engulfed in flames?
Do you wish, in your ignorance, to burn down your own
    temple?
Why do you insult your own parents,
Son of Heracles and Dionysus?'

With this supplication Ismenias cast himself at the feet of King
Alexander.

The Macedonian cast his eye on him
And ground his teeth together
And, fuming with rage, uttered the following words:
'Vilest offspring of the sons of Cadmus,
Vilest of beasts, hateful to the gods,
Vulgar branch of a barbarian stem,
You, the last relic of Ismene's sorrow –
Do you think you can deceive Alexander by telling
These clever fabrications of mythology?
Now I am going to destroy the whole city by fire
And turn it to ashes;
Now I am going to uproot all of you with your precious
    ancestors.
If you knew the history of my descent,
My origins, and who were my forefathers,
Should you not have proclaimed this to the people of Thebes?
"Alexander is our kinsman," you should have said,
"Let us not revolt against a fellow-citizen,
Let us make him our general and enter into alliance with him.
We are citizens and brethren of Alexander,
It will bring glory to our ancient race

If the Macedonians embrace the Thebans."
But since your power was too slight to defend you,
And your temerity has been shamed in battle,
Your change of heart and your entreaties are senseless;
You cannot turn away the doom that has come on you
Because you lost your fight with Alexander.
But as your end is now near, both for you and for the Thebans,
And I am going to raze and burn the city,
I order you, Ismenias, the best of the pipers,
To stand beside the houses as they burn
And accompany the destruction of your city
With the shrilling of your instrument's double reed.'
So he ordered the soldiers to tear down
The seven-gated walls and the citadel of Thebes.
Cithaeron danced again for the Thebans,
The waters of Ismenus itself ran red with blood.
The walls and citadel of Thebes were razed.
The whole land was horror-struck at the slaughter,
And fearful groans echoed from the houses
As they fell down among wild laments.
Meanwhile, Ismenias, within the ruins,
Had tuned his double reed, as the Macedonian had commanded
    him.
When all the walls of Thebes were fallen –
The palace of Lycus and the house of Labdacus –
Alexander, out of respect for his education,
Preserved the house of Pindar alone,
In which as a boy he had shared the gifts of the Muses,[53]
Pursuing his studies with the aged lyrist.
He slaughtered many men in their homes,
He left only a few of them alive,
He wiped out the name of their race.
He ordered that Thebes should no longer be known by that
    name,
That the city should become no city,
That the name of those men should become no name.

Thus the end of Thebes was determined by its beginning.

When it was first built, the lyre of Amphion accompanied the construction of its walls; and the pipe of Ismenias accompanied their destruction. That which was built to the sound of music was also demolished to the sound of music.

Nearly all the Thebans were destroyed along with their city. To the few who were left, Alexander announced that if they should ever approach the city of Thebes, they would be dead men. Then he marched on to other cities.

47. The surviving Thebans went to Delphi to consult the oracle, as to whether they should ever get their city back. Apollo's response was as follows:

'Hermes, Alcides[54] and the boxer Polydeuces,[55]
Three athletes, will rebuild the city of Thebes.'

When the Thebans had received this oracle, they began to wait for its fulfilment.

Meanwhile Alexander had arrived at Corinth and found the Isthmian Games in progress. The Corinthians asked him to conduct the Games; he agreed and took his seat. As the competitors marched in, and the winners were crowned by Alexander – he also gave gifts to the best performers – one of the athletes, a very remarkable man called Clitomachus, who was a Theban, entered for three events: the wrestling, the pankration and the boxing. His performance on the wrestling-ground was so skilful and versatile that his defeat of his opponents won especial praise from Alexander. When he came to receive the garland for victory in wrestling, Alexander said to him, 'If you win the other two events for which you have entered, I will crown you three times with garlands, and will give you whatever you ask.' Clitomachus did win the boxing and the pankration, as well as the wrestling, and he came to receive his three garlands from Alexander. The herald asked him, 'What is your name and what is your city, so that I may proclaim it?'

'Clitomachus is my name,' was the reply, 'and I have no city.'

Then the king said, 'Brave man, you are a fine athlete, and have won in the same arena three victories, in wrestling, the pankration and boxing, and have received from me three crowns of wild olive; how can it be that you have no city?'

'I had one before Alexander became king,' replied Clito-machus, 'but when Alexander became king he destroyed my city.'

Then Alexander realized what he meant and what he was going to ask for, and said, 'Let Thebes be rebuilt to the honour of the three gods, Hermes, Heracles and Polydeuces: thus you shall receive this as a gift from me and not as your request.'

And so the oracle of Apollo was fulfilled:

'Hermes, Alcides and the boxer Polydeuces,
Three athletes, will rebuild the city of Thebes.' *A-text*]

BOOK II

1. [From Corinth Alexander advanced to Plataea, an Athenian city, where Kore is worshipped. He entered the sanctuary of the goddess and found there a priestess weaving a robe for the goddess. The priestess said, 'You have come at a good moment, great king: you will be famous and glorious throughout the city.' Alexander rewarded her with gold.

Some days later, Stasagoras, the general of the Plataeans, entered the goddess's sanctuary, and the priestess said to him, 'Stasagoras, you are to fall from power.' He was very angry.

'Unworthy prophetess,' he said, 'when Alexander came here you offered him honours, but you tell me that I am to fall from power.'

'Do not be angry about that,' she said. 'The gods reveal everything to men through signs, and especially to the great. When Alexander came here, I happened to be weaving a purple thread into the robe of the goddess; and that is why I prophesied as I did. But when you came in, the robe was finished and was being taken down from the loom: this makes it plain that you too are to be hauled down.'

Then Stasagoras had the woman removed from the priesthood, saying, 'The omen referred to yourself.' But when Alexander heard about it he at once removed Stasagoras from his generalship, and restored the priestess to her former position.

Stasagoras went away to the Athenians (who had appointed him to his generalship) without Alexander's knowledge, and, with many tears, told them about his demotion. They were very angry and rebelled against Alexander; but when he learnt of it, he sent them a letter, as follows:

'King Alexander to the Athenians. After the death of my

father I inherited his kingdom and brought order to the western cities and many regions by my instructions. Although they were ready to come and fight alongside me, I advised them to stay where they were. My kinsmen the Macedonians enthusiastically acclaimed me as sovereign. By their bravery I subdued the regions of Europe; I destroyed the Thebans who had behaved evilly towards me, and tore down their city to its foundations. Now that I have crossed into Asia,[56] I require the Athenians to welcome me. I have written to you first – not a long letter, or one of many words, as is the custom of your undisciplined scribes – but brief and to the point: it is not for the conquered but for the conquerors to give orders and instructions. I mean that you must obey Alexander. Therefore, either make yourselves the stronger or yield to those who are stronger, and pay me tribute of 1,000 talents a year.'

2. When the Athenians had read this letter, they replied:

'The city of Athens and the ten best orators say to Alexander: While your father was alive we suffered greatly, and we rejoiced when he died. Philip is thrice evil in our memory. Our opinion of you, most audacious son of Philip, is exactly the same. You are asking the Athenians for a tribute of 1,000 talents a year: this means you have come to us in the spirit of one who wants war. If that is your plan, come on; we are ready for you.'

Alexander's reply to the Athenians was as follows:

'I have already sent on to you my man Leo, who will cut out your tongues and bring them to me, and take away your foolish orators ⟨to stop them deceiving you⟩. I will do my best to destroy you and your city of Athens by fire, because you do not do what I tell you. Hand over your ten chief orators; then I will decide what to do about my differences with you, and will spare your city.'

They replied, 'We will not.'

Some days later they held an assembly to discuss what to do. In the course of the debate the orator Aeschines stood up and said:

'Men of Athens, why are we so slow to debate? If you choose to send us to Alexander, we will go eagerly. Alexander is not

Philip. Philip was brought up in the arrogant lust for war, but
Alexander was brought up on the teaching of Aristotle and
stretched out his hand for discipline. He will be docile when he
sees his teachers, and will blush at the sight of those who instructed him in the art of kingship. Then he will relent and make
his attitude to us one of gentleness.'

While Aeschines was still speaking, Demades, a fine orator,
stood up and cut him short.

'How long, Aeschines, will you continue to offer us these
effeminate and cowardly arguments, urging us not to stand up
to Alexander in war? What god has driven you out of your wits,
that you speak like this? You urged the Athenians at such length
to fight against the Persians; and now will you inspire the Athenians to cowardice, and make them tremble at a tyrant who is
no more than a hot-headed youth, who has assumed the audacity
of his father? We chased out the Persians, we defeated the Lacedaemonians and conquered the Corinthians, we put the Megarians
to flight and overcame the Phocians, we sacked the Zacynthians.
And are we afraid to fight Alexander? But Aeschines says: "He
will remember that we were his teachers and will be ashamed
when he sees us." What a joke. He has insulted all of us and
removed Stasagoras from his command, whom we appointed;
he has imposed my enemy Cithoon as chief general in his stead,
although the city belongs to us. He has already staked his claim
to Plataea; yet you say he will be ashamed when he sees our
faces? More likely he will strip us naked and beat us. Let us,
therefore, go to war with Alexander and place no trust in him,
young as he is. Youth is untrustworthy: it can fight bravely, but
not reason soundly. You say he sacked the Tyrians; that is because
they were weak. You say he destroyed the Thebans who were
not so weak; but they were tired from many wars. And you say
he took the Peloponnesians prisoner; it was not he, but plague
and famine that destroyed them. Xerxes bridged the sea with
ships and sowed the whole land with armies, his arrows darkened
the air and he filled Persia with captives; yet we drove him back
and burnt his ships, because we had Cynegirus, Antiphon and
Mnesochares fighting on our side. Yet now are we afraid to
make war on Alexander, a headstrong child, and on his satraps

and bodyguards who are still more witless than he? So you want to send us, the ten orators, whom he has asked for? Consider whether that is sensible. I proclaim to you, men of Athens, that many a time ten dogs, barking bravely, have saved the flocks of sheep which were running in their cowardice towards the wolves.'

3. After Demades had made his speech, the Athenians called Demosthenes to the podium to give them his advice about their common cause. He stood up and said:

'Gentlemen, citizens – I will not say Athenians; if I were a foreigner, I would have called you Athenians, ⟨but now I call you fellow-citizens⟩ – the matter in question is the safety of all of us, and we must debate whether we are to surrender or to fight Alexander. Aeschines presented us with mixed arguments, neither advising us to fight nor urging against it. He is an old man and has addressed many assemblies. Then Demades, who is a young man, gave the advice characteristic of his youth: "We drove back Xerxes through the heroism of Cynegirus and the others." Well, Demades, if you give us those men again, we will fight again; we will entrust ourselves to the might of those you have named. But if we cannot have them back again, let us by no means fight: every occasion has its own implications and requirements. We orators are good at public speaking, but not at waging war. Although Xerxes was superior in numbers, he was a barbarian, and was defeated by the intelligence of Greeks. But Alexander is a Greek and has already fought thirteen wars and never been defeated; even the larger cities yielded to him without a fight. Then, Demades says, the Tyrians were weak, but they fought Xerxes at sea, conquered him and burnt his ships. Were the Thebans weak? – who have been at war ever since their city was founded and have never been defeated; but now they are slaves to Alexander. The Peloponnesians, he says, were defeated not by Alexander but by famine. Yet Alexander sent them grain from Macedonia. When Antigonus the satrap asked, "Why do you send grain to those on whom you make war?" the Macedonian replied, "Just so that when I defeat you it will be a military victory and not a defeat by famine." Now you are angry because

Stasagoras has been removed by him from office. But he rebelled
first: he said to the priestess, "Because of the omen, I shall have
you removed from your priesthood." When Alexander heard of
his foolishness, he removed him from his generalship. Was it not
right for the king to be angry? "But," Demades says, "Stasagoras
was opposed to Alexander, and a general is the equal of a king."
Then why do you blame Alexander for deposing Stasagoras?
You say, "Because he is an Athenian." Was not the priestess
deposed by Stasagoras also an Athenian? In that case, Alexander
acted to avenge us, because Stasagoras had taken away the priesthood from our priestess.'

4. The Athenians applauded Demosthenes' speech enthusiastically and there was a tremendous hubbub. Demades was silent,
but Aeschines approved the speech; Lysias added his testimony
and so did Plato. The Amphictyons voted for it and Heraclitus
did not oppose it. All the people supported what Demosthenes
had said.

Then Demosthenes went on:

'I have a further argument. Demades says that Xerxes made a
wall across the sea with his ships, sowed the land with armies
and darkened the air with weapons, filling Persia with Greek
captives. Now it is right for Athenians to praise a barbarian for
taking Greeks prisoner; but Alexander is a Greek, and though he
has won control of the Greeks who opposed him, rather than
make them prisoners, he has thought fit to make even those who
fought against him allies in war. He has himself stated publicly:
"I shall make myself master of all by doing good to my friends
and harm to my enemies." Now, Athenians, as friends of Alexander, and his teachers as well, it is impossible for you to be
referred to as his enemies. It is shameful for you the teachers to
appear ignorant, while your pupil shows himself more intelligent
than you.

'None of the kings of Greece has entered Egypt except for
Alexander; and he did not do so to make war, but to seek an
oracle concerning the site for the everlasting city that bears his
name. He received the oracle, laid the foundations for the city
and built its walls: every task that is begun with enthusiasm is

swift to reach its completion. He entered Egypt when it was under Persian rule. When the Egyptians begged to fight with him against Persia, the cunning boy answered, "It will be better for you Egyptians to concern yourselves with the flooding of the Nile and the cultivation of the land than to arm yourselves for the fortunes of war." And so he made Egypt subject to him: a king is nothing if he does not have a productive land. Alexander was the first of the Greeks to overcome Egypt, and thus he made himself first among both Greeks and barbarians. How many armies can that country support? Not only those that are based near by, but also those that are away at war. How many empty cities can it fill with men? As it is rich in wheat, so it is rich in men: whatever the king asks it for, it can willingly supply. ⟨He asks for funds, and they are made available; he needs gold, and its taxes and rents are plentiful; he asks for soldiers, and they come forward with enthusiasm.⟩ Do you Athenians still want to fight Alexander, who has such resources to call on for everything his army needs? Even if you are eager and anxious to do so, still this is not the time for it.'

5. After this speech of Demosthenes everyone was won over. They agreed to send to Alexander, in the care of a number of distinguished ambassadors, a crown of victory, weighing fifty pounds, and a decree of congratulations. They did not send him the orators. The ambassadors came to Plataea and handed the decree to Alexander. When he had read it, and learnt of Aeschines' advocacy and Demosthenes' arguments, as well as the agreement of the Amphictyons, he sent them a letter, as follows:

'Alexander, the son of Philip and Olympias – I will not call myself king, until I have subjected all the barbarians to the Greeks. I sent to you asking you to send me the ten orators, not to punish them but to greet them as my teachers. I did not presume to approach you with an army – in which case you would have regarded me as an enemy – but wished to put the orators in place of an army, to free you from all fear. But you have had a very different attitude to me: you have been shown up by your own foolishness in seizing the occasion to settle your score with the Macedonians.[57] When my father, Philip, was fighting the Zacynthians, you became their allies; but when you were being attacked by the Corinthians, we Macedonians became your allies and drove them back. Then you tore down the statue of ⟨my mother which stood in the temple of Athena in Athens, although I erected in Macedon a statue of⟩ Athena. We have taken from you a just payment for the things we have done for you. Do not be encouraged by my attitude to your misdeeds; you ought to be afraid that I shall rise up in my kingly dignity and retaliate. I was almost ready to do this, but for the fact that I am myself an Athenian. When have you ever made a generous decision about your most celebrated citizens? You imprisoned Euclid who had very sensible advice to offer you; you exiled Demosthenes who acted as a wise ambassador to Cyrus; you insulted Alcibiades, excellent general though he was; you murdered Socrates who was an education to all Greece; you were ungrateful to Philip who took your side in three wars; and now you are angry at Alexander on account of Stasagoras who wronged both you and me. He removed from office the priestess of the goddess, who was an Athenian, and I restored her to her post. I approve the counsel your orators gave you. Aeschines gave you proper advice; Demades spoke bravely; Demosthenes advised the best course of action. You shall be Athenians again, and may expect no harm from me. It would seem monstrous to me to destroy Athens, who fought against the barbarians and made herself the theatre of freedom.'

6. After sending this letter, Alexander took his army and marched to Lacedaemon. The Lacedaemonians were eager to demonstrate their bravery and to shame the Athenians who had been afraid of him. So they shut their gates and manned their ships: they were better warriors at sea than on land. When Alexander heard of their preparations, he sent them a first letter:

'Alexander to the Lacedaemonians. First of all I advise you to preserve the reputation that you have inherited from your ancestors. Greetings will come later, if you deserve them. You are brave warriors and have never been defeated. Look out that you do not destroy your reputation and, by attempting to show up the feebleness of the Athenians, make yourselves a laughing-stock by being yourselves defeated by Alexander. Disembark from your ships of your own accord, or you will be consumed by fire.'

When the letter was read out, the Lacedaemonians were not won over; instead they hastened to battle, so that those who fought on the walls were brought down by missiles, and those in the ships were burnt. When the survivors came as suppliants, begging not to be made prisoners, Alexander said, 'When I came to you in conciliatory fashion, you were not conciliated; now that your ships have been burnt, here you are pleading with me. But I do not blame you: you thought that, because you had driven back Xerxes, you could do the same to Alexander. But you could not stand up to my armoury.'

After these remarks, Alexander sacrificed alongside the generals. He refrained from sacking the Lacedaemonians' city and imposed no tribute on it. Then he hastened on through Cilicia to the regions of the barbarians. *A-text*]

7. Darius, meanwhile, had assembled the Persian leaders, and they were holding a discussion about what they should do. Darius said, 'I see that the war is growing in intensity. I thought that Alexander had the mind of a bandit, but in fact he is attempting the deeds of a king. Great as we Persians believe ourselves to be, Alexander turns out to be more astute. We sent him a whip and a ball to play with and ordered him to go back to school. Let us therefore consider what must be done to set matters to rights; if we go on despising Alexander as insignificant, and continue to indulge our own pride, we shall find ourselves being removed from this great Empire of the Persians which rules over all the world. I am afraid that the greater may turn out to be weaker than the less, when Opportunity and Providence concur in the transfer of a crown. It is better for us, then, to rule over our own barbarians and not, by seeking to free the Greeks, to lose the whole of Persia.'

Then Darius' brother Oxydelkys[58] said to him, 'Now you are over-estimating Alexander and, by yielding Greece to him, encouraging him to attack Persia. You must rather imitate Alexander, and in that way hold on to your kingdom. He did not entrust the conduct of the war to generals and satraps, like you, but has always been the first to enter the cities and has fought at the head of his army. During battle he sets aside his kingly nature, and resumes it when he has won.'

'How am I to imitate him?' asked Darius.

'Just so,' replied the other; 'Alexander has been successful in everything because he has not put anything off; he has done everything bravely, as is his nature. Even in appearance he resembles nothing so much as a lion.'

'How do you know?' asked Darius.

'When I was sent by you, your majesty, to Philip, I saw the respect the Macedonians paid to Alexander, and his appearance, his intelligence and his character. So, your majesty, send now for your satraps and all the peoples who are subject to you: the Persians, the Parthians, the Medes, the Elymaeans, the Babylonians in Mesopotamia and the land of the Odyni, not to mention the Bactrians and Indians[59] (for there are many races under your rule), and raise an army from them. If you can keep the gods on your side and defeat the Greeks, we shall by the very numbers of our troops be a source of astonishment to our enemies.'

'Good advice,' replied Darius, 'but worthless. A single resolute Greek army can conquer a horde of barbarians, just as one fierce wolf can put a whole flock of sheep to flight.'

With these words, Darius gave orders to assemble his troops.

8. Alexander passed through Cilicia and came to the river called Ocean.[60] The water was very fast-flowing. When Alexander saw it he was very eager to bathe, and he undressed and leapt in; the water turned out to be extremely cold, and he got into difficulties. He developed a chill, his head and all his body were in pain and he was ill for some time. When the Macedonians saw Alexander lying on his bed in pain, they were themselves sick at heart, and were afraid that Darius might discover Alexander was ill and attack them. Thus the single soul of Alexander disturbed the souls of the entire army.

Soon a physician named Philip announced that he could give Alexander a draught which would cure him of his sickness. Alexander was very keen to take it, and Philip prepared the medicine. Then a letter was sent to Alexander from Parmenio, one of his generals, saying, 'Darius gave orders to Philip the physician to watch for an opportunity to poison you with a drug, and promised to give him his own sister in marriage and to make him a partner in his kingdom. Philip has agreed to this. Be on your guard, therefore, your majesty, against Philip.' Alexander took the letter and read it without alarm; for he knew what Philip's real feelings were towards him. Then he put the letter under his pillow. When Philip came and gave him the cup with the draught to drink, with the words, 'Drink, your majesty, and be cured of your sickness,' Alexander took the cup and said, 'See, I am drinking it.' And he did so. After he had drunk it, he showed Philip the letter. When Philip had read what the letter said about him, he said, 'King Alexander, you will find I am not as I am here represented.'

When Alexander had recovered from his illness, he embraced Philip and said, 'You see what view I take of you, Philip. I received the letter before you gave me the drink, and then I drank the draught, trusting in your name. I knew that Philip would do nothing to harm Alexander.'

'My lord king,' Philip replied, 'punish Parmenio, the man who sent the letter, in some fitting manner. It was he who many times tried to persuade me to destroy you with poison, with the promise that I should have Darius' sister Dadipharta as my wife. But I refused, and you see how he has tried to trap me.'

Alexander examined this claim, and, finding that Philip was blameless, he had Parmenio removed from his post.[61]

9. Then Alexander took his army and marched on into the land of the Medes. He was keen to conquer Greater Armenia. After he had subdued it, he marched on for many days through waterless country full of ravines, until he eventually came via Ariane to the river Euphrates. Here he built a bridge with iron arches and bands, and ordered the army to cross it. When he saw them hesitating, he ordered the wagons and the beasts of burden, with all the provisions, to be conveyed across first, and then the army. But they were frightened by the swiftness of the river, thinking the arches might give way. Since they did not dare to cross,

Alexander took his bodyguard with him and crossed over first. Then the rest of the army crossed over too. At once he ordered the bridge over the Euphrates to be dismantled. The army was very reluctant to do this, and complained, 'King Alexander, if we should be turned back in our fight against the barbarians, how shall we find a way of crossing to safety?' But Alexander, seeing that they were frightened and hearing their complaints against himself, summoned the whole army and made the following speech:

'Fellow-soldiers, you are filling me with confidence of victory with all your talk of defeat and retreat. It was for this reason that I ordered you to dismantle the bridge, so that when you fight you will win, and not be defeated and turn tail. War goes not to the one who flees but to the pursuer. When we are victorious, we shall all return together to Macedonia; battle is like play for us.'

After this speech, the army acclaimed him and they marched on to war. Presently they put up tents and made a halt.

Darius' army had likewise pitched camp, beyond the river Tigris. The two armies met and fought bravely against each other. One of the Persians came up behind Alexander, wearing Macedonian armour and pretending to be an ally, and he struck at Alexander's head and cracked his skull. At once he was seized by Alexander's soldiers and brought to him in chains.

Alexander, thinking he was a Macedonian, asked him, 'My brave fellow, why did you do that?'

The other replied, 'King Alexander, do not be deceived by this Macedonian uniform of mine. I am a Persian, one of Darius' satraps, and I went to Darius and said, "What will you give me if I bring you the head of Alexander?" He promised to give me part of his kingdom and his daughter in marriage. So I crept up on you wearing Macedonian uniform, but as I missed my mark I stand now in chains before you.'

When Alexander heard this, he sent for the whole army and in their presence set the man free. Then he said to his own soldiers, 'Men of Macedon, you too must be as brave in battle as this man.'

10. The barbarians' supplies had now run out and they retreated to Bactria. Alexander, however, stayed and subdued the whole country. Then another of Darius' satraps came to him, and said, 'I am a satrap of Darius and I have done many great deeds for him in war and have received no reward from him. Give me 10,000 armed soldiers and I will bring you my own king, Darius.' But Alexander replied, 'Go and help your own king, Darius; I will not entrust to you the troops of another when you can thus betray your own.'

Then the satraps[62] of the provinces wrote to Darius about Alexander:

'Greetings to Darius the great king. In our anxiety we have already informed you about Alexander's march against our people; now we are writing to inform you that he has arrived. He is besieging our land and has killed many of us Persians. We are in danger of being destroyed. Come in haste now with a great army to meet him, and do not allow him to come nearer to you. The Macedonian army is extremely strong and numerous, and superior to ours. Farewell.'

When Darius had read their letter, he sent a letter to Alexander, as follows:

'I call the great god Zeus to witness what you have done to me. I suppose that my mother has gone to be with the gods, that I no longer have a wife, and that my children might as well not have been born. I will not cease seeking vengeance for the harm you have done me. It was written to me that you were behaving justly and properly to my family; but if you were really to act justly towards me, you would have shown me a just respect in the first place. You have my family in your power to do as you like: punish them with mishandling, for they are the children of your enemy. You will not make me your friend by treating them kindly, nor your enemy just through ill-treating them.'

When Alexander had read this letter from Darius he smiled, and wrote back to him as follows:

'King Alexander greets Darius. Your empty ravings and your vain and babbling sermons are hateful to the gods, through and through. Are you not ashamed of your blasphemous and vain invectives? It was not through fear of you that I honoured your family, nor out of hope of a reconciliation with you, of your coming to me to thank me. Do not come to me. My crown is not worth yours to gain. You will not prevent me from being respectful in my treatment of all people, but I shall show even greater courtesy to the family that was yours. This will be my last letter to you.'

11. After writing this letter to Darius, Alexander made ready for war and wrote to all his satraps:

'King Alexander to all the satraps who are subject to him in Phrygia, Cappadocia, Paphlagonia, Arabia, and to all the rest of them, greetings. I want you to prepare tunics for a great multitude, and to send them to us in Antioch in Syria. Send us also all that you have in your armouries. We have 3,000 camels drawn up between the Euphrates and Antioch, ready to do our bidding, so that you can carry out your task the more quickly. Hasten therefore to us.'

The satraps of Darius wrote:

'To Darius the great king. We write to you after considerable hesitation, but are compelled to do so by our circumstances. Know, O king, that Alexander the leader of the Macedonians has put to death two of our number, and some of the other princes have gone over to Alexander with their harems.'

When Darius heard this, he wrote to the generals and satraps who were in the vicinity, telling them to make ready and assemble their troops. He also wrote to the nearby kings, as follows:

'Darius, king of kings, greets you. Like a man who wipes away his sweat, we are going to make war against this tiresome race of Macedonians.'

Then he ordered the Persian army to be in readiness. And he wrote to Porus the king of the Indians, to ask for his help.

['Darius the unfortunate greets King Porus, the great god among gods. It is impossible even to write about our great misfortunes; but I suppose that you, my lord, have heard the bare essentials – that the Macedonian boy has attacked us like a bandit and has exiled us from our home, putting aside the slavish station that belongs to him. He is eager to make us his subjects and to extend his rule from east to west. The Persians were afraid of him and – I do not know why – were unable to resist him in battle. Therefore, I beg you in your magnificence not to put up with this, but to extend the hand of salvation to Darius your slave: then let me join battle once more with the Macedonians, so that they may learn not to take up arms against the gods. I know that the Indian army is unconquerable. Be moved by my letter, fulfil my heartfelt plea and agree to drive back the Macedonians who are pressing me hard. Take pity on my misfortunes. Farewell.' *γ-text*]

12. When King Porus received Darius' letter, he was distressed by his misfortunes, and answered as follows:

[Supplement E]

'Porus, the king of the Indians, greets Darius the king of the Persians. When I read your letter to me, I was greatly distressed. I am in a quandary, because I would like to help you and to give good advice about these events, but I am prevented by this chronic illness of mine. But take heart, we shall be with you, even if we cannot hold off this assault. Write to me, therefore, what you require. My own forces are at your service, and the more distant nations will also obey my summons.'

When Darius' mother heard of these goings-on, she secretly sent a letter to Darius, as follows:

'Greetings to Darius, my son. I hear that you are gathering the peoples and preparing to go to war with Alexander again. Do not turn the world upside down, my son. The future is invisible to us. Let us hope for a turn for the better, and do not, by rash action in a critical moment, lose your life. We are held in great honour by King Alexander, and he has not treated me as the mother of an enemy, but has given us steadfast protection, as a result of which I hope we shall reach a good understanding.'

When Darius read this, he wept as he thought of his dear ones, but at the same time he was stirred up again to thoughts of war.

13. Alexander arrived with a great army in the land of Persia. The high walls of the city[63] were visible to the Macedonians

from a long way off. Then the cunning Alexander thought of a trick: he rounded up the flocks of sheep which were grazing there on the meadows, and tied branches from the trees to their backs; he then made the flocks march behind the army. The branches dragging behind them on the ground stirred up the dust, and the sandstorm reached up to Olympus, so that the Persians, as they looked out from their walls, thought that a vast army was coming against them. When evening came, Alexander ordered torches and candles to be tied to the horns of the sheep and set alight. The land was very flat, and the whole plain appeared as if it were on fire. The Persians were terrified.

Soon they came within five miles of the Persian city. Alexander was looking for someone to send to Darius to inform him when the battle was going to take place. While Alexander was asleep that night, he had a dream vision of Ammon standing by him in the guise of Hermes, with his messenger's staff and his short cloak and stick, and wearing a Macedonian cap on his head. Ammon said, 'Child Alexander, when you need help, I will be beside you; but if you send a messenger to Darius, he will betray you. So be your own messenger and go dressed just as you see me dressed now.' Alexander replied, 'It is dangerous for a king to be his own messenger.' But Ammon said, 'With god as your helper, no harm will attend you.' Alexander obeyed the oracle; he got up delighted, and told his satraps about it. They advised him against the enterprise.

14. Alexander set off, however, accompanied by a satrap named Eumelus. He took three horses and went to the river called Stranga.[64] This river freezes over when it snows, so that its surface becomes as firm as a stone road, and beasts and wagons can cross over it. Then a few days later it melts and becomes fast-flowing again, and sweeps away in its current any who are caught crossing it.

Alexander found the river frozen. Putting on the garments that he had seen Ammon wearing in his dream, he mounted his horse and crossed over alone. Eumelus begged to be allowed to cross with him, in case he needed help, but Alexander said, 'Stay here with the two horses. I have as my helper the god whose oracle told me to wear these clothes and to go alone.'

The river was about two hundred yards wide. Alexander rode on and came right up to the gates of Persia. The sentries, seeing him dressed as he was, took him for a god. They seized him and asked him who he was. But Alexander replied, 'Bring me to King Darius; it is to him that I shall reveal who I am.'

Darius was outside the city on a hill, building roads and drilling his phalanxes for a fight against the Macedonian heroes. Alexander drew all eyes by his strange appearance, and Darius almost fell to his knees before him, thinking that he was one of the gods, who had come down from Olympus and dressed himself in barbarian garments. But Darius sat still, wearing his crown set with precious stones, his silk robes woven with gold thread in the Babylonian style, his cloak of royal purple, and his golden shoes studded with gems which covered his shins. He held a sceptre in either hand, and the troops around him were innumerable. [When Alexander saw him, he was somewhat afraid, but he remembered the oracle and did not turn tail. γ-text]

Seeing his visitor wearing clothes the like of which he had never seen before, Darius asked him who he was.

'I am a messenger from King Alexander,' Alexander replied.

'Why have you come to us?' asked Darius.

'To inform you,' replied Alexander, 'that Alexander is close by. When are you going to join battle? You must know, your majesty, that a king who hesitates to go into battle makes plain to his opponent that his martial spirit is weak. So do not delay, but tell me when you intend to join battle.'

Darius was angry and said, 'Am I making war against you or against Alexander? You are as impudent as Alexander himself, and make your replies as boldly as if you were a friend of mine. I am going now to have my accustomed meal; you shall dine with me, since Alexander served dinner to my messengers.'

So saying, Darius took Alexander by the arm and led him inside the palace. Alexander took it as a good omen that the tyrant took him by the arm. When they got inside the palace, Alexander was given the place of honour next to Darius at table. [Darius' couch was at the head of the table. The second was taken by Darius' brother Oxyathres, the third by Ochus the

satrap of the Oxydracae; then there was Adulites the satrap of
Susa, and Phraortes; next to him, the sixth, was Mithridates, and
Tiridates the chief of the archers, then Candaules the black, . . .
the lord of the Ethiopians, and next to him Polyares the great
general. Also present were Orniphatos, Hodiones, Karterophotos,
Sobarites and Delealkides. Opposite all these, all alone on a
separate couch, was the magnificent Macedonian. *A-text*]

15. The Persians looked in amazement at Alexander because of
his small stature, but they did not know that the glory of a
celestial destiny was hidden in that little vessel.

As they began to drink more deeply, Alexander had an idea:
he concealed every cup that he was given in the folds of his
cloak. Those who saw him mentioned it to Darius. Darius stood
up and asked him, 'My good man, why are you concealing
those cups as you dine at my table?' Alexander thought quickly
and replied, 'Great king, whenever Alexander holds a dinner for
his squadron leaders and adjutants, he gives them the cups as
presents. I assumed that you would do as he does, and I supposed
that this was the right thing to do.' The Persians were quite
astounded when they heard what Alexander said. Any old tale
can carry its listeners, if it is told with conviction.

Silence fell on the company, and a certain Paragages,[65] who
was a prince of Persia, looked searchingly at Alexander. In fact
he had recognized Alexander by his face, because the first time
he had gone to Pella in Macedonia as ambassador from Darius to
demand the tribute, he had been prevented from collecting it by
Alexander. So after he had looked at Alexander for some time
he said to himself, 'This is the son of Philip, even if he has
altered his appearance. Many men may be recognized by their
voices, even in darkness.' When he had finally assured himself
that this was Alexander, he sat down beside Darius and said,
'Great King Darius, ruler of all lands, this messenger from Alexander is in fact Alexander himself, the king of Macedon, the brave
son of Philip.' Darius and his fellow diners were already very
drunk. But Alexander heard what Paragages said, and realizing
that he had been recognized, he slipped out without anyone
noticing, still carrying the golden goblets in his cloak, and left

unobtrusively. He mounted his horse to escape the danger. At the gate he found a Persian sentry with a torch in his hand. He snatched this, killed the sentry, and left the Persian city.[66]

When Darius noticed that he had gone, he sent some armed Persians to capture him. But Alexander spurred his horse on and made swift progress. It was late at night and the sky was quite dark. A large number pursued him, but they did not capture him. Some kept to the passable country, but others fell over cliffs in the darkness. Alexander, however, was as bright as a star that rises alone in the sky, and so he led the Persians astray as he fled.

Darius was sitting on his bed, deeply disturbed. Then he saw an evil omen. A statue of King Xerxes, of which he was particularly fond because of its high artistic quality, suddenly fell through the ceiling.

Meanwhile Alexander, saved by the darkness, came at about dawn to the river Stranga. Just as he had crossed it, and his horse had placed its forefeet on the firm earth of the bank, the river melted in the sunshine. The horse was seized by the current and swept away, throwing Alexander to the ground as it slipped. The Persians who were in pursuit of Alexander came to the river after Alexander had crossed it; but they were unable to cross themselves and had to turn back. That river was impassable for any man. So the Persians returned to Darius and told him of Alexander's lucky escape. Darius was stunned by the miraculous omen, and was deeply distressed.[67]

Alexander walked away from the river and found Eumelus waiting with the two horses as he had left him, and he told him all that had happened.

16. Alexander then went into the camp and immediately called all the phalanxes of the Greeks by name, ordering them to arm and be ready to fight Darius. He stood in their midst, encouraging them. When the whole army was assembled, he found that it numbered 120,000. He stood on a high place and made the following speech:

'Fellow-soldiers, even if our numbers are small, our intelligence, our bravery and our strength are great in comparison with those of our foes the Persians. So let none of you allow thoughts of inferiority to enter his mind when he gazes at the multitude of the Persians: one of you with a naked sword can kill a thousand of the enemy. Let none of you be afraid: there may be 10,000 flies swarming in a field, but when the wasps arrive, they frighten the flies away simply by the buzzing of their wings. Numbers are nothing against intelligence; and the flies are nothing against the wasps.'

With these words Alexander encouraged his army; and they in turn became brave and cheered their king.

He then marched on towards the river Stranga, and indeed right up to its banks. Darius with his army also marched to the Stranga. Seeing it low, and frozen over, he began to cross, hastening over its wastes. He hoped to take Alexander's army by surprise and find them unprepared, so that victory would be easy. Heralds went into the middle and called out the champions to battle. Darius' whole army was in full armour. Darius himself was riding in a high chariot, and his satraps were mounted in chariots armed with scythes, while the rest carried cunningly-made weapons and mechanical spear-throwers. Alexander led the Macedonian troops, mounted on his horse Bucephalus; there was no other horse to match him.

Both sides played the trumpet-call for battle. Some began to throw stones, others to shoot arrows, which dropped from the sky like rain; others threw hunting spears, and others hurled lead slingshots until the sky was dark.

There was a tremendous mêlée of soldiers striking and soldiers being struck. Many were wounded with missiles and killed; others lay half-dead on the ground. The air was dark and reeked of blood. When many of the Persians had been horribly killed, Darius in terror pulled round the reins of his scythed chariot; as the wheels whirled, he mowed down a multitude of the Persians, like a harvester cropping the stalks of corn.

When he reached the river Stranga, he and those who were with him found the river frozen over. But so great were the numbers of the Persians and barbarians who wanted to cross the river and escape, that when they all poured on to the ice at once, it broke beneath them and the river bore away as many as it engulfed. The remaining Persians were killed by the Macedonians.[68]

Darius, however, got away safely to his own palace. There, throwing himself on the floor, he began to wail and weep, lamenting his misfortune, the loss of so great an army and the devastation of all Persia. Overcome by this catastrophe, he said, 'King Darius, who was so great and ruled over so many peoples, and had made all the cities his slaves, he who was enthroned with the gods and rose up every day with the sun, has now become a friendless fugitive. True it is that no one can count on the future: if fate's balance slips just a little to one side, it exalts the humble above the clouds and hurls others from their heights into Hades.'

17. So Darius lay, the loneliest of men, who had been king of so many nations. But after a while he pulled himself together and got up. He then composed a letter to Alexander, as follows:

'Darius greets Alexander, my master. My father who gave me life, in his pride, had a great passion to make war on Greece, unsatisfied as he was with the gold and the other blessings he had inherited from our fathers. But although he was richer than Croesus, king of Lydia, he lost much gold and silver, and many tents before he died, and neither could he escape the death that awaited him. You, Alexander, have seen good fortune and disaster; renounce your ambitious plans. Pity us who flee to you as suppliants, now that we have lost all the nobility of Persia. Return to me my wife, my mother and my children; think of the tender hopes of a father. In exchange, I promise to give you all the treasure that is in Mysia and in Susa and in Bactria, which our father stored up for our country. I promise also that you shall be king over the lands of the Medes and Persians and the other nations for ever and ever. Farewell.'

When Alexander had learnt the contents of this letter, he assembled all his army and his commanders and ordered them to read out Darius' letter. When the letter had been read, one of the generals, by name Parmenio, said, 'If I were you, Alexander, I should accept the gold and the land that is offered to you, and should give back to Darius his mother and his children and his wife, after sleeping with them.'

Alexander smiled and replied,[69] 'No, Parmenio, I shall take
everything from him. I am amazed that he proposes to ransom
his family with what is my property, and even more that he
promises to surrender to me a land that is already mine. He
clearly does not realize that unless he defeats me in battle, all
these things will be mine as well as his family. It is shameful and
more than shameful that a man who has defeated men through
his manliness should be defeated by women. So we shall continue
to make war on him for what is ours: I should not have entered
Asia at all, if I had not believed it to be mine. If he was ruler of
it before me, let him count his gain, in that he held another's
land for so long without suffering anything untoward.'

So saying, Alexander ordered the ambassadors from Darius to
go back to him and tell him all this; but he would not give them
a written letter. Then Alexander ordered those who had been
wounded in the war to be nursed with every care, and those
who had been killed to be buried with proper obsequies. He
spent the winter in that place, and ordered the palace of Xerxes,
which was the finest in the country, to be burnt;[70] but a little
later he changed his mind and ordered his men to stop.

18. Alexander saw that the tombs of the Persians were adorned
with a great deal of gold. He saw the tomb of Nabonasar, who
is called Nabuchodonosor[71] in Greek, as well as the dedications
of the Jews and the golden mixing bowls, so large as to be the
work of heroes. Near by he saw the tomb of Cyrus. It was a
twelve-sided free-standing tower, and Cyrus lay on the topmost
floor in a golden coffin roofed over with glass, through which
his hair and every feature could be seen.[72]

At the tomb of Cyrus were Greeks who had had their feet,
noses or ears cut off, and were bound in fetters that were nailed
fast to the tomb. They were Athenians. They begged Alexander
to rescue them. Alexander wept when he saw them, for it was a
terrible sight. He was deeply moved, and gave orders that they
should be released, presented with 2,000 drachmas and repatriated
to their own country. They took the money, but asked Alexander to allot them land there rather than sending them home to
their country; looking as they did, they would shame their

relatives. So he ordered allotments of land to be made for them, and grain and seed to be given to them, as well as six oxen each, sheep and everything that is necessary for farming, and other items besides.

19. Darius, meanwhile, was rearming for the continuation of the war with Alexander. He wrote to Porus the king of the Indians, as follows:

'King Darius greets Porus, king of the Indians. After the disaster that has befallen my house, I write with further news. The Macedonian, who has the soul of a wild beast, has overcome me, and refuses to return my mother, wife and daughters to me. I have promised to give him treasure and all kinds of things, but he is inflexible. Therefore, I have decided to fight him again in order to destroy him for what he has done, until I have punished him and his nation. It is right that you should be angry at what has happened to me, and should come to help me against my insolent opponent. Think of the bonds of blood that bind us. Collect as many of the nations as possible at the Caspian Gates,[73] and organize gold and provisions for the men, and fodder for the animals. I will give you half of all the spoils that I win from the enemy, as well as the horse called Bucephalus, the royal lands and the king's concubines. As soon as you receive this letter, muster your men and send them to me. Farewell.'

When Alexander learnt of this from one of Darius' men who had crossed over to his side, he took all his forces and marched on Media. There he heard that Darius was at Batana,[74] near the Caspian Gates. He continued the pursuit immediately and with all his energy. [Alexander thought he would never rule Asia if he did not despise the name of Darius. Then he was told that Darius had departed for the Caspian Gates. He immediately set off in pursuit until he was informed that Darius was near by: Bagistanes the eunuch arrived and told him everything that happened, which made his pursuit the more enthusiastic. A-text]

20. Two of Darius' satraps, Bessus and Ariobarzanes, knew that Alexander was approaching. They treacherously planned to kill Darius. For, they said to each other, 'If we kill Darius, we shall

receive a great deal of money from Alexander for destroying his enemy.' So with this evil plan they went to Darius, swords in hand. When Darius saw them approaching him with their swords drawn, he said to them, 'O my masters, who were once my servants, how have I wronged you, that you wish to destroy me in this reckless and savage way? Do not act worse than the Macedonians. Let me lie here upon the floor and bewail the unfairness of my fate. If Alexander, the king of the Macedonians, comes here and finds me slain, as a king he will avenge the blood of a king.'

But they took no notice of Darius' pleas and raised their swords. Darius defended himself with both hands: with the left he held Bessus down and drove his knee into his groin, and with the right he held off Ariobarzanes so that he could not bring his sword close to him, and its blows fell aslant. The traitors found they could not finish him off, however much they struggled; for Darius was a strong man.

The Macedonians now found the Stranga frozen over and crossed the river. Alexander went straight to Darius' palace. When the traitors heard that Alexander was coming, they fled, leaving Darius dying. So Alexander found him, blood pouring from his wounds. He cried out and began to shed tears, lamenting him as he deserved; then he covered Darius' body with his cloak. Placing his hands on Darius' breast, he spoke these words, pregnant with pity:[75] 'Stand up, King Darius. Rule your land and become master of yourself. Receive back your crown and rule your Persian people. Keep your kingdom to its full extent. I swear to you by Providence above that what I say is honest and not feigning. Who was it who struck you? Tell me their names, so that I may give you peace.'

When Alexander had so spoken, Darius groaned and stretched out his hands to Alexander, clutching at him and drawing him to himself.

'Alexander,' he said, 'do not become too proud of the glory of your kingship. Even if what you achieved is godlike, and you are ready now to grasp heaven with both hands, have a thought for the future. Fate recognizes no kings, however powerful they are, and swerves hither and thither, quite without reason. You can see what I was, and what I have become. When I am dead, Alexander, bury me with your own hands. Let the Macedonians and Persians carry me to my grave. Let the families of Darius and of Alexander be one. I commit my mother to you as if she were your own, and I ask you to sympathize with my wife as if she were one of your relatives. As for my daughter Roxane, I give her to you for a wife, to start a line of descendants that will preserve your memory. Be proud of them, as we are of our children, and, as you grow old together, preserve the memory of your parents – you of Philip, and Roxane of Darius.'

With these words Darius laid his head on Alexander's breast and died.

21. Alexander raised up a great cry and wept for Darius. Then he ordered him to be buried in the Persian manner. He had the Persians march in front, followed by the Macedonians in full armour. Alexander put his own shoulder to the carrying of the bier, along with the other satraps. They all wept and mourned, not so much for Darius as for Alexander, at the sight of him shouldering the bier. After the burial had been carried out in the Persian manner, he dismissed the crowds.

Immediately he issued an order to all the cities, as follows:

'I, King Alexander, son of King Philip and of Queen Olympias, inform all those in the cities and regions of Persia, that I do not want many tens of thousands of people to die in misery. I give thanks to Providence above, whose goodwill has made me victorious over the Persians. Be informed that I propose to set up satraps over you, whom you must obey as you did in the days of Darius. You shall know no other king but Alexander. Keep to your ancestral customs, festivals, sacrifices and holy days, as you did in the days of Darius. But if anyone leaves his own city or region to dwell in another, he shall be given as food to the dogs. Each of you shall retain all his own possessions, except his gold and silver. I order that the gold and silver be brought to our cities and regions, but we allow you to keep any coined money that you have for your own use. I order every weapon of war to be delivered to my armouries. The satraps are to remain at their posts. No nation will now come to you,

except for the purposes of trade, and then no more than twenty
men at a time. I will exact the same taxes as in Darius' days. I
wish your lands to be established in prosperity, and the roads of
Persia to remain peaceful for trade and travel, so that merchants
may come from Greece to you, and you to them. I shall build
roads and erect signposts from the Euphrates and the crossing to
the Tigris, as far as Babylon.

['As for the road tolls that were customary in Darius' days, I
make a present of these to the gods, especially Sarapis and Zeus.
Since you wish to celebrate my birthday with honours instead of
that of Cyrus, I have commanded Moschylus the satrap to ensure
that you celebrate both my birthday and that of Cyrus with
festivals and contests. Let the Persians be spectators of the contests, and let prizes be offered, whatever you wish, to the Persians.
I wish a virgin to be crowned as priestess of my mother. She is
to continue to receive her annual salary,[76] and to retain her
priesthood until the end of her life; but if she yields to nature
and ceases to be a virgin, let her be given the same amount as a
dowry. These regulations shall apply also to her successor in the
priesthood. Let the gymnasium be built in a conspicuous place,
just as it is in Pella. I shall make the selections for the contests, as
long as I am alive; after my death, it shall be the task of the
rulers to whom I have given the country. For the war-chariot
race the prize shall be a golden goblet weighing twelve [thou-
sand] staters, and five silver goblets, each holding a sufficient
measure for a moderate man to get drunk on. For the war-horse
race the prize shall be a similar goblet and a Persian robe, and
free dinners in the sanctuary of Alexander for life. But if the
winner prefers rewards in the Persian style, he shall have a
golden crown . . . a plain Persian robe and a golden belt and two
cups weighing 170 staters. All my satraps in Persia shall join in
the festival meal at the sanctuary of Alexander. They will be
rulers, not tyrants. The presidents of the games shall all be my
"Alexandrians", that is, the priests of the sanctuary of Alexander.
Moschylus, the founder of the sanctuary of Alexander, is to
receive a golden crown and a purple robe, for wear on special
days. Let no prostitutes enter the temple; and let none of the race
of the Medes enter it. I wish that you be not judges in your own

affairs, no matter who the other party is, and especially not in capital matters: if anyone is found calling an assembly of satraps or others, except in the council chamber, he shall be treated as an enemy.'

When he had finished settling all these matters, Alexander wrote a speech:

'They have destroyed the great king, my enemy, your lord, Darius. *A-text*] I did not kill Darius. Who they were who slew him, I do not know. I owe them great honours, and will present them with much land, because they have killed my enemy.'

The Persians were perturbed at these words of Alexander, because they supposed he wanted to ruin Persia. But Alexander noticed their distress and said, 'Why do you suppose, men of Persia, that I am seeking out the murderers of Darius? If Darius were alive, he would have made war against me, but now the war is over. Whether it was a Persian or a Macedonian who killed him, let him come to me with confidence, and receive whatever he wishes from me. I swear by Providence above, and by the safety of my mother, Olympias, that I will raise those men up and make them conspicuous among men.'

The crowd wept at this oath of Alexander. Then Bessus and Ariobarzanes came to Alexander, expecting to receive lavish gifts from him, and said, 'Lord, it was we who killed Darius.' At once Alexander ordered them to be seized and crucified on the grave of Darius. They protested violently: 'You swore that you would make those who killed Darius exalted and conspicuous among men. How can you now betray your oath and order us to be crucified?'

'It is not for your benefit,' replied Alexander, 'that I shall answer your question, but for the benefit of the assembled soldiers. There was no way to find you so easily and bring you to light, except by praising the murder of Darius. I was determined to subject his murderers to the severest penalty. How could I suppose that those who killed their own master would spare me? I have not broken my oath, you villains. I swore that I would raise you up and make you conspicuous among men – by which I meant that I would crucify you, so that all can look upon you.'

Then everyone praised Alexander's cunning, and the wicked murderers were crucified on the grave of Darius.

22. When Alexander had restored peace to the whole land, he asked the people, 'Whom do you want as the satrap of your city?' 'Adulites,[77] the brother of Darius,' came the reply. So he appointed him satrap.

He had left Darius' mother, wife and daughter in a city two days' journey away. Now he wrote to them, as follows:

'King Alexander greets Stateira, Rodo and Roxane, my wife.[78] We fought against Darius but did not revenge ourselves on him. I would rather have had him remain alive under my rule. But I found him at the point of death; I pitied him and covered him with my cloak. I asked him who had struck him down, but he said nothing to me except this: "I commit to you my mother and my wife, but especially my daughter Roxane, your wife." He had no chance to tell me how he had been slain. However, I have punished the murderers in a suitable manner. He required me to bury him in the grave of his ancestors, which has been done. I expect that you have heard about that. Cease now from your grieving. I shall re-establish you in your royal palace. Remain for the moment where you are, until everything is properly settled here. According to the last wishes of Darius, I claim Roxane as my bride, if this is agreeable to you. I wish and command her from now on to be shown obeisance as wife of Alexander. Farewell.'

When they received this letter from Alexander, Stateira and Rodo replied as follows:

'Greetings to King Alexander. We have prayed to the gods in heaven, who brought low the name of Darius and the pride of Persia, and have revealed you as eternal ruler of the world, full of cunning, wisdom and power. We know that we shall live in safety under your protection. So we prayed to Providence above to grant you many years of flourishing and a reign of endless duration. Your achievements are the proof that you are from an exceptional family. Now we are no longer like prisoners, and we know that Alexander is our new Darius. We fall at Alexander's feet because he has not disgraced us. We have written to everyone, "O people of Persia, know that the dying Darius chose King Alexander as his successor. Fate has given Roxane as wife to Alexander, king of all the world. All of you, show your gratitude to Alexander, for the fame of Persia has been even further exalted. Rejoice with us in proclaiming Alexander our great king!'' This is what we have written to the people of Persia. Farewell.'

Alexander replied to this letter as follows:

'I commend your good sense. I will try to make my achievements worthy of your love, for I too am only mortal. Farewell.'

In another letter he wrote to Roxane and told her what he had decided.

['King Alexander greets his wife, Roxane. I have written to my mother, Olympias, about some other matters that concern us, and I have asked her in my letter to send us the jewellery and robes of Darius' mother and your mother, Rodo, and to send the bridal gifts on my behalf. Try to adopt a suitable attitude to Alexander and to fear him and to respect Olympias. If you do this, you will bring great distinction to both yourself and us. My dearest, farewell.' γ-text]

Then he wrote a letter to his mother, Olympias, as follows:

'King Alexander to his sweet mother, greetings. I am writing to ask you to send me the garments and jewellery of Darius' mother and his wife, and the royal robes for Roxane, the daughter of Darius, who is now my wife.'[79]

When Olympias received this letter, she sent him all her royal garments, and all her jewellery of gold and precious stones. When Alexander received them, he began preparations for the wedding in Darius' palace. Who could describe the joy of that event!

[Supplement F]

23. Alexander wrote again to his mother, as follows:[80]

'King Alexander to my mother, whom I miss sorely, and to my most honoured tutor Aristotle, greetings. I thought I ought to write to you about my recent battle with Darius. I heard that he was at the Gulf of Issus with a vast army of his own and the other kings. I took a large number of goats and tied torches to their horns; then I set off and marched forward by night. When the enemy saw the torches from afar, they supposed it to be a countless army, and became so frightened that they were

defeated. And that is how I won my victory over them. I
founded a city there and called it Aegae.[81] I also founded another
city on the Gulf of Issus, and called it Alexandria. Darius was
deserted, and then seized and murdered by his own satraps. I was
very sorry for him. I did not want him to be killed after his
defeat, but to live under my rule. I came upon him still alive,
and took off my cloak to cover him. Then I reflected on the
uncertainty of fortune, as exemplified in the fate of Darius, and I
lamented him. I buried him royally, and gave orders to cut off
the noses and ears of those who guarded his grave, as is the
custom here. I had the murderers of Darius crucified on his
grave. Then I went and conquered the kingdom of Ariobarzanes
and Manazakes. I subdued Media and Armenia, Ebesia and all
the kingdom of Persia that had formerly belonged to Darius.

32. 'Then I took guides, intending to go deep into the desert, in
the direction of the constellation of the Plough. They counselled
against going that way because of the numbers of wild beasts
that live in those regions. However, I took no notice of them
and set out. We soon came to a land full of ravines, where the
way was very narrow and precipitous, and it took us eight days
to cross it. In this place we saw beasts of all kinds, all quite
unfamiliar to us. After we had crossed it, we came to an even
more desolate place. Here, we found a great forest of trees called
anaphanda, with a strange and unfamiliar fruit: they were like
apples, but of the size of melons. There were also people in the
wood, called Phytoi, who were 36 feet tall, their necks alone
being 2 feet in length, and their feet of equally enormous size.
Their forearms and hands were like saws. When they saw us
they stormed our camp. I could not believe my eyes when I saw
them, and gave orders to capture one; but when we charged
them, shouting and blowing our trumpets, they ran away. We
killed thirty-two of them, and they killed 100 of our soldiers.
We spent some time there, eating the fruit of the trees.

33. 'Then we set out and came to a green country where there
were wild men like giants, spherical in shape, with fiery
expressions like lions. After them were another people, the

Ochlitae, who had no hair at all on their bodies, were 6 feet tall and as broad as a lance. When they saw us, they ran towards us. They were dressed in lions' skins, very strong and ready to fight without weapons. We fought them, but they struck us with logs and killed a good many of us. I was afraid they might put our men to flight, and so I ordered fires to be lit in the forest. When these mighty men saw the fire, they ran away. But they had killed 180 of our soldiers.

'The next day I decided to visit their caves. We found wild beasts, resembling lions but with three eyes, tethered at the entrances. There we saw fleas jumping about, as big as frogs in our own country. Then we marched on and came to a place where an abundant spring welled out of the ground. I ordered the army to halt, and we stayed there two months.

'Then we advanced and reached the country of the Apple-eaters. There we saw a huge man with hair all over his body, and we were frightened. I gave orders to capture him. When he was taken, he gazed at us ferociously. I ordered a naked woman to be brought to him; but he grabbed her and ate her.[82] The soldiers rushed up to rescue her, but he made a gnashing noise with his teeth. The rest of the natives heard him, and came running towards us out of the swamp: there were about 10,000 of them. Our forces amounted to 40,000. I ordered the swamp to be set alight; and when they saw the fire they fled. We gave pursuit and overpowered three of them, but they would not take any food and died after eight days. They had no human intelligence, but barked like dogs.

36. 'We marched on from there and came to a river. I ordered my men to pitch camp and lay aside their armour in the usual way. In the river there were trees which began to grow at sunrise and continued until the sixth hour, but from the seventh hour they shrank again until they could hardly be seen. They exuded a sap like Persian myrrh, with a sweet and noble aroma. I had cuts made in a few of them, and the sap soaked up with sponges. Suddenly the sap-collectors began to be whipped by an invisible spirit: we heard the noise of the whipping and saw the marks of the blows on their backs, but we could not see those

who were beating them. Then a voice was heard, telling them neither to cut the trees nor to collect the sap: "If you do not cease," it said, "the army will be struck dumb." I was afraid and gave orders not to cut or collect any more of the sap.

'In the river there were black stones. Anyone who touched one of them became as black as the stone itself. There were also many snakes and many kinds of fish, which could not be cooked by fire, but only in freezing cold water. One of the soldiers, in fact, caught one of these fish, washed it and put it into a bucket, and shortly found it cooked. There were also many kinds of birds in this river, closely resembling our own; but if any of our people touched one of them, flames shot out of it.

37. 'The next day we lost our way. The guides said to me, "We do not know where we are going, your majesty. Let us turn back, for fear we find ourselves in an even worse place." But I was reluctant to turn back. Many wild animals shared our march: they had six feet, and some had three eyes and some five, and they were 15 feet long; these were just a few of the species that accompanied us. Some of them shrank back from us, but others attacked us. Then we came to a sandy place, where we encountered animals like onagers, but 30 feet long. They had not two eyes but six; but they only used two of them for seeing. They were not fierce but tame. The soldiers shot a great many of them with bow and arrow.

[Supplement G]

'After that we came to a place where there were men without heads. They were hairy, wore skins and ate fish; but they spoke with human voices and used their own language. They used to hunt fish in the nearby sea and brought them to us; others collected mushrooms for us, each of which weighed 25 pounds. We saw a large number of large seals crawling about on land. Our friends repeatedly urged us to turn back, but I was reluctant because I wanted to see the end of the world.

38. 'We set off again and made for the sea through the desert. On the way we saw nothing – no bird or beast, nothing but sky

and earth. We could not even see the sun, and the sky remained black for a period of ten days. Then we came to a place by the sea and pitched our tents; we stayed in camp here for several days. In the middle of that sea, there was an island. I was eager to see it and to explore its interior, and so I gave orders for the construction of a number of small boats. About 1,000 men set off in those boats, and we crossed over to the island, which was not far from the land. There we heard human voices uttering the following words:

'"O son of Philip, seed of Egypt, the name you received is a sign of the success of your future achievements. You were named by your mother, Alexander. You have hunted men down and defeated them; you have swept kings from their seats. But soon you will find yourself without men,[83] when the second letter of your name, that is, l,[84] has been fulfilled."

'We heard these words, but could not see those who spoke them. Some of the soldiers in their foolishness swam from the ships to the island to investigate. But at once crabs came to the surface, dragged the men into the water and killed them. Frightened, we turned back towards the shore.

'When we had got out of the boats and were walking along the seashore, we found a crab emerging from the water on to the land. It was about the size of a breastplate, and its forefeet or claws were each 6 feet long. We at once took our spears and killed it. It was hard work, because the iron made no impact on its shell, and the spears were broken by its claws. When we had killed it, we opened it up and found in its shell seven pearls of considerable value. None of our men had ever seen pearls like them before. When I saw them, I supposed that they must originate in the inaccessible depths of the sea. So I then made a large iron cage, and inside the cage I placed a large glass jar, 2 feet wide, and I ordered a hole to be made in the bottom of the jar, big enough for a man's hand to go through. My idea was to descend and find out what was on the floor of this sea. I was going to keep this opening in the bottom of the jar closed until I reached the seabed, and then uncover it and quickly push my hand out to gather up from the sandy bottom whatever I could find, and then withdraw my hand and cover the hole up again.

And this is what I did. I had a chain made, 1,848 feet long, and ordered the men not to pull me up until they felt the chain shake. "As soon as I reach bottom," I said, "I will shake the jar and you are to pull me up again."

'When everything was ready I stepped into the glass jar, ready to attempt the impossible. As soon as I was inside, the entrance was closed with a lead plug. When I had descended 180 feet, a fish swam by and struck the cage with its tail. At once the men hauled me up, because they had felt the chain shake. The next time I went down the same thing happened. The third time I got down to a depth of 464 feet, and saw all kinds of fish swimming around me. And behold, an enormous fish came and took me and the cage in its mouth and brought me to land a mile away. There were 360 men on the ships from which I was let down, and the fish dragged them all along. When it reached land, it crushed the cage with its teeth and cast it up on the beach. I was gasping and half-dead from fright. I fell on my knees and thanked Providence above which had saved me from this frightful beast. Then I said to myself, "Alexander, now you must give up attempting the impossible; or you may lose your life in attempting to explore the deeps!" So I immediately ordered the army to strike camp and march on.[85]

39. 'After we had advanced for another two days, we came to a place where the sun does not shine. This is, in fact, the famous Land of the Blessed. I wanted to see and explore this region; I intended to go with just my personal servants to accompany me. My friend Callisthenes, however, advised me to take 40 friends, 100 slaves and 1,200 soldiers, but only the most reliable ones. So I left behind the infantry with the old men and the women, and I took only hand-picked young soldiers, giving orders that no old men should accompany us.

'But there was one inquisitive old man who had two young sons, real soldiers, and he said to them, "Sons, heed the voice of your father and take me with you; you will not find me a useless burden on the journey. In his moment of danger King Alexander will have need of an old man. If he finds that you have me with you, you will receive a great reward."

'"We are afraid of the king's threats," they replied. "If we are found disobeying his orders, we may be deprived not only of our part in the expedition, but of our lives."

'"Get up and shave my beard," the old man replied. "Change my appearance. Then I will march with you in the midst of the army, and in a moment of crisis I shall be of great use to you." So they did as their father ordered.

'After we had marched for three days we came to a place filled with fog. Being unable to go further, because the land was without roads or paths, we pitched our tents there. The next day I took 1,000 armed men with me and set off to see whether this was in fact the end of the world. We went towards the left, because it was lighter in that direction, and marched for half a day through rocky country full of ravines. I counted the passing of time not by the sun, but by measuring out the leagues we covered and thus calculating both the time and the distance. But eventually we turned back in fear because the way became impassable. So we decided to go instead to the right. The going was much smoother, but the darkness was impenetrable. I was at a loss, for my young companions all advised me not to go further into that region, for fear the horses should be scattered in the darkness over the long distance, and we should be unable to return. Then I said to them, "You who are so brave in war, now you may see that there is no true bravery without intelligence and understanding. If there were an old man with us, he would be able to advise us how to set about advancing in this dark place. Who among you is brave enough to go back to the camp and bring me an old man? He shall be given 10 pounds of gold."

'Then the sons of the old man said to me, "Lord, if you will hear us without anger, we have something to say to you."

'"Speak as you wish," I replied. "I swear by Providence above that I will do you no harm." Then they told me all about their father, and how they had brought him along with them, and they ran and fetched the old man himself. I greeted him warmly and asked him for his advice.

'"Alexander," the old man said, "it must be clear to you that you will never see the light of day again if you advance without horses. Select, then, mares with foals. Leave the foals here, and advance with the mares; they will without fail bring you back to their foals."

'I sought through the whole army and found only 100 mares with foals. I took these, and 100 selected horses besides, as well as further horses to carry our provisions. Then, following the old man's advice, we advanced, leaving the foals behind.

'The old man had advised his sons to pick up anything they found lying on the ground after we had entered the Land of Darkness, and to put it in their knapsacks. There were 360 soldiers: I had the 160 unmounted ones go on ahead. So we went on for about fifteen leagues. We came to a place where there was a clear spring, whose water flashed like lightning, and some other streams besides. The air in this place was very fragrant and less dark than before. I was hungry and wanted some bread, so I called the cook Andreas by name and said, "Prepare some food for us." He took a dried fish and waded into the clear water of the spring to wash it. As soon as it was dipped in the water, it came to life and leapt out of the cook's hands. He was frightened, and did not tell me what had happened; instead, he drank some of the water himself, and scooped some up in a silver vessel and kept it. The whole place was abounding in water, and we drank of its various streams. Alas for my misfortune, that it was not fated for me to drink of the spring of immortality, which gives life to what is dead, as my cook was fortunate enough to do.

40. 'After we had eaten we went on for about another 230 leagues. Then we saw a light that did not come from sun, moon or stars. I saw two birds in the air: they had human faces and spoke in Greek. "Why, Alexander, do you approach a land which is god's alone? Turn back, wretch, turn back; it is not for you to tread the Islands of the Blessed. Turn back, O man, tread the land that has been given to you and do not lay up trouble for yourself."

'I trembled, and obeyed dutifully the order that had been given to me. Then the second bird spoke again in Greek: "The East is calling you, and the kingdom of Porus will be made subject to you." With these words the bird flew away. I prayed, and then removed our guide and placed the mares at the head of

the expedition. Taking the Plough again as our guide, and led
by the voices of the foals, we arrived back at our camp after a
journey of twenty-two days.[86]

'Many of the soldiers were carrying things they had found.
The two sons of the old man had been particularly assiduous in
filling their knapsacks, as their father had told them.

41. 'When we found ourselves back in the light, it turned out
that they had brought with them pure gold and pearls of great
value. Then the others regretted that they had not brought back
more, or in some cases had brought nothing. We all congratulated the old man who had given us such good advice.

'After we had re-emerged, the cook told us what had
happened at the spring. I was consumed with misery when I
heard it, and punished him severely. But then I said to myself,
"What use is it, Alexander, to regret what is past?" I did not of
course know that he had drunk some of the water, or that he
had kept some of it. He had not admitted this, but only how the
dried fish had come to life again. But then the cook went to my
daughter Kale,[87] whom one of my concubines, Unna, had borne
to me, and promised to give her some of the water of immortality; which he did. When I heard of this, I will admit, I
envied them their immortality. I called my daughter to me and
said, "Take your luggage and leave my sight. You have become
an immortal spirit, and you shall be called Neraida because you
have obtained immortality from the water."[88] [Then I ordered
her henceforth to live no longer among men but in the mountains.] She left my presence weeping and wailing, and went to
live with the spirits in the desert places. As for the cook, I
ordered that he have a millstone tied around his neck and be
thrown into the sea. He thereupon became a spirit himself and
went away to live in a corner of the sea, which is called Andreas
after him.

'That is the story of the cook and my daughter.[89] From all
that I had experienced, I was sure that this place was the end of
the world. I had a great arch built there and inscribed with the
words: "If you want to get to the Land of the Blessed, keep to
the right, or you will get lost."

'Then I began to ask myself again if this place was really the end of the world, where the sky touched the earth. I wanted to discover the truth, and so I gave orders to capture two of the birds that lived there. They were very large white birds, very strong but tame; they did not fly away when they saw us. Some of the soldiers climbed on to their backs, hung on tightly, and flew off. The birds fed on carrion, with the result that a great many of them came to our camp, attracted by the dead horses. I captured two of them and ordered them to be given no food for three days. On the third day I had something like a yoke constructed from wood, and had this tied to their throats. Then I had an ox-skin made into a large bag, ⟨fixed it to the yoke⟩ and climbed in, holding two spears, each about 10 feet long and with a horse's liver fixed to the point. At once the birds soared up to seize the livers, and I rose up with them into the air, until I thought I must be close to the sky. I shivered all over because of the extreme coldness of the air, caused by the beating of the birds' wings.

'Soon a flying creature in the form of a man approached me and said, "O Alexander, you have not yet secured the whole earth, and are you now exploring the heavens? Return to earth as fast as possible, or you will become food for these birds." He went on, "Look down on the earth, Alexander!" I looked down, somewhat afraid, and behold, I saw a great snake curled up, and in the middle of the snake a tiny circle like a threshing-floor. Then my companion said to me, "Point your spear at the threshing-floor, for that is the world. The snake is the sea that surrounds the world."

'Thus admonished by Providence above, I returned to earth, landing about seven days' journey from my army. I was now frozen and half-dead with exhaustion. Where I landed, I found one of the satraps who was under my command; borrowing 300 horsemen from him, I returned to my camp. Now I have decided to make no more attempts at the impossible. Farewell.'[90]

[After travelling for the whole day, he[91] arrived at a lake. There he built a fortified camp and halted. The water of the lake was like honey. Because it was so clear, Alexander waded in: a fish saw him and made for him. When he saw it, Alexander at once jumped out of the lake. The speed of the fish was so great that it was lifted up and hurled right out of the water; when Alexander saw that, he turned round and speared it. Its size was spectacular. He ordered it to be cut up into sections, so that he could see the arrangement of its internal organs. When this was done, a gleaming stone was seen in its belly, as bright as a lantern. Alexander took the stone, set it in gold and used it at night instead of a lamp.[92]

That night, women came out of the lake and circled around the camp, singing a most lovely song; everyone saw them and heard the singing.[93]

When dawn came he continued his journey. After travelling for a day, he reached a level place. Here animals resembling men appeared: from their heads to their navels they were like men, but below they were horses. There were a great number of them, carrying bows in their hands; their arrows were not tipped with iron but with a sharp stone. They were eager for battle.

When Alexander saw them, he ordered a camp to be constructed, with a deep ditch around it, covered over with reeds and grass. At dawn he stationed a few archers near the ditch, telling them to fix no iron barbs to their arrows, but to carry the shafts only. 'When the battle begins, aim your arrows well. When the arrows strike, they will do no harm but will excite their valour. When you see them charging towards us, do not be afraid, but pretend to flee inside the camp. In this way we shall perhaps be able to capture some of them.'

This was done. When day broke, the horse–men had already surrounded the camp, and were shooting their arrows at it. When the Macedonians began to shoot back and their weapons did them no harm, the horse–men gathered into a mob and decided to charge on the Macedonians from all directions, whom they now despised for their cowardice. This was in keeping with their nature. Just as their human part was incomplete, so too were their reasoning powers. As men they despised the arrows because of their harmlessness, but as beasts they were incapable of understanding the devilment of men. So they charged regardless towards the camp, thinking that their opponents were on the run, and plunged and tumbled straight into the ditch. At this point Alexander ordered a large number of armed men to go out to them; and then they discovered what sort of swords the Macedonians really used – strong and murderous ones after all.

Alexander wanted to capture some of them and bring them back to our world. He brought about fifty out of the ditch. They survived for twenty-two days, but as he did not know what they fed on, they all died.[94]

After travelling for sixty days Alexander and his men regained the world, and ceased from their labours.

44.[95] After five days' rest the army recovered its strength. Then they set off towards India, reaching the country of the Sun and entering his city. There was said to be a shrine of the Sun there and certain sacred trees, where Apollo gave oracles. Alexander went into the shrine and sat down; he heard a voice, though he saw no one. The voice was an oracle, and the oracle revealed to Alexander his death. Alexander was very sad when he came out again, and went off into a lonely place.

While the army was resting, little men came out of the bushes growing near by. They had one foot rather like a sheep's, but the other foot, as well as their hands and head, were like a man's. They went very lightly on their feet as they approached. The soldiers ran and surrounded them, and with some difficulty captured a few and brought them to Alexander. Alexander told his men to go and fetch some more. When these creatures were brought near to him, they addressed him plaintively: 'Have mercy on us, lord, because we are men like you. It is because of our timidity that we live in this lonely place.' At this, Alexander relented and ordered them to be released. When this was done, they went up on to some high cliffs and began to mock Alexander. 'Silly fool,' they cried. 'How inept you are. See how we have escaped. You cannot even touch us in judgement. Because your wits are inferior to ours, you were unable to capture us.' So they jumped about and danced and made sport of Alexander. But when he heard and saw them, he laid aside his anger and began to laugh. And since he received the oracle, we have not seen him laugh again up to this present moment. Yet what they said deserved a good laugh. γ-text]

BOOK III

1. Alexander then took his army and continued the march against Porus, the king of the Indians. After they had been marching for a long time through barren and waterless country, full of ravines, the officers addressed the men of the army: 'We did enough when we brought the war as far as Persia and subdued Darius for demanding tribute from the Greeks. Why are we wearing ourselves out with this expedition to India, a land full of wild beasts and having nothing to do with Greece? If Alexander's great ambition leads him to go on making war and subduing barbarian peoples, why should we go along with him? Let him go on alone and fight his own wars.' When Alexander heard this, he addressed the Greeks and Macedonians, having separated the Persian troops from their number.

'Fellow-soldiers and allies, Macedonians and all you leaders of the Greeks (after all, these Persians are enemies of yours and of mine), why are you grumbling now? You demand that I go alone and make war on my own against the barbarians. But let me remind you that I won those former wars on my own, and I shall win more if I take with me only the Persians I require. My will alone spurred you on to fight when you were quaking before the forces of Darius. Was I not in the forefront of the army with my sword? Did I not go as my own emissary to Darius? Did I not despise every danger? Well, make up your minds and go back to Macedon on your own; save yourselves and try not to quarrel with one another. Then you will learn that an army can do nothing without a king's intelligence.'

After this speech of Alexander, they begged him to calm his anger, and to keep them with him to the bitter end.[96]

2. Soon he and his whole army arrived at the border of India.[97]
Here messengers met him with a letter from Porus, the king of
the Indians. Alexander took it and read it out to the army. It ran
as follows:

'King Porus of the Indians to Alexander the looter of cities. I
command you to retreat. What can you, a man, do against a
god? Why do you concoct such misfortune for those who are
with you? You think that you are stronger than me, but in fact
your forces are inferior. I am invincible. I am king not only over
men but over gods: Dionysus is here on my side, whom you call
a god. Therefore, I do not merely advise you, I command you
to depart as swiftly as possible for Greece. Your battles against
Darius and the other peoples do not frighten me, because your
success was the result of their weakness. Your strength is only a
matter of appearance. Depart for Greece! If we had wanted
Greece, we would have conquered it long before Xerxes did,
but because it is a worthless country and does not deserve to be
looked at by a king of ours, we have not troubled it. Every man
desires only what is better than his own.'

When Alexander had read to the army this letter from Porus
he said, 'Fellow-soldiers, do not be disturbed by Porus' letter
which I have just read out to you. Remember how Darius used
to write. Truly the only sense one can get out of barbarians is
their own insensibility. Just as animals – tigers, lions, elephants,
which pride themselves on their own strength – are easily brought
to heel by human nature – even among barbarians – so the kings
of barbarians who exult in the size of their armies are easily
worsted by the intelligence of Greeks.'

Alexander heartened his men with this speech, and then he
wrote to Porus, as follows:

'King Alexander greets King Porus. By saying that Greece is
not worth a king's looking at it, while you have all the cities and
regions of India, you have made us even more eager for battle
with you. I know that every man desires what is better than his
own, not what is less. Well, since we Greeks do not have these
things, and you barbarians have got them, we are eager for the
better and would like to wrest them from you.

'You write to me that you are king over gods as well as all men, and that you are more powerful than a god. I, however, am going to make war against a boastful man and a barbarian, not a god. The whole world cannot withstand the weapons of a god, the rumble of thunder, the flash of lightning and the anger of the thunderbolt. The nations I have already defeated did not overawe me, and your boastful words do not frighten me either.'

3. When Porus read this letter from Alexander he was very angry, and at once assembled the barbarian hordes, as well as the elephants and other beasts that fought alongside the Indians. When the Macedonians and Persians approached, Alexander saw the Indian forces and was frightened, not by the men but by the beasts. The strange sight filled him with amazement; he was used to fighting men, not wild animals.

So Alexander once again became his own messenger and went to the city where Porus was, dressed as a soldier, as if he was going to buy provisions. When the Indians saw him, they brought him before King Porus, who said to him, 'How is Alexander?'

'He is alive and well,' came the reply, 'and eager to see such a great king as Porus.'

Then the king went out with Alexander and showed him the troops of elephants. 'Go to Alexander,' he said, 'and tell him that I am bringing wild beasts like himself to fight against him.'

'King Porus,' Alexander replied, 'before I return to Alexander he will himself have heard what you have said about him.'

'From whom?' asked Porus.

'From Porus,' was the reply. 'As son of a god, he is ignorant of nothing that is said.'

Then Porus gave him gifts and sent him away.

As Alexander was leaving, he saw the regiment of Porus' animals. He racked his brains and thought hard, and what do you think the cunning fellow did? He had all the bronze statues he possessed and all the armour he had taken as booty from the soldiers heated up thoroughly until they were red-hot, and then set up in front of the army like a wall. The trumpets sounded the battle-cry. Porus ordered his beasts to be released. As the beasts rushed forward, they leapt on to the statues and clung to them; at once their muzzles were badly burnt and they let go immediately. That is how the resourceful Alexander put an end to the attack of the beasts. The Persian mounted archers were superior to the Indians, and drove them back. There was a fierce mêlée, soldiers both killing and being killed.

[Supplement H]

In the course of the battle Alexander's horse, Bucephalus, collapsed from exhaustion. At once Alexander lost interest in the battle; the armies went on fighting for twenty days, but at the end of that time Alexander's men began to lose heart and give ground.

4. When Alexander realized that they were on the point of defeat, he ordered a cessation of the fighting and sent a message to Porus, as follows:

'It does not befit the power of a king to allow one or other of us to gain the victory only by the destruction of our armies; but it will be a mark of our personal bravery if each of us puts a stop to the general fighting and comes forward to decide the victory by single combat.'

Porus was delighted – he had noticed that Alexander was no match for himself in physical size – and promised to fight him single-handed. Porus was 8 feet tall and Alexander less than 5. Both sides stood around to watch the fight. Suddenly there was a tremendous noise in Porus' camp. Porus was startled, and turned round to see what the cause of the noise was. At once Alexander knocked his legs from under him, jumped on to him and drove his sword through his ribs. That was the end of Porus, king of the Indians.[98]

Then both the armies began to fight again. Alexander called out to the Indians, 'Wretched Indians, why do you go on fighting when your king is dead?' But they replied, 'We fight so as not to be made prisoners of war.' Then Alexander said, 'Stop fighting, turn round and return to your city as free men. It was not you who made this audacious attack on my army, but Porus.' He said this because he knew that his army was no match for that of the Indians.

Immediately he ordered that Porus be given a royal burial. He took all the treasure from the royal palace and marched on to the Brahmans, or Oxydorkai. These were not for the most part warriors, but naked philosophers who lived in huts and caves.[99]

5. When the Brahmans learned that King Alexander was on his way to them, they sent their best philosophers to him, bearing a letter. Alexander took and read the letter, and this is what was in it:

'We the naked philosophers address the man Alexander. If you have come to fight us, it will do you no good. There is nothing that you can take from us. To obtain from us what we do have, you must not fight, but ask humbly, and ask it not of us but of Providence above. If you wish to know who we are – we are naked and we have devoted ourselves to the pursuit of wisdom. This we have done, not by our own decision but through the agency of Providence above. Your business is war, ours is wisdom.'

When Alexander had read this, he approached them in a peaceable manner. He saw great forests and tall trees, beautiful to look at and bearing all kinds of fruit. A river ran round the land, with clear water as bright as milk. There were innumerable palm trees, heavy with fruit, and the vine stock bore a thousand beautiful and tempting grapes. Here Alexander saw the philosophers themselves, entirely without clothing and living in huts and caves. A long way off from them he saw their wives and children, looking after the flocks.

6. Alexander asked them some questions. 'Do you have no graves?' was the first.

'This ground where we dwell is also our grave,' came the reply. 'Here we lie down and, as it were, bury ourselves when we sleep. The earth gives us birth, the earth feeds us, and under the earth when we die we spend our eternal sleep.'

'Who are the greater in number?' he asked next. 'The living or the dead?'

'The dead are more numerous,' they replied, 'but because they no longer exist they cannot be counted. The visible are more numerous than the invisible.'

Next he asked, 'Which is stronger, death or life?'

'Life,' they replied, 'because the sun as it rises has strong, bright rays, but when it sets, appears to be weaker.'

'Which is greater, the earth or the sea?'

'The earth. The sea is itself surrounded by the earth.'

'Which is the wickedest of all creatures?'

'Man,' they replied.

And he, 'Why?'

'Learn from yourself the answer to that. You are a wild beast, and see how many other wild beasts you have with you, to help you tear away the lives of other beasts.'

Alexander was not angry, but smiled. Then he asked, 'What is kingship?'

'Unjust power used to the disadvantage of others; insolence supported by opportunity; a golden burden.'

'Which came first, day or night?'

'Night. What is born grows first in the darkness of the mother's womb, and at birth it encounters the light of day.'

'Which side is better, the left or the right?'

'The right. The sun rises on the right and then makes its way to the left-hand side of the sky. And a woman gives suck first with her right breast.'

Then Alexander asked them about themselves. 'Do you have a king?'

'Yes, we have a leader,' they replied.

'I should like to meet him.'

So they showed him Dandamis, who was lying on the ground on a thick couch of leaves. Beside him lay some melons and other fruit. Alexander greeted him at once, and he replied, 'Greetings.' He did not stand up, and made no attempt to treat him like a king.

Then Alexander asked him if they had any property.

'Our possessions,' Dandamis replied, 'are the earth, the fruit trees, the daylight, the sun, the moon, the chorus of the stars, and water. When we are hungry, we go to the trees whose branches hang down here and eat the fruit they produce. The trees produce fruit every time the moon begins to wax. Then we have the great river Euphrates, and whenever we are thirsty we go to it, drink its water, and are contented. Each of us has his own wife. At every new moon each goes to mate with his wife, until she has borne two children. We reckon one of these to replace the father, and one to replace the mother.'

Then Alexander said to them all, 'Ask me for whatever you want and I will give it to you.' At once they all burst out, 'Give us immortality.' But Alexander replied, 'That is a power I do not have. I too am a mortal.'

Then they asked him, 'Since you are a mortal, why do you make so many wars? When you have seized everything, where will you take it? Surely you will only have to leave it behind for others?'

'It is ordained by Providence above,' replied Alexander, 'that we shall all be slaves and servants of the divine will. The sea does not move unless the wind blows it, and the trees do not tremble unless the breezes disturb them; and likewise man does nothing except by the motions of divine Providence. For my part I would like to stop making war, but the master of my soul does not allow me. If we were all of like mind, the world would be devoid of activity: the sea would not be filled, the land would not be farmed, marriages would not be consummated, there would be no begetting of children. How many have become miserable and lost all their possessions as a result of my wars? But others have profited from the property of others. Everyone takes from everyone, and leaves what he has taken to others: no possession is permanent.'

After this speech, Alexander gave Dandamis gold, bread, wine and olive oil: 'Take these things, old man, in remembrance of me.' Dandamis laughed and said, 'These things are useless to us. But in order not to appear proud, we will accept the oil.' Then, building a great pile of wood, he set it alight and poured the oil into the fire before Alexander's eyes.[100]

[Supplement I]

17. After these events, Alexander departed from the naked philosophers and returned to the proper road towards Prasiake, which is regarded as the capital city of the land of India and was the site of Porus' palace. Here Porus' men received Alexander. He

organized all Prasiake's affairs properly, and the Indians enthusiastically committed themselves to him. Some of them said to
Alexander, 'Great king, you will capture wonderful cities and
kingdoms, and mountains on which no king of the living has
ever set foot.'

Some of the wise men of the kingdom came to Alexander and
said, 'Your majesty, we have something to show you which
deserves your special attention. We will take you to the trees
that speak with a human voice.' So they brought Alexander to a
place where there was a sanctuary of the Sun and the Moon.
There was a guardpost here, and two trees closely resembling
cypresses. Around these stood trees that resembled what in Egypt is
called the myrrh-nut, and their fruits were also similar. The two
trees in the middle of the garden spoke, the one with a man's
voice, the other with a woman's. The name of the male one was
Sun, and of the female one Moon, or in their own language,
Moutheamatous.[101] The trees were surrounded with the skins of
all kinds of wild animals, male ones around the male tree, and
female ones around the female tree. In their neighbourhood
there was no iron, bronze or tin, not even potter's clay. When Alexander asked them what sort of animals the skins came from, his
companions told him that they were those of lions and panthers.

Alexander wanted to learn more about these trees. They told
him, 'In the morning, when the sun rises, a voice issues from the
tree of the sun, and again when the sun is in the middle of the
sky, and a third time when it is about to set. And the same
applies to the tree of the moon.' The priests, as they evidently
were, of the place came up and told Alexander, 'Enter if you are
pure, make obeisance and receive an oracle. And, Alexander,'
they went on, 'no iron may be brought into the sanctuary.' So
Alexander ordered his men to leave their swords outside the
perimeter wall. A number of men went in with Alexander, and
he ordered them to explore the enclosure in all directions. He
kept some of his Indian companions with him as interpreters,
swearing solemnly to them that if the sun set and no oracle was
heard, he would have them burnt alive.

Just then the sun set; at once an Indian voice was heard in the
tree. The Indians who were with him were afraid and did not

want to translate its words. Alexander became anxious and took them aside one by one. They whispered in his ear, 'King Alexander, soon you must die by the hand of one of your companions.' All those who stood around were extremely disturbed, but Alexander wanted to question the oracle again. As he had heard what was going to happen to him, he went in and requested that he might once more embrace his mother, Olympias. When the moon rose, its tree spoke in Greek: 'King Alexander, you are to die in Babylon, by the hand of one of your companions, and you will not be able to return to your mother, Olympias.'

Alexander was amazed, and wanted to bedeck the trees with the finest garlands, but the priests stopped him, saying, 'This may not be. If you insist, do as you will; a king can make every law unwritten.' Then Alexander was very melancholy.

At dawn he rose with the priests, his friends and the Indians, and went back to the sanctuary. After praying, he approached with one of the priests and laid his hand on the tree of the sun, and asked it if the full span of his life would be completed. That is what he really wanted to know. As the sun rose and the first rays fell on the top of the tree, a resonant voice came forth: 'The span of your life is completed now, you will not be able to return to your mother, Olympias, but must die in Babylon. A short time afterwards, your mother and your wife will be horribly murdered by your own people. Ask no more about these matters, for you will be told no more.'

Alexander was very unhappy when he heard this. He went out and departed from India at once, making for Persia.

18. He was very eager to see the world-renowned palace of Semiramis. The whole of her country was ruled by a woman of remarkable beauty, in her early middle age. So Alexander wrote her a letter, as follows:

'King Alexander greets Queen Candace of Meroe[102] and the princes who are her vassals. When I was travelling in Egypt I heard from the priests there about your houses and tombs, and that at one time you had been queen of Egypt. That is why I am writing to you. [Bring the temple and the image of Ammon to your borders, so that we may sacrifice to him. If you are unwilling to come with him, we shall soon meet in Meroe and discuss the matter together. Send me here what you think proper. *A-text*] Take counsel and send me news of your decision. Farewell.'

Candace's reply was as follows:

['Candace, queen of Meroe, and all her vassal kings, greet King Alexander. At that time Ammon ordered us by an oracle to march into Egypt; but now he orders that he is not to be moved and that no one else is to enter the land. We are to defend ourselves against all comers and treat them as enemies. *A-text*] Do not despise us for the colour of our skin. In our souls we are brighter than the whitest of your people. We have eighty flame-throwers ready to do harm to those who attack us. My messengers will bring you 100 solid-gold ingots, 500 young Ethiopians, 200 sphinxes,[103] an emerald crown made of 1,000 pounds of gold, 10 strings of unweighed[104] pearls, [10 staters], 80 ivory chests, and all kinds of animals that are common among us: 5 elephants, 10 tame panthers, 30 bloodhounds in cages, 30 fighting bulls; also 300 elephant tusks, 300 panther skins, 3,000 ebony wands. Send immediately people to collect all these goods, and send further news of yourself, when you have made yourself king of the whole world. Farewell.'

19. When Alexander had read Candace's letter, he sent an Egyptian named Cleomenes to collect the gifts. But as Candace had heard how Alexander had defeated the mightiest kings, she called one of her courtiers, a Greek painter, and told him to go to Alexander and to paint his portrait without his realizing it. He did so. Candace took the portrait and put it in a secret hiding-place.

Some days later the son of Candace, by name Candaules, accompanied by a few horsemen, was attacked and beaten by the king of the Bebryces. He ran for safety to Alexander's tents. At once the sentries seized him and brought him to Ptolemy Soter, who was Alexander's second-in-command.

'Who are you, and who are your companions?' Ptolemy asked him.

'The son of Queen Candace,' replied Candaules.

'Why have you come here?'

'I was on my way,' explained Candaules, 'with my wife and a few troops to take part in the annual mysteries held by the Amazons. But the king of the Bebryces saw my wife and came down with a great army to seize her, and killed most of my soldiers. Now I am on my way home to collect a larger force and overrun the land of the Bebryces with fire.'

When Ptolemy heard this, he went to Alexander, woke him up, and told him all that he had heard from Candace's son. Alexander got up at once, took his crown and set it on Ptolemy's head, threw his cloak around his shoulders and said to him, 'Sit on the throne as if you were Alexander and tell the secretary, "Call Antigonus, my chief bodyguard." When I come, tell me what you have just told me and say, "Give me your advice, what shall we do?"'

So Ptolemy took his place on the throne, dressed in the royal robes. The soldiers were puzzled when they saw this, and asked one another what Alexander was up to now.[105] But when Candace's son saw Ptolemy in the royal robes, and supposed him to be Alexander, he was afraid that he might order him to be killed. Then Ptolemy said, 'Call Antigonus, my chief bodyguard.' Alexander came in, and Ptolemy went on, 'Antigonus, this is the son of Queen Candace. His wife has been carried off by the king of the Bebryces. What do you advise me to do?'

'I advise you, King Alexander,' replied Alexander, 'to arm your men and make war against the Bebryces, so that we can free his wife and hand her back to him. This will be a mark of respect towards his mother.'

Candaules was delighted when he heard this. 'If you wish, Antigonus,' went on Ptolemy, 'you may do this yourself, as my chief bodyguard. Give the army orders to get ready.'

20. These were the orders Ptolemy gave to Antigonus, while pretending to be Alexander; and so they were carried out. Antigonus and Ptolemy arrived in just one day at the tyrant's city. Then Antigonus said to Ptolemy, 'King Alexander, we should not let the Bebryces see us by day, in case the tyrant discovers us and kills the woman. Let us invade the city at night and set fire

to the houses; the people themselves will then rise up and give back the wife of Candaules. After all, we are not fighting for a kingdom but for the return of a wife.'

Then Candaules threw himself at Antigonus' feet, and said, 'Oh, how clever you are, Antigonus! If only you were Alexander, and not just his chief bodyguard.'

When night came and everyone was asleep, they invaded the city and set fire to the suburbs. When the people woke up and began to ask what was the cause of the fire, Alexander had an announcement made in a loud voice: 'Here is King Candaules with a great army. I order you to give back my wife, before I burn down the whole of your city.' The people, seeing that they were caught, burst into the king's palace in great numbers and opened the gates. They dragged out the wife of Candaules from the tyrant's bed, and handed her over to Candaules; and they killed the tyrant.[106]

Candaules thanked Antigonus for his clever advice and plan, embraced him, and said, 'Entrust yourself to me, and I will bring you to my mother, Candace, and give you many gifts good enough for a king.'

Alexander was delighted and replied, 'Ask Alexander for permission for me to go; I would very much like to see your country.'

So Alexander gave Ptolemy the task of sending him with Candaules as his envoy. Ptolemy said to Candaules, 'I wish to send your mother a letter of greetings. Take my messenger Antigonus with you, and bring him back safely to me, so that I can restore you and your wife safely to your mother.'

'Your Majesty,' Candaules replied, 'I will take responsibility for this man as if he were Alexander himself. I will send him back to you with royal gifts.'

21. So Candaules set off with Alexander, taking a number of troops, beasts of burden, wagons and plentiful gifts. As Alexander travelled along, he marvelled at the spectacular mountains of the Crystal Country, which reached up to the clouds, and at the foliage on the tall trees, laden as they were with fruit; they were strange and wonderful, nothing like the trees of Greece. There

were apple trees which gleamed like gold, weighed down with
fruit like Greek lemons; there were vines with enormous grapes,
nuts as big as melons, apes the size of bears, and many other
animals of diverse colours and unfamiliar shapes.

'Antigonus,' said Candaules, 'this place is known as the Dwell-
ing of the Gods.'[107]

They continued their journey and came to the palace, where
they were met by the mother and brother of Candaules. As they
were about to embrace him, Candaules stopped them:

'Do not embrace me until you have greeted my saviour and
the benefactor of my wife, Antigonus the messenger from King
Alexander.'

'What did he save you from?' they asked him.

Then Candaules described the rape of his wife by the king of
the Bebryces and the help Alexander had given him. After that
Candaules' brothers and his mother, Candace, embraced him. A
magnificent meal was served in the palace.

22. Next day Candace came out resplendent in a royal diadem.
She was above normal human size and almost godlike in appearance, so that Alexander could have taken her for his mother,
Olympias. He saw over the palace, which sparkled with golden-
ceilinged halls and walls of marble. There were coverlets woven
of silk shot with gold by the most exquisite art, laid across
couches with golden feet; even the straps on which the mattresses
were slung were made of gold. The tables were inlaid with
ivory, and there were Persian columns whose capitals gleamed
with ebony. There were countless bronze statues; scythed chariots
carved out of porphyry with galloping horses to match, looking
as natural as if they were really alive; elephants carved out of the
same stone, trampling their enemies with their feet and rolling
their opponents over with their trunks; whole temples carved,
columns and all, from a single stone. Alexander was amazed at
all he saw. Then he had dinner with the brothers of Candaules.
The latter called his mother and asked her to give the messenger
gifts worthy of Alexander's cleverness and to let him return.

Next day Candace took Antigonus by the hand and showed
him rooms with transparent walls made of an unidentified stone,

which allowed one to tell, even when inside, when the sun rose. In one of the buildings was a dining-room of imperishable wood, and a house which did not rest on the ground but stood on gigantic square columns, and was pulled about on wheels by twenty elephants. When the king or queen went out to make war on a city, he or she travelled in this.

'All this would be amazing,' said Alexander, 'if it were found among the Greeks and not here, where there are such fine and varied sources of stone.'

'Yes, indeed, Alexander,' cried Candace angrily.

But he, hearing himself addressed by name, retorted, 'My name is Antigonus, my lady; I am the messenger of Alexander.'

'Yes,' replied Candace, 'be Antigonus if you will, but not here; as far as I am concerned, you are Alexander. Now I will show you how I was able to recognize you.'

She took him by the hand and led him into a room, where she showed him the portrait she had had made.

'Do you recognize your own features?' she asked him.

Alexander was distressed when he recognized the picture, and he trembled.

'Why are you trembling, Alexander? Why are you so upset? You who have destroyed the Persians and the Indians, who have taken trophies from the Medes and Parthians, who have subdued the whole East – now, without a single battle, you have become the prisoner of Candace. Know this then, Alexander, that no matter how clever a man may be, another will be able to outwit him. Now Candace's cunning has outstripped even Alexander's intelligence.'

Alexander was furious and began to gnash his teeth.

'Why are you gnashing your teeth?' asked the queen. 'What can you do? You who were such a great king have now fallen into the hands of a single woman.'

Alexander was all ready to stab himself and Candace with his sword.

'That would be a brave and noble act,' said Candace. 'But do not fret, child Alexander. Because you saved my son and his wife who had been captured by the Bebryces, I will save you from the barbarians, by calling you Antigonus. If they discover that you are Alexander, they will kill you immediately, because you killed Porus, the king of the Indians. The wife of my younger son is the daughter of Porus. Therefore I will call you Antigonus, and will keep your secret.'

23. With these words Candace went outside with him and addressed her son and daughter-in-law:

'Candaules, my son, and Harpisa, my daughter, if you had not encountered the army of Alexander at just the right moment, I should never have got you back, nor would you have found your wife again. Let us repay Alexander's messenger worthily and give him gifts.'

Then her younger son[108] spoke to her.

'Alexander saved my brother and his wife, but my wife is still grieving for her father Porus who was murdered by Alexander. She wants to put his messenger Antigonus to death, now that she has him in her power.'

'What good will that do, child?' countered Candace. 'If you kill this man, will you thereby overcome Alexander?'

'He saved me and my wife,' said Candaules to his brother. 'So I will send him safe home to Alexander. Shall we fight each other over this man?'

'I do not want to, brother,' replied the other. 'But if this is what you want, I am more than ready to go along with you.' So they went off to prepare themselves for a duel.

Candace was very worried about her sons and their decision to fight. She took Alexander aside and said, 'You are a clever man, and have carried out so many plots. Can you not think of some way to prevent my sons from fighting each other?'

'I will go and make peace between them,' Alexander promised. So he went and stood between them.

'Now listen,' he said, 'Thoas and Candaules; if you kill me here it will be of no concern to Alexander, because my name is Antigonus, and messengers are not accounted of much value in war. If you kill me, Alexander has plenty of other messengers. But if you want to take your enemy Alexander prisoner with my help, promise to give me a share of the gifts, so that I can stay here and induce Alexander to come here too, on the pretext that you wish to give him in person the gifts you have prepared for him. Then you will have your enemy in your power, and you can take your vengeance at your pleasure.'

The brothers trusted him and gave up their quarrel. Candace was amazed at Alexander's cunning.

'Antigonus,' she said, 'I wish you were my son, for then I should have conquered every nation. It is not by fighting that you have overcome so many enemies and cities, but by your cleverness.'

Alexander was delighted at the protection he received from Candace's determination to keep his secret.

Ten days later he departed. Candace gave him royal gifts, including a very valuable diamond crown, a breastplate decorated with pearls and beryls, and a cloak of purple threaded with gold, which twinkled like the stars. She sent him off with a large escort of her own soldiers.

24. After marching for the stated number of days he came to the place where Candaules had told him that the gods dwelt. He entered with a few soldiers, and saw indistinct phantasms and flashes of lightning. Alexander was afraid at first, but waited to see what would happen next. Presently he saw some men lying down with light flashing out of their eyes as if from lamps.

One of them said to him, 'Greetings, Alexander. Do you know who I am? I am Sesonchosis, the Lord of the World. Yet I was not so fortunate as you. [I, who subdued the whole world and enslaved so many races, am now without reputation; but you will be favoured because you have founded in Egypt the city of Alexandria, which the gods love. But enter: you will behold the creator and champion of all Nature.'

The king went in, and saw a mist glowing with fire, and seated on the throne the god whom he had once seen in Rhacotis being worshipped by men, namely Sarapis.

'What is this,' he asked, 'incorruptible Lord, source of all Nature? I saw you sitting on your throne in the lands of Libya, and now I see you again here.'

Sesonchosis stood close by Alexander and said, 'This god can be seen everywhere though he remains in one place, just as heaven may be seen everywhere though it remains in one place. *A-text; restored from the Armenian*]

'How many years have I left to live?' asked Alexander.

'It is best for a living man not to know when his end will come,' was the reply. 'As soon as he learns the hour of his death, from that moment he is as good as dead. But if he remains in ignorance, this helps him to forget about his death, even though he must die one day.

'But the city which you have founded will be famous the world over. Many kings will come to destroy it. But you will dwell in it, dead and yet not dead; the city you founded will be your tomb.'

After hearing this speech, Alexander went out again.

25. He took his own soldiers and set off back to his camp. The satraps came to meet him and presented him with royal clothing. Then Alexander and his men marched against the Amazons. When they were close, Alexander sent the Amazons a letter, as follows:

'King Alexander greets the Amazons. I imagine you have heard of my victory over Darius. After that I made war on the Indians, defeated their leaders and enslaved them with the help of Providence above. Then we visited the Brahmans, the so-called naked philosophers. We accepted tribute from them and left them to dwell in their own place, as they requested; we passed on in peace. Now our expedition has brought us to you. Come to meet us rejoicing, for we have not come to harm you, but to see your country and to do you good. Farewell.'

When they had received and read this letter, the Amazons replied as follows:

'The leaders of the Amazons greet Alexander. We are writing to give you some information before you come into our country, lest you afterwards return without glory. This letter will inform you about our country, and about us and our way of life. We live in the hinterland across the river Amazon. Our country is completely encircled by a river, and it takes a year to travel around it. There is only one entrance. We, the virgins who dwell in it, number 270,000, and we are armed. There is no male creature in our land. The men live on the other side of the river and farm the land. We hold an annual festival at which we sacrifice a horse to Zeus, Poseidon, Hephaestus and Ares; the festival lasts six days. Any of us who have decided to be deflowered[109] move to the men's territory. Any female children are returned to us at the age of seven. When enemies attack our country, 120,000 of us ride out on horseback; the rest remain to defend the island. We join battle at the frontier; the men accompany us, drawn up in battle formation in the rear. If any of us is wounded in battle, she receives great honours in our revels; she receives a garland and her memory is preserved for ever. If any of us is killed in battle, her nearest relative receives a considerable amount of money. If any of us brings the body of an enemy on to the island, she is rewarded with gold and silver and dines at public expense for the rest of her life. That is how we fight for our reputation. If we conquer the enemy or put them to flight, that is regarded as a humiliation for them for the rest of time; but if they conquer us, it is only women that they have defeated.

'Now beware, Alexander, that the same thing does not happen to you. Take counsel, write to us again; you will find our camp at the frontier.'

26. When Alexander received this letter, he smiled and wrote back to the Amazons, as follows:

'King Alexander greets the Amazons. We have made ourself lord of the three continents and we have not failed to set up trophies of all our victories. It would be seen as shameful in us if we did not campaign against you too. If you are ready to be destroyed and to see your land made uninhabitable, remain at your frontiers. But if you would rather dwell in your own land without risking the fortunes of war, cross your river and let us see you. Let the men also show themselves in the open. If you do this, I swear by my father and my mother, Olympias, that I will do you no harm, but will accept from you whatever tribute you care to give, and I will not attack your country. Send us as many horsewomen as you think fit. We will pay each of them wages of a gold stater every month, and their food and drink in addition. At the end of a year these shall return to you and you shall send others. Take counsel and inform me of your decision. Farewell.'

When the Amazons received Alexander's letter, they held an assembly and wrote to inform him of their decision, as follows:

'The leaders of the Amazons greet King Alexander. We give you permission to come to us and to see our country. We undertake to pay you 100 talents of gold each year, and we have sent 500 of our strongest warriors to meet you, bringing with them the money and also 100 pure-bred horses. They will remain with you for one year. If any of them is deflowered by any foreigner, she may remain with you. Write and tell us how many choose to remain with you, send us back the remainder and we will send you replacements. We will obey you whether you are near or far. We have heard of your bravery and generosity. We dwell beyond the edges of the world, but still you have come to be our lord. We have determined to write to you and to dwell in our own land, obeying you as lord. Farewell.'[110]

[Supplement J]

27. After this exchange of letters, Alexander wrote to his mother, Olympias, to tell her everything he had done. His letter ran as follows:[111]

'King Alexander greets his sweet mother, Olympias. [As far as concerns my first achievements up until we reached Asia, I am sure that you are fully informed by my previous letters. I thought it would be best to tell you about our journey to the interior also. We made a journey to Babylon, taking with us 150,000 soldiers. And then we made another journey ... arriving at the Pillars of Heracles in ninety-five days. The local inhabitants told us that Heracles, in order to mark the limits of the lands he travelled, had set up two columns, one of gold and one of silver; and each of them was 20 feet high and 3 feet broad. I did not believe that they were solid, so I decided to sacrifice to Heracles and to make a hole in one of them. Then I discovered that it was of solid gold. So I filled up the hole again, which turned out to contain the equivalent of 1,500 gold pieces.

'Then I marched on through a deserted and craggy land,

where it was impossible to see the person standing next to one because of the fog. Enough about these places. *A-text*]

'We mounted an expedition against the Amazons and marched as far as the river Prytanis. When we reached the edge of the city, we saw a river full of wild beasts. The soldiers were very downhearted. Although it was midsummer it rained without ceasing, and many of the infantry had painful feet. There was also a tremendous amount of thunder, flashes of lightning and thunderbolts. While we were waiting to cross the river Prytanis, which I mentioned, many of the natives were killed by our soldiers.

'Then we came to the river called Thermodon, which flows through a level and fertile country. Here dwell the Amazons, who are larger than other races of women, and remarkable for their beauty and strength. They wear flowery garments and carry silver weapons and axes: iron and bronze are unknown among them. They are notable for their intelligence and quick wits. As we approached the river where the Amazons live – it is a very wide river, hard to cross and full of wild animals – they crossed over themselves and lined up against us. But we persuaded them by a series of letters to submit to us.

28. 'We took tribute from them and continued towards the Red Sea as far as the river Tenon. Next we came to the river Antlas, where we could see neither land nor sky. A great variety of races dwelt there. We saw dog-headed men, and men without heads who had their eyes and mouths in their chests; we saw men with six hands, others with bulls' heads, and troglodytes and the wild strap-legs; still others were hairy like goats and had heads like those of lions. There were strange-looking animals of every kind.

'We sailed on from that river to a large island, 14 miles from the shore. There we found the City of the Sun. It had twelve towers built of gold and emeralds. The wall of the city was built of an Indian stone. In the centre was an altar constructed also of gold and emeralds, with six steps leading up to it. On top of this were a horse-drawn chariot and charioteer, yet again of gold and emeralds. It was hard to see these things because of the fog. The priest of the Sun was an Ethiopian, and was dressed in pure linen. He told us in a barbarian tongue to depart from there. After we had left, we marched for seven days until we came to a place of darkness where there was not even a fire to give light.

'We left there and came to the harbour of Lyssos. Here there was a very high mountain, which I climbed and saw beautiful houses full of gold and silver. I also saw a perimeter wall of sapphire, with 108 steps. On top was a circular temple ringed by 100 columns of sapphire. Within and without were carved images of almost divine artistry: bacchants, satyrs, maenads playing pipes and raving in trances, and the old man Maron[112] sitting on his mule. In the middle of the temple was a couch of polished gold, covered with cushions, on which a man lay, clothed in thin muslin. I could not see his shape because he was covered up, but I could see his strength and the size of his body. Also in the middle of the temple hung a golden chain weighing 100 pounds and a golden crown. Instead of a fire there was a precious stone that lit up the whole place. There was a golden birdcage hanging from the ceiling, and in it was a bird somewhat like a dove, which called to me in a human voice, in Greek, and said: "Alexander, desist now from struggling against the gods; return to your own palace and do not strive to climb the paths of heaven." I wanted to take down the cage and the candelabrum to send them to you, but then I saw the man on the couch move as if he were about to get up. My friends said, "Stop now, your majesty; this is sacred property." When I went out into the temple precinct I saw two engraved golden mixing bowls, each holding sixty measures – as we discovered at dinner time. I ordered the army to pitch camp there and enjoy themselves. There was a very large mansion, which contained the finest goblets imaginable, carved from precious stones. As we and the army settled down to dinner, there was a sudden tremendous sound, loud as thunder, of pipes and many cymbals, of fifes and trumpets and drums and lyres. The whole mountain began to smoke as if we had been struck by lightning.

'We were afraid and left the place at once, and came to the royal palace of Cyrus. We came across a great many deserted cities and one very fine city, in which there was a large building where the Persian king himself used to conduct business. They told me that a bird was there that spoke with a human voice. When we entered the building we saw a great many things worth seeing. It was built entirely of gold. In the middle of the ceiling hung a golden birdcage, like the previous one, and in it was a bird like a golden dove. They said that this bird could speak to the kings in tongues. There I also saw, inside the palace of Cyrus, a large engraved golden mixing bowl, which held 160 measures. The craftsmanship was amazing: on the rim it had statues, and on the upper band of decoration a relief of a sea battle. Inside the bowl there was an honorific inscription, and the exterior was adorned with gold. They said that this vessel had once been in the Egyptian city of Memphis, and had been brought here when the Persians conquered that city.

'There was also a house built in the Greek style, where the king used to conduct his business. In this was depicted the sea battle fought by Xerxes. There were also a throne of gold and precious stones, and a lyre which played of its own accord. Around the throne was a sideboard 24 feet long, and standing at the top of a flight of eight steps. Above it was an eagle of gold which spanned the entire circuit with its wings. There was also a golden vine with seven branches, all made of gold. But why should I tell you so much about all the other sights of the palace?[113] They are such that their very quantity prevents us from describing their astonishing excellence. Farewell.'[114]

30. Alexander also wrote another letter to his mother, Olympias, after he had reached Babylon, and was close to the end of his life. It ran as follows:[115]

It is said that the gods have great powers of foresight. One of the women here bore a child whose upper body was human as far as the flanks, but from the hips downward it had the legs and paws of a wild beast; it resembled the monster Scylla. The paws were those of a lion and of a wild dog. These extremities moved and could be clearly seen, so that their distinctive forms could be recognized; but the upper body of the baby was lifeless. As soon as the mother had given birth, she wrapped the child in a cloth and went to Alexander's palace, saying to his servant, 'Tell

King Alexander of a great wonder; I have come to show him
something.' Alexander happened to be having his afternoon rest
in his room. When he woke up, he was told of the woman and
ordered her to be brought in. He told all those who were with
him to leave. Then the woman showed him the prodigy and
explained that she had given birth to it.

When Alexander saw it, he was amazed and at once sent for
his magicians and his interpreters of omens. When they arrived,
he asked them to give a judgement about this miraculous birth,
and threatened them with death if they did not tell him the
truth. They were the most famous and learned of the Chaldaeans,
in number five;[116] but the one whose skill was greater than that
of any was not at that time in the city. Those who were there
told Alexander that he would be stronger than all men and
overcome all his enemies, and be lord of all the world. For, they
said, the savage beasts in the lower part of the human body
represented the nations who had been subdued; and that was
their interpretation of the omen.

But later the other Chaldaean came to Alexander. When he
saw the form the omen had taken, he cried out and wept and
tore his clothes, in a frenzy of grief. Alexander, seeing him in
this state, was extremely disturbed and told him to pull himself
together and explain the significance of the omen. 'King,' came
the reply, 'you may no longer be numbered among the living.'
Alexander asked him to explain the omen in detail, and the
Chaldaean replied: 'Mightiest king of all the world, you yourself
are the human part, and the animal elements are those around
you. If the upper part were alive and moved like the animal
parts below, so would you, O king; but just as the animal parts
are, so are those around you: they have no understanding and
are savage towards men, and just so are those around you
disposed to you.' Then the Chaldaean went out, ordering that
the child be burnt. After he had heard this, Alexander began to
put his affairs in order.[117]

31. In Macedonia Antipater had taken over the reins of power
and was treating Alexander's mother Olympias just as he liked.
Olympias wrote frequently to her son about Antipater, as she was

very angry about this. Finally, when she was planning a trip to Epirus, Antipater forbade her to go. Alexander, having received his mother's letter and learned what a difficult position she was in, sent Craterus to Antipater in Macedonia to take charge of the country. When Antipater learnt of Alexander's plan and of the arrival of Craterus, who had brought an army with him to Macedonia and Thessaly, he was afraid. He decided to murder Alexander. Otherwise, he feared, he would be imprisoned because of the way he had treated Olympias. He had heard that Alexander had far exceeded his earlier arrogance as a result of his great successes. So he laid a plot, and prepared a poison which could not be carried in any vessel of bronze, glass or clay, because such a vessel would shatter instantly. Antipater put the poison in a jar of lead, and placed this in another jar of iron; then he gave it to his son and sent it to Babylon to Alexander's cupbearer, Iolaus.[118] He explained to him the ferocity and fatal power of the poison, so that if any of his enemies met him in battle he could take it and make an end of himself.

When Antipater's son arrived in Babylon, he spoke secretly to Alexander's cupbearer, Iolaus,[119] and asked him to give the king the poison. Now Iolaus was nursing a grudge against Alexander because some days earlier he had made some mistake and Alexander had hit him over the head with his stick, injuring him severely. So Iolaus in his anger was very willing to become accomplice to Antipater's son in the crime. Iolaus also took into his confidence a certain Medius who had likewise been assaulted by Alexander. They discussed how they would get Alexander to drink the poison. One day Alexander was sleeping off a large dinner. Medius came to him the following morning and invited him to his house as a guest.

Alexander accepted the invitation and came to dinner; there were several other guests besides him. They included Perdiccas, Ptolemy, Olcias, Lysimachus, Eumenes and Cassander.[120] None of these knew anything about the planned crime; but the others present at the dinner were in the secret of the poison and had sworn oaths to each other and to Iolaus the cupbearer. All of them had reason to be angry at Alexander's acts.

When Alexander was reclining at table, Iolaus brought him

first an uncontaminated cup. As the conversation grew general, and, as a result of their drinking, had been going on for some time, Iolaus brought another cup, this time containing the poison. Alexander, to his misfortune, accepted it and drank it down. At once he gave a loud yell as if he had been pierced by an arrow through the liver. He remained conscious for a time, and fought down the pain enough to return to his own house. He asked the guests to continue with their meal.

32. [They were very upset and at once broke up the party; then they went out to see what would happen next. Alexander wanted to bring up the excess of wine and asked for a feather, for that was how he usually made himself vomit. Iolaus smeared one with some of the poison and gave it to him. In this way the poison infected him all the more quickly, spreading unchecked throughout his body. Alexander was racked with cramps and doubled up with pain. He endured a night of agony with great fortitude. On the next day, seeing how ill he was, unable even to speak clearly because his tongue was swollen, he sent everyone out, hoping to get some rest and to talk privately about the affairs that concerned him. Cassander[121] conferred with his brother and departed by night. He removed to the mountains of Cilicia and waited there for Iolaus to arrive. He had made a pact with Iolaus, that if Alexander died, he would not be implicated. He sent the husband of their nurse by sea to his father in Macedonia, carrying a coded message indicating that the affair was concluded.

When night fell, Alexander ordered all the girls and boys who were attending him to leave the house, including Kambobaphe and Roxane his wife. There was a door leading out of the house towards the river Euphrates, which runs through the middle of Babylon. He ordered this to be opened, and that no one was to stand guard by it, as was usual. When they had all left, and it was the middle of the night, Alexander rose from his bed, extinguished the lamp, and left the house on all fours, heading for the river. As he approached, he looked around and saw his wife Roxane running towards him. She had guessed, when he sent everyone away, that he was going to attempt some deed worthy of his great audacity, and had followed him out by a secret door into the darkness, guided by the sound of his groans, faint though they were. He stopped, and she embraced him and said, ⟨'Alexander, are you leaving me to kill yourself?' He replied,⟩ 'Roxane, it is small benefit to you to take away my glory. Let no one else hear about this.' Then, with her support, he made his way back secretly to the house. *A-text*]

The next day he summoned Perdiccas, Ptolemy and Lysimachus. He instructed that no one else should enter the room until he had made his will. Suddenly there was a great outcry from the Macedonians, who all ran to the courtyard of Alexander's palace, ready to kill his guards if they would not let them see the king. When Alexander asked what the commotion was about, Perdiccas told him what the Macedonians were saying. So Alexander ordered his bed to be positioned where all the army could march past and see him, going out again by another door. Perdiccas did as Alexander commanded, and the Macedonians alone came in and saw Alexander. There was not one among them who did not weep to see their great king, Alexander, lying on his bed at the point of death. One of them, a good-looking man but only a private soldier, came close to the bed and said, 'Your father, Philip, your majesty, ruled as a good king, and so have you done. You are leaving us now; it would be good that we should die with you, for you made Macedon a free country.' Alexander wept, and stretched out his hand with a consoling gesture. [The horse Bucephalus ran into their midst and, standing close to Alexander, began to water the bed with his tears. Both the Persians and Macedonians exclaimed in amazement when they saw the horse weeping. *γ-text*]

[When the Macedonians had filed past, he called back those who were with Perdiccas. He took Olcias by the hand and ordered him to read out the will. What follows is a copy of the will's dispositions, as taken down from Alexander by Olcias.

Alexander's Will [122]

King Alexander, the son of Ammon and Olympias, greets the Rhodian generals and their rulers, the council and people.

Since we have crossed the boundaries marked by the Pillars of Heracles our forefather, and, by the will of Providence above, have reached our fated day, we have decided to send and inform you of our decisions, in the belief that you of all the Greeks will be the most suitable guardians of our achievements, and because we have always loved your city. Therefore, we have written to order that the garrison be removed from your city. Thus you will be able to enjoy free speech and preserve your freedom for ever. Also, we wish you to guard my treasure among you. We know that your city is generous and deserves to be remembered: therefore, we shall make plain that we think no less of it than of our own country, but as a city worthy of us. We have made the following disposition of our affairs, giving each his land with freedom, beginning with the land where we were born to this glory.

We have commanded the administrators of the regions to send 1,000 talents of coined gold from the satrap's palace to the temples in Egypt, and have ordered our body to be conveyed thither. As for the arrangement of our tomb, we shall concur with whatever the Egyptian priests decide. We have ordered Thebes to be rebuilt with royal money, in the belief that it has suffered enough and its people have now repented of their misdeeds. Grain is to be given by the Macedonians to the Thebans who will come from Thebes, until the city's strength is restored. We have commanded that you be given for the adornment of your city 350 talents of gold and 77 triremes to protect your freedom; you are to receive from Egypt in grain 20,000 bushels of wheat a year, and from the stewards of Asia and the regions near you 20,000 of barley. Land is to be allotted to you, so that in future times you shall be self-sufficient in grain and shall lack for nothing, and can live as your city deserves.

I have appointed Craterus the ruler of Macedon, Ptolemy the satrap of Egypt, and Perdiccas and Antigonus[123] to rule the regions of Asia. I instruct you to take this letter from Olcias who will give it to you, and not to neglect these dispensations, because it has been made your responsibility to guarantee these matters, in order that your city shall prosper. I am quite sure that you will obey my instructions. Ptolemy my bodyguard will take

care of you: we have indicated to him what he must do for you.
Do not think this legacy was made to you lightly. The administrators of the kingdom will ensure that there is no deviation
from the instructions.

King Alexander, the son of Ammon and Olympias, appoints
Arrhidaeus, the son of Philip, to be king of Macedonia for the
present.[124] But if Roxane bears a son to Alexander, he is to be
king of Macedonia and to be given whatever name the Macedonians please. But if Roxane's child is female, let the Macedonians
elect as king whomever they choose, if they do not want Arrhidaeus, the son of Philip. Whoever is elected, let him preserve
the rule of the Argeads, and let the Macedonians pay tribute to
the Argeads in the accustomed way. It shall be permitted to
Olympias, the mother of Alexander, to dwell in Rhodes, if the
Rhodians are agreeable. But under no circumstances is this to be
done without their consent. If she does not want to live on
Rhodes, let her live wherever she likes, and receive the same
income as she received while her son Alexander was alive.

Until the Macedonians decide to appoint a king, King Alexander, the son of Ammon and Olympias, appoints as administrators
of all his kingdom of Macedonia Craterus and his wife Cynane,
the daughter of Philip the former king of Macedonia; as ruler of
Thrace, he appoints Lysimachus with his wife Thessalonike, the
daughter of Philip the former king of Macedonia; he gives the
satrapy of the Hellespont to Leonnatos and his wife Cleodice, the
sister of Olcias, and he gives Paphlagonia and Cappadocia to
Eumenes his secretary. The islanders he leaves free, with the
Rhodians as their masters. Pamphylia and Cilicia go to Antigonus, who is to rule all that country as far as the river Halys.
Babylon and its territory go to the warrior Seleucus. Phoenicia
and Hollow Syria, as it is called, go to Meleager. Egypt goes to
Perdiccas; Libya to Ptolemy and his wife Cleopatra, the sister of
Alexander. The regions beyond Babylon are to have as general
and administrator Phanocrates and his wife Roxane the Bactrian.[125]

I command the administrators of the kingdom to build a
golden sarcophagus, weighing 200 talents, to hold the body of
Alexander, the king of Macedonia. Those of the Macedonians

who are old or feeble are to be sent to Macedonia, as are the Thessalians in the same condition; and they are to be given 3 talents of gold. The armour of Alexander is to be sent to Argos, along with 50 talents of coined gold as first-fruits of the war for Heracles. The elephants' tusks and the snake-skins are to be sent to Delphi along with 130 gold cups, first-fruits of the expedition. The Milesians are to be given 150 talents of coined gold for the adornment of their city, and [the same] for the Cnidians.

I wish Perdiccas, whom I leave as king of Egypt in the city I have founded named Alexandria, to keep it in good fortune and pleasing to the great Sarapis, ruler of all. There is to be an administrator of the city, who will be known as the priest of Alexander and will attend all the city's great festivals, adorned with a golden crown and a purple cloak; he is to be paid 1 talent per annum. His person is to be inviolate and he is to be free of all civic obligations; the post shall be the preserve of the man who excels all in nobility of family, and the honour shall remain in his family thereafter.

King Alexander appoints Taxiles king of India as far as the river Hydaspes, and Porus king of the part of India beyond the Hydaspes; he appoints Oxydrakes of Bactria, the father of Alexander's wife Roxane, king of the Paropanisadae. Arachosia goes to . . ., Drangiana to . . ., Bactria and Susiana to Philip, Parthyaea and the parts of Hyrcania which we hold to Phrataphernes, Carmania to Tlepolemos, Persis to Peucestas . . . is to replace Oxyntes in Media.

King Alexander appoints Olcias king of Illyria; he is to have 500 horses from Asia and 300 talents. With these he is to construct and dedicate statues of Ammon, Heracles, Athena, Olympias and Philip. The administrators of the kingdom are to set up statues of Olcias ⟨at Olympia⟩ and golden statues at Delphi. Perdiccas is to set up bronze statues of Alexander, Ammon, Heracles, Olympias and Philip.

Witnesses of these provisions shall be the Olympian gods, and Heracles the first ancestor of King Alexander.

Then Ptolemy came to him and said, 'Alexander, to whom do you leave your kingdom?'

'To him who is strong, who is willing, who can keep it, and who can maintain it,' was the reply. A-text]

33. Then he dictated the following letter to his mother:

'King Alexander greets his sweet mother. When you have received this, my last letter, prepare a fine banquet in honour of Providence above which gave you such a fine son. But if you wish to honour me, go out by yourself and invite all, both great and small, both rich and poor, to the banquet, and tell them, "See, the banquet is prepared; come in and enjoy yourselves. But let no one come who knows of past or present sorrow; for I did not make this banquet for sorrow but for joy." Mother, farewell.'

Olympias did as she was bidden; but no one could be found, great or small, rich or poor, who had known no sorrow, and so no one came. Then Olympias perceived Alexander's wisdom, and realized that Alexander had written this as a consolation to those whom he was leaving, so that they should realize that what had happened was nothing unusual, but something that had happened and would happen to everybody.

[When he had finished greeting everybody, Charmides the son of Polycrates came in. He was a strong lad, well-reputed even among his enemies, and Alexander was in love with him. He embraced Alexander and did not want to leave him. He wailed terribly and poured forth a long lament. Even the earth seemed to mourn with him. At last the boy turned to the horse Bucephalus, and addressed him tearfully, 'You too, I imagine, are just as unhappy; you are a Pegasus who has lost his Bellerophon; but you were stronger than Pegasus among horses, just as Alexander is mightier than Bellerophon. Alas, who will ride you now? Who could look Bucephalus in the eye with another rider on his back?' So said Charmides, weeping as he spoke; and the crowd beat their breasts. Alexander did not want to let the lad go, but flung his arms around his neck. On the point of death, Alexander made the following speech:

'I, who crossed all the inhabited earth,
And the uninhabited places, and the places of darkness,
Was unable to evade fate.
A small cup can yield a man to death,
And send him down among the dead with a drop of poison.

The army, seeing me compelled to die,
Wish to help and are powerless.
For the rest – I shall lie buried in Hades.'

Then he called everyone and asked them to have him buried
in Alexandria, and to accompany him to his grave, and after the
funeral to depart, each of them, to his allotted kingdom. He
called them and made them swear an oath not to disregard any
of his dispensations, if he was in charge of Macedonians and was
troubled in his soul about them. All the while he clung to Charmides.

Alexander stroked Bucephalus, who was standing at his feet,
and said, 'You were born to share my fate, and now you suffer
ill-fortune on my account. You were always my companion in
war; but now you cannot fight for me in this my last battle with
death. You look as if you wish to help me, but you cannot.'

When Alexander spoke like this to Bucephalus, the whole
army howled, making a tremendous noise. The treacherous slave
who had prepared the poison and who had plotted against their
lives thought that Alexander was dead, and came running to see.
When Bucephalus saw him, he cast off his morose and dejected
look, and, just as if he were a rational, even a clever man – I
suppose it was done through Providence above – he avenged his
master. He ran into the midst of the crowd, seized the slave in
his teeth and dragged him to Alexander; he shook him violently
and gave a loud whinny to show that he was going to have his
revenge. Then he took a great leap into the air, dragging the
treacherous and deceitful slave with him, and smashed him
against the ground. The slave was torn apart; bits of him flew all
over everyone like snow falling off a roof in the wind. The
horse got up, neighed a little, and then fell down before Alexander and breathed his last. Alexander smiled at him. *γ-text*]

Then the air was filled with mist, and a great star was seen
descending from the sky, accompanied by an eagle; and the
statue in Babylon, which was called the statue of Zeus, trembled.
When the star ascended again to the sky, accompanied by the
eagle, and had disappeared, Alexander fell into his eternal sleep.

34. There followed a struggle between the Persians and the Macedonians: the former wanted to bring him to their country and honour him as Mithras; the latter, on the contrary, wanted to bring his body back to Macedonia. Then Ptolemy addressed them:

'There is in Babylon an oracle of the Babylonian Zeus. Let us consult the oracle about the body of Alexander; the god will tell us where to lay it to rest.'

The god's oracle was as follows:

'I tell you what will be of benefit to all. There is a city in Egypt named Memphis; let him be enthroned there.'

No one spoke against the oracle's pronouncement. They gave Ptolemy the task of transporting the embalmed body to Memphis in a lead coffin. So Ptolemy placed the body on a wagon and began the journey from Babylon to Egypt. When the people of Memphis heard that he was coming, they came out to meet the body of Alexander and escorted it to Memphis.[126] But the chief priest of the temple in Memphis said, 'Do not bury him here, but in the city that he founded in Rhacotis. Wherever his body rests, that city will be constantly troubled and shaken with wars and battles.' So Ptolemy at once brought the body to Alexandria and built a tomb in the temple, which is now called Alexander's Monument; and there he deposited Alexander's mortal remains. [They set up there a statue of moonstones, representing Alexander as he laughed at the moment of his death, leaning his arm on Charmides. It was so like him that Alexander himself seemed to be displaying his fear and sorrow.

So Alexander, in his wars and battles, was elevated in glory, wisdom and bravery above all the race of kings. But in his journey through life he was unable to anticipate his death. The greatest king of the greatest kingdom abandoned the honours attaching to his glory, and departed this life. γ-text]

35. Alexander lived thirty-two years. His life ran thus: he was king for ten years; he made war for twelve years, and was victorious in his wars. He overcame twenty-two barbarian nations and fourteen Greek peoples. He founded these twelve cities: Alexandria-in-Egypt, Alexandria-among-the-Horpae,

Alexandria-the-Strongest, Alexandria-in-Scythia, Alexandria-on-the-river-Crepis, Alexandria-Troas, Alexandria-Babylon, Alexandria-in-Persia, Alexandria-for-the-horse-Bucephalus, Alexandria-by-Porus, Alexandria-on-the-Tigris, Alexandria-among-the-Massagetae.

Alexander was born in January at the new moon, at the rising of the sun; he died in the month of April at the new moon, at the setting of the sun. The day of his death was called Neomaga,[127] because Alexander had died young. He died in the year of the world 5176,[128] in the last year of the 113th Olympiad.[129] (One Olympiad is four years, and the first Olympiad began in the fourth year of King Ahaz.) From the death of Alexander to the Incarnation of the Word of God by the Virgin is 324 years.

[Supplement K]

SUPPLEMENTS TO THE TEXT

A: THE SCYTHIAN AND THESSALONIAN CAMPAIGNS (I.23, p. 54)

The γ-text has a different sequel here, at the end of which it resumes the story at ch. 25, after the death of Philip.

Some days had passed, the situation remaining unchanged, when the Scythians started preparing for war against the Macedonians. When Philip heard of it, he looked at his own army and realized it was insufficient to withstand them. For there were about 400,000 of the Scythians. Philip was at a loss, and summoned all his chieftains and friends to discuss what to do about the war.

'Your Majesty,' said Aristotle, 'entrust the campaign to Alexander and let him fare as fortune wills.'

At once Philip summoned Alexander.

'Now, Alexander,' he said, 'is your opportunity to fight for your country. War is your lot, by fate's decree. Consider how you are going to deal with it. The saying, "Consider the affairs of war," shall be the prologue to your success.'

Alexander stood up, and so did the others; then he smiled, took heart and replied to his father with an eager expression on his face.

'Why did you not tell me this long ago? Have you plunged yourself into such despondency and grief because of the gathering of a number of ants? I will go out and beat them and obliterate their mighty ones. Victories are not won by numbers but by the grace of Providence above.' They all fixed their eyes on Alexander and were amazed: he stood in the midst of them like a shining star.

'Go, child,' said Philip, 'and do whatever Providence prompts you to.'

Alexander set out accompanied by 300,000 young men and went to war with the Scythians. The number of Scythian troops was huge, but Alexander's fortune was unbeatable. He took a few men with him and captured a ridge. When he saw their camp, he spied out a suitable stronghold that the Scythians did not know about. Then he turned round and brought with him the whole army and, in the course of the night, stationed them in a circle around the Scythian camp some distance off. He let his men go as they pleased in the difficult terrain, but hid 2,000 picked men. Then he ordered the encircling troops to light thirty or more bonfires. When the Scythians saw this huge number of fires, they decided to flee under cover of darkness and save their skins. At once they abandoned all their equipment and fled. When Alexander observed this, he followed them silently with all his army. When the Scythians reached the appointed place and stepped into the ambush,[130] Alexander sounded the trumpets behind them, and the Macedonians started to shout, and the Scythians began to jostle one another; those in ambush came forward and began to bombard them. The Scythians stood still, expecting nothing but death, and crying out for mercy. Virtually all of them were slaughtered by the Macedonians. Alexander advanced his men and told them to keep up the pressure; he had all the Scythians bound and brought to his camp while he decided what to do with them. When they arrived at the appointed place, Alexander ordered their leaders to stand forward. They did so, trembling. Alexander addressed them:

'You know that Providence has given you into the hands of the Macedonians and you cannot stand against our coming. Will you be my slaves or not?'

'We will be your slaves, lord,' they replied in fear, 'for ever, just as you wish.'

They threw themselves before him and made obeisance to him. Alexander, to show he was well disposed to them, ordered their fetters to be struck off, and marched them with him into the city of Philip his father, to show them off in triumph.

24. When they reached the city, there was a great noise and commotion. People came to meet Alexander and tell him what had happened. A certain Anaxarchus, king of the Thessalonians, had once come to visit Philip, and while he was his guest had seen Olympias and fallen in love with her. Knowing of the Scythian expedition against Macedonia, he had set out with 12,000 men for Macedonia, with the idea of entering into alliance with Philip. Then, if he could, he would seize Olympias, but if he could not, he would renew the alliance and return home. As it fell out, he captured Olympias, in the following way. When Philip learnt of Alexander's victory against the Scythians, he took Olympias with him and went out to meet Alexander. He left her in a villa and went out with his troops, full of confidence. When Anaxarchus learnt of this, he came down and seized Olympias and made off with her. Philip at once set off in pursuit with his few troops. When Alexander learnt what had happened, he hastily extended his line and set off in pursuit of Anaxarchus, taking 8,000 horsemen with him. Philip caught up with him first. There was a battle, in which Philip was struck on the chest and fell from his horse. Alexander found him lying on the ground. Seeing that he was still alive, he left him and went off to battle. He surrounded Anaxarchus' men and trounced them soundly, so that they ran away; but they took Olympias with them. Alexander got hold of a prisoner and said, 'Show me where Anaxarchus is and I swear by Providence that I will spare your life.' The man showed him. 'Look in the middle of the phalanx. When you see someone wearing a white robe and a gold crown, sitting on a finely apparelled horse, that is Anaxarchus.'

With these indications, Alexander soon spied him, and set off into the middle of the phalanx with 400 horsemen. They killed everyone there, and only Anaxarchus was left. Alexander got hold of him with only one thing in mind, to bring him alone back to his father. But Philip was at his last gasp.

'Father,' Alexander said to him, 'stand up and take your revenge on your enemy who is in your hands.'

Anaxarchus was brought before him in chains. Philip, still breathing, leant on his hands and got up; then he took a sword and killed Anaxarchus. He anointed Alexander with the blood and spoke to the Macedonian army:

'Let this be the fate of all who oppose Alexander and the Macedonians.'

Olympias was standing by, grieving. He looked at her and spoke with difficulty:

'You too deserve admiration for having borne such a son.'

Then he cast his eye on Alexander, flung his arms round his neck, rested his head on his breast, and expired. The Macedonians mourned for him and carried him into the city on a golden bier. Then they buried him with the customary rites.

When the period of mourning was over, the Scythians came to Alexander to ask him for his decision. He sent them away to their own homes:

'Depart, and conscript 30,000 distinguished warriors for my army, all archers. When I summon them, send them to me at once. If you will not do this, they will become my soldiers anyway because I shall come and raze your country.'

Then the Scythians made obeisance to Alexander and acclaimed him as a god. They went home and prepared to be his slaves, even to the fifth generation.

B: THE EMBASSY FROM DARIUS (I.26, p. 57)

The γ-text inserts here the embassy from Darius (this episode occurs in ch. 23 in the main text):

While affairs in the east were in this state, Darius, the king of the Persians, sent messengers to Macedonia to collect the annual tribute and return with it to him as quickly as possible. When they reached the city of Philip, they expected the king to come out to them in the usual way, and make obeisance to Darius' letter, and receive the messengers with the appropriate honours. But Alexander did none of these things; instead he sent to them a man named Antiochus who happened to be with him. He was, like Alexander, a young man of about thirteen. With him went several of the chieftains, all wearing golden breastplates. Antiochus was carrying in his hand the spear of Alexander.

When they had left the city, Antiochus sent on an envoy with the following message from the king's ambassadors: 'Let this be a sign to you, you who have been sent by Darius, to come to us. Fall on your faces and pay homage to the spear of Alexander. If you refuse, you will be put to death at once.'

When Darius' ambassadors heard this unaccustomed and unexpected speech, they were astonished. Reluctantly they did as they were told; they approached, paid homage to the spear of Alexander and kissed Antiochus' feet. They did this in a spirit of fair exchange: they expected that whatever they did, the king would in return do to them. But Alexander took his seat on high, surrounded by Macedonian children who were dressed in silk robes and golden girdles. Alexander himself was dressed in the garments of the sun; on his head was a crown of gold, precious stones and pearls, with a victory on top of it. He resembled no one so much as Zeus himself. Those around him shone like stars, and between Alexander and the gates of the city there stretched a great multitude of armed men. All around there were cries, crashes, the sound of trumpets, blessings and jostling crowds. When Darius' ambassadors were about to enter the city, Antiochus ordered the people to make way for them to approach Alexander, and they did as they were told. The messengers were both amazed and terrified: the unexpected is frightening to simple people. As they crossed the city, they did not know what to look at first, for everything was so amazing.

When they reached Alexander and set their eyes on him, they imagined they must be looking at a god; they fell down and worshipped him, and when they stood up again, they were reluctant to take their eyes off him; nor could they do so even if they wanted to: having forced their eyes to look down towards the ground, the eyes lifted up again of their own accord to Alexander, and could not get enough of the sight of him. They kissed the letter three times and handed it to Alexander. Antiochus took it and read it out to him. The contents were as follows:

'Whereas the power of monarchy has been granted by god to Darius alone – and what god is there besides Darius? – who has become lord of all that is below heaven by virtue of his limitless

might. He rules kings and satraps. Nevertheless, be it known
that our power does not forget Macedonia. If it has been forgotten up to now, these heavenly mortals present here, who have
been sent by us, will demonstrate everything that concerns us.
Though you have tried to rule Macedonia independently of our
divine Providence, you will submit as slaves and in reverence to
our power. You will hand to these my ambassadors the annual
tribute, and concur in the rule of my divine majesty from hence-
forward.'

*The γ-text continues with Alexander's refusal of the Persians' demands,
the story as in ch. 23, and then moves to the numbering of the army in
ch. 25.*

C: ALEXANDER IN ROME (I.27, p. 61)

The γ-text adds here:

Leaving there, Alexander went on to capture Rome. Near there,
ambassadors of all the nations came and made obeisance before
him, bringing him gifts of gold and silver, countless in number,
and promising him their allegiance. He captured Rome; the
Romans came out to meet him with drums and dances, bearing
branches of bay in their hands, and went up to him and addressed
him as ruler of all the world. He entered the city and went to
the temple of Capitoline Jupiter, where the priest welcomed him
and made him his guest.

While they were in Rome, Laomedon, who had ridden in the
chariot with Alexander, arrived with 50,000 men to make himself
Alexander's ally, bringing gifts of gold and precious stones and
pearls. Alexander welcomed him with generous enthusiasm: 'My
brave fellow,' he said, 'you have come to be my ally in the war
against Darius.' Then he left Rome at sunset, and no one stood
in his way. All the kingdoms of the west came to meet him,
flattering him with gifts and inviting him to come and visit their
countries. Alexander accepted the gifts and turned about, leaving Laomedon in charge of all those places; the latter assessed
tribute for all of them for the next twelve years.

Then Alexander changed direction and headed for the south: there he subdued many diverse races, passed through the inhabited world and came to the uninhabited regions, reaching as far as Ocean. In those regions he found men with two heads, whom he fought and defeated; they ran away from him. There he also found very large and ugly women, fiercer in battle than any others he had encountered. When they ran, they rested their breasts on their shoulders; and they were clothed only in their own shaggy pelts. They made their attack flying in the air on wings – the Macedonians were quite bewildered when they saw the women flying into battle. When Alexander saw them, he ordered fires to be lit and held up on high; the women, who were ignorant of fire, swooped down on them, had their wings burnt and were unable to take off again. They were finished off where they had fallen by the soldiers' swords, although killing 100 of the soldiers with their claws. That is how the soldiers escaped, though only with difficulty. As they could not go any further, since Ocean blocked their way, they took the left bank of Ocean, headed for the north and regained the inhabited regions. After many wars against the barbarians, Alexander subdued the whole of the west.

D: ALEXANDER IN SYRIA (I.35, p. 70)

The γ-text adds here:

Opposite them General Seleucus built a city called Nicatoria. Antiochus built Antioch-in-Asia. Alexander was angry and said to them: 'We have left Macedon and traversed the whole world; now that we have arrived in Asia, are we going to learn how to found Macedonian cities and abandon our military good sense?'

36. He set off again and passed Syria. He turned his footsteps to the East. All those he encountered begged him for forgiveness; but if any dared to resist him, he had their cities destroyed to the foundations, and his broad sword mowed them down. Fear and trembling ran through all the East, so that the people left their cities and fled. The news reached Darius through those who

were fleeing home. 'O king,' they said, 'there is no hope of safety for us from this race of Macedon: we are lost. Very soon he will have reached even here.'

E: PORUS (II.12, p. 100)

The γ-text adds here:

When Porus had received Darius' letter and read it, he shook his head and said, 'Now Darius, who was once the equal of the gods, is on the run before the Macedonians.' He called together his generals and regional commanders, and said, 'Take 50,000 horsemen and go to Darius as allies. If you get the Macedonians in your power and capture Alexander, bring him to me alive, so that I can see him. I have a yearning to set eyes on the boy.'

F: ALEXANDER IN JUDAEA AND EGYPT; THE INTERIOR AND THE RIVER OF SAND (II.22, p. 114)

The γ-text continues with a section that deals with Alexander's relations with the Jews and his reception in Egypt (it is the only version to contain this account); and it repeats adventures that occur in II.8.

When this became known to everyone in Persia, the Persians entered into concord with the Macedonians and they regarded each other as brothers.

23. In the meantime, Alexander ordered his general, Seleucus, to assemble the whole Persian army. Seleucus gathered the troops together with all speed: there were found to be 1,030,000 horsemen and 4,000,000 foot-soldiers; the rest had been killed in the war. Alexander united these men with his Macedonian army and marched towards Egypt.

24. On the way he reached Judaea. The Jews wanted to resist him and sent out spies, who presented themselves as ambassadors. But Alexander was not deceived. He ordered some of the most

warlike young men of the Macedonian phalanx to ambush them in a nearby ravine; they hastened to carry out their orders. The Macedonian troops were always swift to obey Alexander. Then he turned to the would-be spies.

'See,' he said, 'you ambassadors of the Jewish race: death is as nothing to a Macedonian soldier. Go therefore and do what is appropriate. I shall come to you tomorrow and shall do whatever is approved by Providence.'

They went away and told their leaders: 'It would be best to save our skins and yield to Alexander; otherwise there is no hope of safety. The Macedonian army is of superhuman nature. While we are afraid of death, the Macedonians are not at all; they simply despise it. It seems to us that they make death a matter of competition, so that you would think it was actually a necessity to them. The sons of Macedon surprised us in a ravine and poured arrows down like rain: no sooner had Alexander given the orders than it was done. It was not their bravery in the face of death that astonished us, so much as their lack of expectation of any reward. They simply marched of their own free will towards death. If there is profit to be made as well, no one will be able to resist them. Well, we have told you what we saw: now you can make up your minds how to deal with Alexander when he arrives; let all indecision be put aside.'

When the leaders had heard this, they gave orders to surrender to Alexander. The priests dressed themselves in their priestly robes and went out to meet him, together with a multitude of followers. When Alexander saw them, he was frightened at their appearance, and ordered them to approach no further but to return to the city. Then he summoned one of the priests.

'Your appearance is like that of gods,' he said. 'Tell me, what god do you worship? I have never seen priests of any of our gods dressed like this.'

'We serve one god,' the priest replied, 'who made heaven and earth and all that is visible and invisible. No mortal man can discover him.'

'You are worthy priests of the true god,' responded Alexander. 'Go in peace. Your god shall be my god and my peace shall be with you. I shall not treat you as I have done the other nations, because you are servants of the living God.'

Then they brought quantities of gold and silver to Alexander. He was reluctant to accept it.

'Let these gifts, as well as the tribute I decreed, be dedicated to the Lord God. I myself will take nothing from you.'

25. Then Alexander crossed Judaea and reached Egypt. The Egyptians decided not to give in to Alexander, and they fortified their city and got ready for a battle. Alexander extended his phalanx and surrounded the city; then he constructed trenches and gave his troops some rest. As the summer heat was very intense, he went out with a few horsemen to cool down. He came to a pure lake of crystal-clear water, got down from his horse and washed in it. But the cold of the water made him ill. As his sickness worsened, the Macedonians were distressed, and so were the Persians. Soon the Egyptians realized that Alexander was ill: they sent some men from the city to Philip, Alexander's doctor, saying, 'If you can kill Alexander with a poison, you shall be our king.'[131]

'What is this you are saying about Alexander?' retorted Philip. 'The whole universe is not worth one hair of his head.'

They took counsel, and, seeing that Philip was not going to co-operate with them, they made another plan. Pretending to be well-disposed to Alexander, they wrote him a letter and passed it secretly through the walls to Antiochus, with the words, 'Give this letter to Alexander in person.' The letter was chock-full of wickedness, claiming that Philip had been suborned by the Egyptians to murder Alexander. Antiochus took the letter to Alexander, read it out and put it on his pillow. At dawn, Philip came with a cup of medicine.

'Get up, your majesty, drink this medicine which will drive away your sickness.'

Alexander stood up, took the cup and said, in tears, 'Shall I drink it, Philip?'

'Drink, your majesty,' replied the doctor. 'It will drive away your sickness.'

Alexander looked at him again and said, 'Then I will drink it.'

'Yes, your majesty, I told you: it will drive away your sickness.'

Alexander drank it. He then picked up the letter and gave it to Philip.

'I could see,' he said, 'that Philip is without guile towards Alexander.'

Philip took the letter and read it.

'Your majesty,' he said, 'the whole universe would not repay the destruction of a single hair of your head. Where in the world should I find another Alexander? Why should I plot against your life? Far be it! Do not take any notice of all this, your majesty. Nevertheless, since this is what the Egyptians decided to do, see, you have drunk the medicine. Rise up now and show them what we are like, so that they will learn not to despise the Macedonians.'

Then Philip went out, instructing him to keep silence on the matter.

After this, Alexander fell into a deep sleep, which lasted the whole day. When evening came, he woke up completely cured. He called Antiochus to him.

'Antiochus, I have seen Philip's medicine, and he is a trustworthy man, worth many others. Call him.'

Antiochus went out and called Philip. Alexander told him that he was now quite well, and fell on his neck and embraced him.

26. He got up and ordered the army to prepare for war. As the sun was rising and casting its flaming rays against the mountain ridges, the Macedonian and Persian army, fully armed, surrounded the city, all dressed in their golden breastplates, so that when the sun's rays fell on them they seemed to gleam back as bright as the day itself. The multitude of their arrows darkened the rays of the sun. The hoplites with their raised spears looked like walking mountains. When they shouted, you would have thought the sky was falling in pieces. So all the wisdom of Egypt was destroyed.

When the Egyptians saw this, they had no idea what to do, so they went to the oracle of Apollo to inquire how they should escape their danger and be saved. The oracle ran: 'Let be, let be. The mind of man is inconstant. When you were young, you obeyed an old man; now that you are old, you obey a young one. Go to my house. Remember how things used to be. I order you to submit to Alexander.'

Then they remembered the old oracle given when Nectanebo fled the country, and guessed that Alexander was Nectanebo's son.

The Macedonian soldiers and the captains close to the walls heard voices from within which were acclaiming Alexander: 'Long live King Alexander,' they said. And the cries were heard beyond the walls, but none of those inside dared show their faces because of the quantity of missiles raining down. When the Macedonians heard these voices, at once they began to laugh; the laughter spread to the whole army and the sound of warfare was mingled with laughing. Word was brought to Alexander that those within the city were acclaiming him, and at once he relented and gave orders to cease the bombardment. When this was done and the battle had eased off, the Egyptians dared to poke their heads over the walls, and began to beseech Alexander in submissive tones: 'Have mercy, your majesty, on your own country. Do not persist in your anger towards your slaves.' When Alexander heard the bit about 'your country', he understood, and ordered the battle to cease altogether; he ordered those who wished to come out of the city to do so and explain this statement.

'I am not an Egyptian. I am from Macedonia. Why do you say that Egypt is my country?'

They fell at his feet and told him about the oracle, and how Nectanebo had once been their king, in the days when Egypt saw good fortune. 'But now all Egypt is divided into tribes, as is the custom with us. Take your city, therefore, and do what seems proper to you.'

When Alexander was told about the oracle, he took to heart what concerned himself and ordered the war to cease, and the leaders of the city to go in with him and lead him to the palace of Nectanebo. This was done with all speed.

27. The Egyptians all rushed and fell at Alexander's feet, and accompanied him to Nectanebo's palace. Now they had exchanged their sorrow for rejoicing: for when a besieged city is captured, endless oppression is the lot of its inhabitants, as they see their country taken over by the enemy. But in this case the Egyptians were joyful because they had been liberated from oppression. They did not lead Alexander as a conquering enemy but as a king, acclaiming him and cheering and shouting, 'Egypt rules again.'

When Alexander entered the palace, there was a statue of Nectanebo standing before the door, with an inscription on it, and a crown in its right hand and a sphere in its left. On this was portrayed the creation of the world. On the statue's breast was inscribed: 'Whoever enters my house, I will place this crown on his head. You shall all recognize this man as my son. He will travel over the whole earth. His name shall be given to this city.' And just as Alexander entered the gate, the statue placed the crown on Alexander's head. Alexander swivelled around in amazement, and stretched out his hand to the crown that had just been placed on his head. And then the statue placed in Alexander's hand the globe that was in its left hand. Everyone who was there was astonished. Alexander embraced the statue and recognized the features of Nectanebo; then he looked down at the inscription on the statue's chest and rubbed it out with his own hand. He honoured the statue that had thus prophesied his rule by gilding it all over. Alexander did not want to be considered the son of Nectanebo, but of Philip and the gods. That was the story that became known to everyone.

28. Alexander spent some time there rebuilding the city, adorning it with numerous columns and strengthening the walls with high towers. The highest of all he built at the eastern gate, and placed on top of it a statue of himself, surrounded by Seleucus, Antiochus and Philip the doctor. The statue of Seleucus had horns, and the sculptor made it distinctive by its brave and ferocious expression; Philip's was distinguished by his military doctor's attire; and Antiochus was holding a spear. When all this was finished and the city had been made exceedingly beautiful in the

eyes of all, Alexander ascended the tower, stood up and condemned all the gods of the country. He proclaimed the one true God, who cannot be known nor seen nor sought out, who is surrounded by the seraphim and glorified with the name of the 'thrice holy'. Alexander made a prayer: 'O God of gods, creator of all that is visible and invisible, be my helper now in all that I intend to do.' Then he came down from the tower and went to his palace.

He made Seleucus ruler of the Persians, and set Philip up over the Egyptians, while he himself was in charge of the Macedonians, who were devoted heart and soul to him.

29. Then he assembled all his army and marched towards the nations of the Interior. All the nations became his servants and paid him tribute. Not one of them resisted, because they were all afraid of him. He crossed all the land beneath the sun – no habitable part was omitted. He ordered his people to wait for six months, deliberating whether to enter the uninhabited regions. When this time expired, they made a ten-day expedition in these level and deserted regions. Suddenly there appeared women of terrifying appearance and ferocious countenance, their whole bodies covered with hair like a wild pig.[132] The hair of their heads reached down to their knees, and their eyes shone like stars. They looked like humans only from their foreheads to their chins; their nails were very long on one hand and their feet were like a wild donkey's; their bodies were the size of three men. When the soldiers saw them and without thinking charged at them, the women turned about and killed four by tearing them apart with their nails; then they ate them up before the army's eyes, and even licked up the blood where it had fallen. Alexander's men were quite at a loss. Then Alexander had the idea of collecting all the dogs from the camp – for all the soldiers had dogs which they took out when they went hunting. When the women saw the dogs they turned and fled *en masse*. The dogs killed a few, but the rest escaped and disappeared.

After this escape, the soldiers marched on for thirty days until they reached a sandy country. As they crossed, ants came and seized the men and horses and disappeared. They saved themselves from this danger by lighting fires.

Next they reached a very large river, so broad that it took three days to cross it. When they came to it and looked at this immense divide, Alexander was at a loss.

30. Alexander sat down on the bank and ordered the men to build a rampart across it. When this had been done according to Alexander's plan for crossing the river, the water suddenly dried up and became sand instead. Then Alexander saw how to cross the river. He ordered square containers to be constructed of wooden planks. These were then placed on the river-bed, and when the first one was in place, it was filled with stones so that it would not move. Next, he ordered his men to bring very long planks, 24 to 36 feet long, and to place them on the first box, stretching over to the second. So they put them on top of the wood, and nailed them down. Then he put down in the stream of sand a second box 24 feet from the first, and filled this with stones; and that likewise remained immobile. And so with the third and subsequent ones, until they had bridged the river. It took the army sixty-six days to cross the river. When they had crossed it, Alexander named it the River of Sand; it flowed three days with water and three days with sand.

31. When they had crossed the river, they came to another world, where they found very small and insignificant men, of such a size that even a full-grown man was only 3 feet high. When these creatures saw the soldiers, they came and fell at the soldiers' knees, begging them to be kind. Alexander, seeing their miserable stature, sent them away with promises of peace: 'Go, you will receive no harm from us.'

From there he travelled again for several days through the uninhabited world: after ten days he reached a wide plain of immeasurable breadth and extent. He decided to halt his army there, and looked around in search of water. He saw a lake: as he approached it, he saw a huge statue set in a pile of stones. The statue was inscribed with Greek letters; the writing on it said that it was of Sesonchosis, ruler of the world. It represented a young man strongly resembling Alexander. It was inscribed: 'He who has traversed the whole world may reach this far; but beyond this he may not go, just as I was stayed here and could go no further. Here I, Sesonchosis, ruler of the world, turned back and departed this life.' When Alexander had read this, he immediately covered the inscription with his cloak, pretending to honour the statue; but in fact he did it so that none of the Macedonians would see the writing and become frightened. He claimed instead that he had received an oracle from the statue: 'If you cross this place, Alexander, you will find another, better world, which you have not yet traversed.' That is what he said, to make the army more enthusiastic. They stayed three days there, and then continued their journey.

32. *(As in main text, p. 115.)*

33. After marching for ten days he reached a level place. When the army was exhausted with marching, and the Macedonians were out of breath, suddenly wild men appeared, sitting on the rocks, naked and hairy, terrifying, enormous, black, but not strong. Their hair was like stretched gristle, and they were larger than any man. At once the Macedonians approached them; but the wild men kept their distance. When the Macedonian troops were sleeping, the wild men kept watch. The Macedonians came and told Alexander about it. Alexander left the army and went to the place where the wild men were encamped. They were keeping watch in blithe unconcern.[133] Alexander had an attractive young woman brought to him and told her, 'Go up to that man, so that you can observe the wild man's nature and see if he is human in all respects.' The woman went up to him, but when he turned round and saw her, he leapt up, seized her and straightaway began to eat her. Alexander at once ordered some soldiers to go and rescue her from the beast. The soldiers ran up to him; he took no notice of them at all, but had his mouth clamped on her leg and was chewing her like a dog. One of the soldiers struck him with his spear, at which the beast ran off barking like a dog, leaving the girl half-dead. They brought the girl back to Alexander at the camp. Suddenly an enormous number of the wild men appeared, holding branches and stones in their hands, and they went up to the first phalanx and fought fiercely with it.

Seeing this, Alexander ordered the hoplites and archers to join the battle. In its course, when one of the wild men was wounded, the others immediately tore him apart and ate him. As long as the battle continued, they kept their numbers up and became stronger and bolder. The Macedonians were overcome with fear and trembling. Alexander stood pondering how to rout the enemy. In the whole engagement thirty Macedonian soldiers were killed; but although countless numbers of the enemy perished, as fast as they died more reinforcements arrived, and the more fiercely they fought. Then the clever Alexander ordered fires to be lit and carried towards them at a run. When they saw this strange marvel, they fled at once. The army chased the whole gang but did not capture one of them; they were as swift on their feet as a swallow swooping over the ground. Alexander, mounted on Bucephalus, caught up with one boy with difficulty and brought him back to the camp. He seemed to be about twelve years old, but was larger than a man.

Night fell and the tents were erected within the palisade; the soldiers turned to rest. They were exhausted with fighting, and very badly disposed towards Alexander. They came to him and said, 'King Alexander, we will go no further. We cannot deal with men like these. We are afraid that the end of our good fortune will come on us when we have subdued the whole world; that we shall be satiated with human food and will turn to that of beasts; and the evil is compounded, because no one in the world will remember us.'

Alexander was angry and said, 'It is not up to me to turn back, but is in the hands of fate. I often wanted to, but could not. We must yield to fate and not delay.' At this they were all silent and surrendered themselves to fate.

34. At dawn they rose and continued their march. Crossing the land of the wild men, they came after five days to another land, where two golden statues had been erected, the one of a man, the other of a woman. When he came upon these, Alexander said: 'These are statues of Heracles and Semiramis.' After going on for a bit they found the palace of Semiramis, but it was deserted. Alexander entered it with only the Macedonian army; the Persians and Egyptians stayed outside and waited three days.

From there they journeyed for ten days and found men with six hands and six feet, countless in number and all naked, who seemed to gather together when they saw the size of the phalanx. When Alexander saw them, he ordered fires to be lit and carried against them. At once they all fled and hid in caves below the ground. The soldiers caught one of the men, and he was a wonderful sight to see. They kept him with them for one day's journey, but because he had none of his fellows to accompany him, suddenly he shivered, gave a great cry and expired.

After three days' journey they reached the land of the Dog-heads. They were men except that their heads were those of dogs; their voices were partly human and partly canine. They drew themselves up ready for battle, but Alexander drove them back with fire. It took them a full ten days to traverse the country of the Dog-heads.

Then they reached a place by the sea. They built a camp and decided to rest there. They piled their weapons up around the palisade, and he ordered them to keep guard with their shields above the ditch. One of the horses chanced to die, and was thrown into the sea. A crab came out of the sea, seized the dead horse in its claws and dived back into the sea. This was told to Alexander, and he ordered fires to be lit all around the palisade. In this way they were saved from the attacks of the sea-creatures.

35. They continued on their journey and came to a marshy but beautiful place, where there were fruits of all kinds; it was close to the sea. When Alexander saw it, he ordered the army to halt there. When a palisade had been built, Alexander went out along the shore.[134] He saw an island in the sea, about a mile from the shore. He ordered wood to be brought and a ship built. He wanted to get into it and sail over to the island, but Philo his friend prevented him with the words, 'Do not do that; I will go first and look at the island. If I return safely, then you can embark and do as you see fit.'

'I do not want you, my friend, to go first,' Alexander replied, 'in case something happens to you. What other friend do I have in the world, and who will console me in my grief for you?'

'If Philo, the friend of the king, were to die,' said Philo, 'the king would find another Philo for a friend; but if something untoward were to happen to Alexander, all the world would be plunged into grief.'

With these words Philo entered the ship and sailed to the island. There he found men resembling us in all respects, and speaking to one another in Greek. When Philo had looked, he sailed back at once to Alexander and described the island. When Alexander heard about it he took fifty men and entered the ship, leaving Antiochus to lead the army in his stead until his return. He told him to remain where they were because it was convenient for obtaining supplies for the people.

35A. When Alexander reached the island, he saw men like himself, but naked. When they saw him on the island, they came up to him.

'Why have you come to us, Alexander? What did you wish to obtain from us? We are naked and entirely without possessions, except the faculty of reason. If this is what you want, you do not need to fight for it.'

Alexander was startled at being called by his name.

'Nothing is stronger than reason,' he said, 'by Providence. Reason is of more value than thousands of gold pieces and precious stones.'

At this point γ inserts a substantial portion of the work by Palladius, On the Brahmans, *which includes a dialogue of Alexander with the Brahmans, differing from the account given in the main text (III.6, p. 131). Thereafter, γ continues with the story of the trees which grow all morning and decline all afternoon, as in the main text (II.36, p. 116).*

G: ALEXANDER'S ARCH (II.37, p. 117)

The γ-text adds here:

From there they advanced to a flat plain; the plain was divided in the middle by a ravine, whose depth was immeasurable. There Alexander erected an arch to bridge the ravine; and on the arch he inscribed in Greek, Persian and Egyptian the following words: 'Alexander came here and erected an arch over which the whole army crossed; his intention was to reach the end of the earth, if Providence approved his plan.'

γ continues with an abbreviated version of the story of the cook and the Water of Life (II.39, p. 121).

H: THE BATTLE WITH PORUS (III.3, p. 130)

The chapter has a different ending in the γ-text:

As they joined battle, the Persians and Macedonians fought bravely against the Indian army: they chased them back with volleys of arrows and cavalry charges. Alexander's experience defeated their strength of numbers. When they joined battle on the following day, elephants came to join the Indian ranks, carrying wooden castles on their backs, in which stood armed men holding spears in their hands. When the Macedonians saw these, they were alarmed and fell into a panic. But night put an end to the battle.

When they regained their tents, they were thoroughly downhearted. They decided to betray Alexander into the hands of Porus, and beg the latter for their lives and a safe return to Macedonia. Philo, the king's friend, realized this and informed Alexander. Alexander summoned the whole multitude, and stood in their midst with a scowl on his face and tears pouring down his cheeks; but even his tears added beauty to his appearance. He begged them, 'Men of Macedon, if you hate me, take my life from me. Split my limbs with your broadswords, I beg you; I would rather die at your hands, my friends, than submit my neck to the enemy yoke. Yes, yes, kill me, I beseech you all, if you are thinking of betraying me to the Indians.'

When the Macedonians saw Alexander, they made a tremendous noise. 'Lord,' they cried, 'all of us will die at once tomorrow; we should value the loss no more than that of a single hair. Be brave and strong and do as you wish; we should easily prefer to die on your behalf.'

Then he greeted them all, and they all embraced him cordially. Tears can turn the heart and change the soul of the most unbending, they can encourage the cowardly and turn their spirits to courageousness. Where there is a spirit of friendship, there is no stronger weapon with which to oppose the enemy.

When dawn arrived, the Indian army marched out to battle. On their elephants, as I said before, were structures like walking walled cities. When Alexander saw these and realized their strength, he was struck with amazement and admiration. He ordered his hoplites, as soon as the elephants approached, to spear a number of tiny piglets in front of them. When the elephants saw the creatures squealing before their feet, they reared up, shaking the little castles off their backs, and then bolted precipitately.

The Indians were very frightened as a result of this. 'What are we to do against this young man?' they said. 'He puts lions to flight and chases away elephants. What hope is left for us?'

After these events, they joined battle again, the Indians being superior in strength to Alexander's army. Alexander fought magnificently, and almost succeeded in turning the Indian line; but then he was surrounded by the Indians and it was only because he was mounted on the horse Bucephalus that Providence was able to save him. The battle went on unremittingly all day, but when evening came the darkness separated the two sides. Alexander spent the whole night encouraging his men and urging them to bravery in the battle; he recommended them neither to be shamed by unfounded imaginings, nor to be easily turned to flight.

I: THE LETTER TO ARISTOTLE ABOUT INDIA (III.7–16, p. 133)

The A-text inserts at this point a letter of Alexander to Aristotle about India. The Greek text is somewhat corrupt and very lacunose; the version given here is substantially supplemented from the Armenian version (marked by angle brackets). [135]

Then Alexander wrote a letter to Aristotle about the affairs he had been engaged in.

'King Alexander greets Aristotle. I must describe to you the remarkable things that happened to us in India. When we reached the city of Prasiake, which is, as it were, the capital of India, we occupied a conspicuous promontory in the sea. I went off with a few men to the places mentioned above. We discovered people living there who looked like women and fed on fish. When I called some of them to me, I discovered that they were barbarian in speech. I asked them about the region, and they pointed out an island that was visible to all of us in the middle of the sea; they said it was the grave of an ancient king, and that much gold had been dedicated there. ⟨I was very keen to cross over to the island, but the barbarians resisted fiercely; then they withdrew⟩ and disappeared. But they left behind their boats, of which there were twelve. My closest friend, Pheidon, Hephaestion, Craterus and the rest of my friends did not want me to go over there. "Let me go instead of you," said Pheidon; "if there is any danger, I will run it for you; but if not, then I will send the boat over to you afterwards. If I, Pheidon, should die, you will find other friends; but if you, Alexander, die, all the world will be saddened." I was persuaded and allowed them to cross over. They disembarked, but after an hour the island dived into the depths, for it was a creature and not an island. We shouted out when the beast vanished and all the men perished, along with my best friend. I was very angry; I looked for the barbarians, but could not find them anywhere.

'We remained eight days on the promontory, and on the seventh we saw the beast. It had tusks. We made the journey back to Prasiake in a few days. On the way we saw many wonderful things, which I must describe to you. We saw many strange beasts ... and reptiles. The most amazing thing of all was the disappearance of the sun and moon and the bitter weather.

'After we had conquered Darius the king of Persia and his men, and had subdued the whole country, we made a journey to see all its wonders. There was gold, and urns decorated with precious stones, ... and many other marvels besides.

'We began our journey from the Caspian Gates. At the tenth hour the trumpets sounded the call for dinner ... everyone went to sleep. As soon as the sun rose, the trumpets sounded . . . until the fourth hour. The preparation of the soldiers was so complete that each had his own sandals, greaves, thigh armour of leather, and breastplates. The natives had warned me about the deadly serpents on the road, so I ordered no one to go abroad without this protection.

'After we had travelled for twelve days, we arrived at a city in the middle of a river. In the city there were reeds, 45 feet in circumference, from which all the buildings of the city were made. It was built not on the ground but on top of these reeds. I ordered the men to pitch camp there. We arrived at about the third hour of the day. Going down to the river, we found its water more bitter than hellebore. We tried to swim over to the city, but hippopotamuses came and seized the men. The only thing to do was to leave that place. The trumpets sounded. From the sixth to the eleventh hour we were so short of water that I saw soldiers drinking their own urine. Then we chanced to come to a place where there was a lake and trees with all kinds of fruit. We rushed to enjoy the sweet water, which was more delicious even than honey.

'We were exulting about this when we saw on the cliff a stone statue with this inscription: "Sesonchosis, the ruler of the world, made this watering-place for those who sail down the Red Sea."136

'I ordered the men to pitch camp, to prepare the beds and to light fires. About the third hour of the night, when the moon was high, the beasts that lived in the wood came out to drink from the lake. There were scorpions 18 inches long, sand-burrowers, both white and red. We were very frightened. Some of the men were killed, and there was tremendous groaning and wailing. Then four-footed beasts began to come out to drink. Among them were lions bigger than bulls – their teeth alone were 2 feet long – lynxes, panthers, tigers, scorpion-tails [?], elephants, ox–rams, bull–stags, men with six hands, strap-footed men, dog–partridges and other kinds of wild animals. Our alarm grew greater. We drove some of them off with our weapons. ⟨We set fire to the woods. The serpents ran into the fire. Some we stamped on and killed with our swords, but most were burnt; and this lasted until the sixth hour of the night, when the moon set. Shaken by fear and terrible dread, we stood wondering at their varied forms. And suddenly a wild animal came that was larger than any elephant, called the Odontotyrannos;[137] and it wanted to attack us. I ran back and forth and beseeched my brave companions to make fires and protect themselves lest they met a horrible death. The beast in its eagerness to hurt the men ran and fell into the flames. From there it charged into the army, killing twenty-six men at once. But some of our other brave men struck down and slew this one-horned beast. Thirteen hundred men were hardly able to drag him away. When the moon went down⟩ night foxes leapt out of the sand, some 8, and some 12, feet long; and crocodiles emerged from the wood and killed the baggage-carriers. There were bats larger than pigeons, and they had teeth. Night crows were perching by the lake; we hunted them down and cooked a large dinner. ⟨The creatures never attacked humans nor did they dare to approach the fire. When it was day, all these animals went away. Then I ordered that the local guides, of whom we had fifty and who had led us to those evil places, be tortured and taken and thrown into the river. Then we collected our things, and moved on 12 miles.⟩

   'We followed the usual road to Prasiake.[138] When I was ready to move on – about the sixth hour on the third day of the month of Zeus – the following sight was seen in the air: first there was a sudden breeze, so that our tents were blown down and we were knocked over on to the ground. ⟨I immediately ordered that the tents be set right and everything else secured. While we were getting organized, a cloud happened to come over; it became so dark that we could not even see one another. After the cloud disappeared, the sky darkened and thickened without cause; then we saw in the sky a great wind and various objects. On the ground before us for over a mile we saw all the clouds heaped together. Suddenly they turned red. This lasted for three days. For five days the sun was invisible, and there was much snow. Soldiers who dared to go out were buried upright. When the sun rose, we had lost many possessions and many of our men. The accumulation of snow made the field 5 feet higher.⟩

'After thirty days the road was clear again and we marched on. After five days we conquered the city of Prasiake along with its king, Porus, and his men.'

The A-text continues with the story of the wise men and the trees of the Sun and Moon, as narrated in the main text (III.17, pp. 133–5).

J: THE UNCLEAN NATIONS (III.26A, p. 145)

The γ-text adds here:

Leaving those regions, he went to war against Eurymithres the leader of the Belsyrians, because he refused to bow to the might of Macedonia. When Eurymithres discovered this, he took 1,800 men and hastened to war against Alexander. When he approached Alexander's advance lookouts, they spotted him, and so Alexander discovered what Eurymithres was up to. Alexander reinforced his lookouts to a number of several thousands, all armed with golden breastplates, ordered the most trusted soldiers to stay behind on guard, and put Seleucus in charge of the troops. As night drew on Eurymithres sent spies to Alexander's camp, who reported back that Alexander was quite unaware of their presence.

Meanwhile Alexander was arming a huge army against him. Eurymithres' counsellors advised him: 'Eurymithres, we cannot fight successfully against Alexander unless we capture the advance posts and hurl ourselves against him with full force. If we do, they will be bewildered by the unexpected clash and will be put to flight, each thinking only of his own safety.'

This was their advice, though they had no idea of Alexander's position. They surrounded Alexander's advance posts by night, expecting to hunt them all down while they were ignorant of the attack. But when the Belsyrians caught sight of Alexander's dispositions, they forgot all about fighting and their thoughts turned to flight: it was too much for them. At this point Seleucus brought his phalanx up against them; at once they turned tail, exemplifying the Homeric phrase: 'He came on like a lion and went off like a deer.' Seleucus' men charged and captured Eurymithres. Some of the enemy Alexander's men killed, others they pursued northwards for fifty days, until they came to two mountains in the unseen world, which they called the Breasts of the North.

When they got there, Alexander stopped pursuing them. He saw that the two mountains would be suitable for closing up their exit, so he stayed there and prayed to God to help him close up the mountains to keep them out. He stood and prayed as follows:

'God of gods, lord of all creation, who made all things by your Word, both heaven and earth. Nothing is impossible for you, all things are slaves to the word of your command. You spoke and they were created, you commanded and it was done. You alone are eternal, supreme, invisible, sole god, and there is no other but you. Through your name and your will I have done what you wished, and you have placed the whole world in my hands. I call now upon your name that is so often praised: fulfil this request of mine and cause these two mountains to come together, as I have asked of you, and do not look askance at me, wretched as I am, who have been so bold as to speak in this way. I know you care for me and your supreme goodness.'

Immediately the mountains came together, though they had previously been 18 feet apart. When Alexander saw what had happened, he praised God. Then he built bronze gates, fixed them in the narrows between the two mountains and oiled them. The nature of the oil was such that it could not be burned by fire nor dislodged by iron. Within the gates, stretching back to the open country [for a distance of 3,000 miles] he planted brambles, which he watered well so that they formed a dense mane over the mountains.

So Alexander shut in twenty-two kings with their subject nations behind the northern boundaries – behind the gates that he called the Caspian[139] and the mountains known as the Breasts. These are the names of those nations: Goth, Magoth, Anougeis, Aigeis, Exenach, Diphar, Photinaioi, Pharizaioi, Zarmatianoi, Chachonioi, Agrimardoi, Anouphagoi, Tharbaioi, Alans, Physolonikaioi, Saltarioi, and the rest.[140] These were the nations that dwelt behind the gates that King Alexander built so as to be indestructible. They used to eat worms and foul things that were not real food at all – dogs, flies, snakes, aborted foetuses, dead bodies and unformed human embryos; and they ate not only animals but the corpses of humans as well. Alexander, seeing all this, was afraid that they would come out and pollute the inhabited world; so he shut them in and went on his way.

K: THE OBITUARY (III.35, p. 159)

The γ-text adds here:

He subdued a multitude of nations: the Greeks, Iberians, Abari, Slavs, Moors, Mauretanians, Onogouroi, Tetragouroi, Tetrakatoi, One-horns, Sikiones, Kanziotes, Kanzetes, Rysperetes, Charourites, Snake-charmers, Elephant-feet, Skebryotes, Examaroi, Lombards, Lebesentianoi, Ebrides, Dermatesioi, Abasgoi, Armenians, Russians, Ochloi, Saracens, Syrians, Alans, Ebrepaoi, Ebrexaoi, Six-hands, Six-rows, Strap-feet, Under-fingers, Priskoi, Lakoi, Multi-feet, Patesophoi, Lebeis, Wolf-heads, Dog-heads, Lokomites, Ostrikoi, Panzetes, Deleemes, Sandaleis, Kansadeis, Kasandriotes, Aigiotes, Hyopobiotes, Hypobotioi, Indians, Sindians, Sogdians, Barmaioi, and Egyptians as well as the inhabitants of the lands of darkness, Hebrews, Thrymbetes, Kouskoi, Khazars, Bulgars, Khounaboi, Pinsai, Ethiopians and Romans, those victorious warriors. The rest he subdued without a battle; and they paid tribute. Amen.

Iambic lines on Alexander

The bright world's glory, O my friend, is nothing.
Before they even appear, they are swiftly gone
Like flowers or grass, a shadow in a dream.
The worse love better than the good.
Before its season what is lovely vanishes.
There's nothing new in all this, foreign guest:
Acanthus flowers and flourishes, and quickly
It passes on; it may be foul of smell
Or thick with thorns, its fame is just as bright.

Often one day sees all this disappear
And leaves the kings bereft of all their goods.
Virtue alone remains, imperishable
In fame, and even Time that conquers all
Cannot destroy a noble reputation.
You wish to know, O stranger, what this means
That I have told you? Listen, then, and hear:
King Alexander, ruler of the world,
Olympias' son, the fair-bloomed rose.
Baptized with drenchings of the blood of kings,
The mighty hero, noble, like a lion,
Whose sword affrighted even the fiercest nations,
Whose javelin made the Persian army tremble,
Who swept the barbarians like a hurricane,
Where they dwelt in the four quarters of the earth;
He was illustrious among the Macedonians,
Alack. He died untimely, and was hidden
Like a brilliant light beneath a bushel.

NOTES

1. These opening sentences are not in A.
2. Nectanebo II was the last Pharaoh of Egypt, who fled the country after the Persian conquest of 343 BC under Artaxerxes Ochus.
3. 'So-called' only in B.
4. The list of peoples varies in the different recensions. A has: 'Scythians, Arabs, Oxydrakai, Iberians, Seres, Kaukones, Lapates, Bosporoi, Agroi, Zalboi, Chaldaeans, Mesopotamians, Wild-game-eaters, Euonymitae'.
5. The Greek word is *aerinos*. γ has *aerios*; A has *aitherites*. The expression is translated as 'the ethereal astrologer Aramazd' (i.e., Zeus) by the Armenian translator; he did not understand it either.
6. *karpisetai* might also mean: 'will make you free'.
7. L has: 'sewing up a papyrus roll and sealing it'. The sequel makes it clear that my text, translated from A, is the correct one.
8. This odd clause is not in A.
9. A inserts here Nectanebo's detailed astrological arguments. The rest of the chapter differs slightly in A.
10. A Greek father, at the birth of his child, customarily examined the newborn infant for deformities and made a decision as to whether the child was to be reared, or exposed to die. 'Let it be reared' (*trephestho*) was the formal expression of his favourable decision.
11. The asymmetry of Alexander's eyes is a traditional attribute: in A one eye is black, the other white, and the Armenian text describes Alexander's eyes as 'heavy-lidded'.
12. Literally 'cauldron'.
13. Literally 'black'.
14. The Julius Valerius version adds that these details are confirmed in the 'learned histories' of Favorinus (*c.* AD 200). As Favorinus is mentioned in the Armenian version, he may have been mentioned in the Greek recension as well. But in the interpolated state of the recensions, this is of no value for determining the date of any of the versions.
15. γ adds here: 'without Philip's knowledge'.

16. *boos kephale*.

17. The Armenian version (39–46) inserts here some letters from Zeuxis the painter and Aristotle to Philip and Olympias, and the replies. This correspondence is not given in any of the Greek texts.

18. In γ the Games are held not at Pisa where the sanctuary of Olympia was situated, but at Rome, and Alexander is invited by the princes, with the promise, 'The winners will receive prizes from Jupiter Capitolinus; but the defeated will be put to death by the victors.' In the passages from γ in chs. 19 and 20 I have not attempted to iron out the contradiction.

19. Nicomachus in A.

20. In A Cleopatra is the sister of Antalos, not of Lysias.

21. The tribute of golden eggs is not mentioned in A, but is prominent in Firdausi's *Shahnameh*. The whole episode occurs later in γ, after the death of Philip.

22. The name literally means 'dwellers round about'. Amphictyonies were leagues, centred on a temple, which had some political standing. Philip II acquired the votes of Phocis in the Delphic Amphictyony.

23. The error in the addition is that of the Greek text.

24. In the true historical sequence the events of I.43–II.6 belong here. They were displaced into the middle of the Asian campaign at an early stage in the formation of the *Romance*. As a result the campaign against Thebes is recounted twice in L – briefly in I.27 and at greater length in I.46. I have filled out the narrative here with the γ-text, with the result that there are now two versions of the debate in Athens: I.27 (γ) and also II.3.1–5 (A). The campaign against Lacedaemon appears there (briefly) in L and at greater length in A at II.3.6. There is no way of rationalizing these confusions and I offer both versions of each event.

25. The Cynic philosopher. In Plutarch and other historical accounts his meeting with Alexander (see p. 60) took place in Corinth.

26. At this point the γ-text abandons the siege of Athens without explanation and continues with the events that are narrated here in L.

27. The events of this chapter are described in the historical accounts. The place where the sea drew back was on the Cilician coast near Mount Climax, where the cliffs fall precipitously into the sea. See Freya Stark, *Alexander's Path* (London, 1958), pp. 73 ff.; A. B. Bosworth, *Conquest and Empire* (Cambridge, 1988), p. 51.

28. It is only the *Romance* that puts the visit to Ammon before the foundation of Alexandria. C. B. Welles, *Historia*, 11 (1962), pp. 271–98, argues that for once the *Romance* tradition is historically superior;

it was natural to seek an oracle before founding a city. The following chapters clearly derive from local histories of Alexandria and are an important clue to the place of origin of the *Romance*.

29. The Greek for 'wide of the mark' is *paratonon*.

30. *taphos* means 'grave', 'tomb'.

31. The fuller A-text names sixteen villages. The L-text names none.

32. These details, given only in A, are very corrupt and were probably left out in later recensions because of their obscurity.

33. The Greek word is *hormei*.

34. Europhoros and Eurylichos; A has Eurylochos for both.

35. See n. 34.

36. Sarapis was often portrayed accompanied by the three-headed dog, Cerberus.

37. Zeus and Hera were identified in antiquity with Sarapis and Isis.

38. The numbers are expressed in Greek by the letters forming the name of Sarapis. The riddle is corrupt in A's verse version, so I have given it in L's prose. The rest of the section given here from A (pp. 66–8) is altogether lost in L.

39. The usual Greek name for Ptah.

40. The Greek word *tyros* means 'cheese'.

41. Actually the Pinaros, which flows through the plain of Issus, site of Alexander's second great battle with Darius.

42. Chronology and geography are given another violent jerk. The river Scamander in the Troad was one of the first places Alexander came to after crossing into Asia.

43. Alexander's reply is omitted in γ. The Armenian and Julius Valerius versions add here that so far Olympias had travelled with Alexander, but that he now sent her back to Macedon. None of the Greek texts contains this detail.

44. Like a film running in reverse, the narrative now brings Alexander back to Europe and recapitulates the Greek campaigns of chs. 26 ff. See n. 24.

45. I.45 and I.47–II.6 are not in L. The narrative goes directly from the end of I.46 to the end of II.6. I have omitted L's ch. 46 in favour of the much fuller narrative in A, I.45–II.6.

46. Tripod of Phoebus. Though the *Romance* places this event in Acragas it clearly belongs, in geography and sense, at Delphi.

47. Thebes was founded by Cadmus, after an oracle had told him to follow a white ox and to found a city where she lay down.

48. Antiope.

49. Zeus prevented the sun from rising in order to extend his night of

pleasure with Amphitryon's wife Alcmena, who then gave birth to Heracles.

50. An *outré* name for the god Dionysus, born of Semele by Zeus' thunderbolt.

51. The story is that of Euripides' *Bacchae*. Pentheus' mother was Agave, who in Bacchic ecstasy mistook her son for a wild beast and tore him apart.

52. The Cadmeia was the Acropolis of Thebes.

53. The text of this line is corrupt and the meaning of the sentence obscure. Alexander did not study with Pindar, but perhaps the author of the *Romance* thought he did?

54. i.e., Heracles, whose grandfather was Alcaeus.

55. The twin of Castor, one of the Dioscuri.

56. The author's geography is confused. See Introduction, pp. 5–6.

57. The meaning of this sentence is uncertain.

58. 'Oxydelkys' also in γ; A has 'Oxydarkes'.

59. γ adds here the Iberoi, Tabaktoi and Taeroi.

60. So in all versions. This is actually the river Cydnus. The story has already been told, very briefly, in I.41.

61. Parmenio's role in this story has a historical basis: see Introduction, n. 21. The correct form of his name is Parmenion. A wild version of this story relating to the war against Egypt is told by γ in II.25 ff.: see Supplement F.

62. In A the satraps are named as Hydaspes and Spinther.

63. The author of the *Romance* treats Persia as a city rather than a region. It is not until he has crossed the (fictitious) river Stranga that Alexander reaches Persepolis, the capital (II.14).

64. Stranga. γ calls the river Arsinoe.

65. γ: Parages. A: Parasanges.

66. In γ Alexander demands the torch, and then hits the sentry but does not kill him; with the result that the sentry is able to tell the pursuers which way he has gone.

67. In γ Alexander takes time out to yell mockery at the Persians beyond the river, and Darius' reaction is told at greater length.

68. This battle corresponds to the historical one of Gaugamela or Arbela, in which scythed chariots were used and many of the Persian army were drowned in the Great Zab as they fled (see Bosworth, op. cit., p. 84).

69. None of the versions contains Alexander's famous retort which is in the historians: 'And so would I, if I were Parmenio.'

70. Historians continue to differ as to whether the burning of Persepolis was an act of policy or the outcome of a drunken rampage.

71. i.e., Nebuchadnezzar.

72. The tomb of Cyrus was, and is, actually in Pasargadae, about 25 miles north-east of Persepolis. Its appearance bears no resemblance to this fictional description.

73. The Caspian Gates were the complex of defiles south-east of Rai and the modern city of Tehran which linked Media with the eastern satrapies.

74. Ecbatana (modern Hamadan).

75. This speech of Alexander's, and Darius' reply, are given in verse in A.

76. The meaning of this sentence is very uncertain. The Armenian, Syriac and A versions have differing, but equally obscure, senses.

77. This is the form of the name in all MSS except L, which has 'Lites'.

78. In reality the mother of Darius was Sisygambis, and his wife and daughter were both called Stateira. Alexander did not marry his daughter. Roxane, whom he did marry, was the daughter of the Bactrian prince, Oxyartes. In A Rodo is called Rodogyne.

79. This short letter to Olympias is not in A or γ.

80. This letter to Olympias (II.23–40) is replaced in γ by a third person narrative which is much longer and relates different events (see Supplement F). This account occupies chs. 22–31 of Book II, and, therefore, the numbering in A, B and L goes directly from 23 to 32.

81. Literally 'Goats'.

82. The testing of a wild man with a naked woman is reminiscent of the corruption, or 'civilization', of the Wild Man Enkidu in the *Epic of Gilgamesh*.

83. The Greek for 'without men' is *exandros*.

84. i.e., lambda.

85. The story of the diving bell is not in A. γ has a similar version, but in the third person narrative.

86. This stratagem of using foals to ensure the mares found their way home features also in Rashid al-Din's version of the legend of Oghuz, eponymous ancestor of the Oghuz Turks (see J. Boyle, *Zentralasiatische Studien*, 9 (1965), p. 270). It is also in Marco Polo (IV.21).

87. Kale lives on in modern Greek legend as Kale ton Oreon, the Beautiful One of the Mountains. The Nereids in modern Greece have become mountain spirits.

88. The Greek word is *neros*.

89. The story of the Water of Life is not in A.

90. The story of Alexander's Ascent is not in A. This became one of the most popular pieces of Alexander iconography in the Middle Ages;

e.g., misericords in Wells and Gloucester, and a relief in the museum at Thebes.

91. γ continues the narrative directly in the third person. The events of 41 are not in L.

92. This magic stone assumes a much larger significance in the Syriac and hence the Persian traditions.

93. The Sirens. These too receive more attention in the Syriac narratives.

94. γ inserts as ch. 43 (not in L or A) a letter to Olympias, which repeats in brief all the previous adventures.

95. Chs. 42 and 43 occur in γ only and repeat events of chs. 24–41.

96. The mutiny in India has a historical basis, but it did not take place until after the conquest of Porus (see Bosworth, op. cit., p. 133).

97. γ begins Book III here, omitting ch. 1 and the first sentence of ch. 2. The mutiny appears in γ, III.3.

98. Porus is historical but the single combat is not. In fact, Porus was captured. When brought to Alexander, the latter asked him how he expected to be treated. 'Like a king,' replied Porus; and Alexander reestablished him as a vassal ruler.

99. The meeting with the Brahmans is naturally omitted at this point by γ which includes it in Book II: see Supplement F.

100. A inserts here the monograph by Palladius, De Bragmanibus. Most of this work is also included in the version in γ (Supplement F). I have not translated this work.

101. The sentence seems to be corrupt. The name Moutheamatous may conceal names for each tree – perhaps the Iranian sun and moon deities, Mithras and Mao.

102. Beroe: B, L. Meroe: A.

103. Or 'chimpanzees'.

104. Or 'unbored'.

105. The author of γ was obviously puzzled too, and simplified the story. He has only two characters, Alexander and Antiochus, and the two of them change clothes. The third character is, in fact, unnecessary to the plot.

106. γ has a different account of the rescue of Candaules' wife from the tyrant (who is called Evagrides). Frightened by Alexander's letters, the tyrant commits suicide. The tale in γ is tedious and not nearly as good.

107. γ includes here the events of III. 24, except that the Egyptian king, Sesonchosis, is replaced by the Persian king, Ochus, the father of Darius.

108. As we shall discover later, his name is Thoas. In A and the Armenian version he is called Kargos; and in γ, Doreph.

109. The expression is a strong one: *diakoreusai* literally means 'penetrate'. γ has the more decorous *symmigenai*: 'have intercourse with'. The same divergence occurs in ch. 26 below.

110. In γ the Amazons ask for a portrait of Alexander to revere, and he sends them his spear.

111. The events of this letter are told in the third person in γ, thus making a doublet of the Amazon story.

112. Maron. A son or grandson of Dionysus, raised by Silenus. Here he seems to be identified with Silenus.

113. These wonders of the palace of the Persian kings are also mentioned by Philostratus, *Life of Apollonius of Tyana*, I.25.2; cf. Herodotus, 7.27.2.

114. There is no ch. 29 in A, B or L. Only γ includes the story of the enclosure of the Unclean Nations, Gog and Magog (see Supplement J).

115. The text of the *Romance* tells the tale in the third person, and therefore I have not given it in quotation marks.

116. In γ the number of Chaldaeans is ten.

117. At this point γ (MS C) inserts *another* letter to Olympias, again repeating several of the preceding events.

118. A has Iollas, a more Greek form.

119. Antipater's son is Cassander. In reality Iolaus was Cassander's younger brother.

120. γ adds Seleucus, Philo and Scamandrius. Antipater's son Cassander should not be in this list of those who were ignorant of the plot, and has probably been inserted through carelessness.

121. Antipater's son.

122. The first four paragraphs of the will are in an extremely pompous style, unlike the following ones, and notable for their overriding concern with Rhodian affairs. In the fifth paragraph the will opens afresh. One may suspect a Rhodian hand in the addition of the first four paragraphs.

123. Merkelbach (pp. 277–8), followed by Heckel, emends to Antipater.

124. The arrangements for the administration of Macedon are a puzzle to historians. See Bosworth, op. cit., p. 175.

125. The dispositions of this paragraph reappear, more or less, in γ, which does not have the rest of the will. None of the will appears in L except for the sentence about Roxane's offspring.

126. γ has Alexandria.

127. 'Neomaga' may be a Greek form of an Egyptian word, in which the element 'neo-' was taken to mean 'young'.

128. i.e., 323/2 BC.

129. i.e., 325/4 BC.

130. The Greek expression literally means 'molten metal'.

131. What follows closely resembles the events in Cilicia recounted in II.8.

132. This story is also told by γ earlier (see Supplement C).

133. What follows repeats the story in II.35 in L.

134. What follows repeats the dialogue in A, III.17 (Letter to Aristotle; see Supplement I).

135. The Latin version is fuller, but the denouements differ. A translation may be found at the end of L. Gunderson, *Alexander's Letter to Aristotle about India* (Meisenheim am Glan, 1980).

136. The Red Sea in ancient times referred to all the waters surrounding the Arabian Peninsula. The historical nugget in this section is Alexander's return from India through the Gedrosian desert of south Iran.

137. The name literally means 'Tooth-tyrant'. Various candidates have been proposed for this puzzling monster. They include the mammoth, the kraken, the crocodile and a Ganges water-snake with huge fangs. Or the name may derive from Persian *kerkodon*, the rhinoceros. The tale of Sindbad asserts that the rhinoceros can kill elephants. See J. Zacher, *Pseudo-Callisthenes. Forschungen zur Kritik und Geschichte der ältesten Aufzeichnung der Alexandersage* (Halle, 1867), pp. 153–8.

138. Prasiake seems to be a Greek form of the Sanskrit *prachyaka*, 'the eastern land' (i.e., east of the Ganges).

139. Caspian Gates. Not the same as those of n. 73 but either a defile between the Caucasus and the Caspian Sea, or the Pass of Dariel. The Caliph Wathiq once mounted an expedition to discover these gates.

140. Not much can be made of this exotic catalogue.

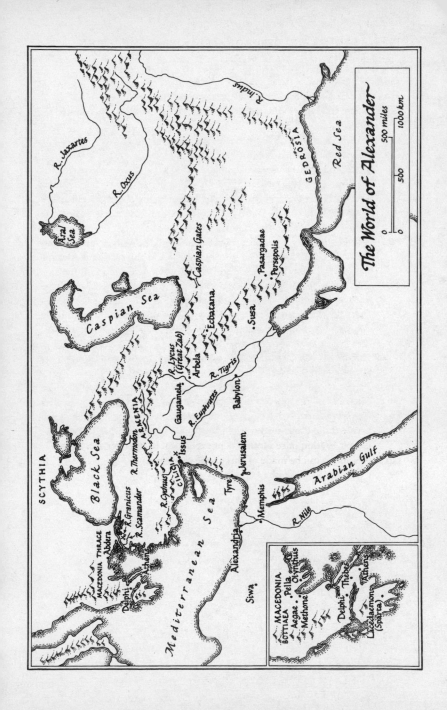

The World of Alexander